# BURGLARY AT BARNARD

*An Oxford Key Mystery*

## LYNN MORRISON

D1160875

The Marketing Chair

Cover design by Emilie Yane Lopes

Published by

The Marketing Chair Press, Oxford, England

LynnMorrisonWriter.com

Paperback ISBN: 978-1-8380391-1-0

# CONTENTS

# Chapter One

I rush down the pavement, pausing only long enough to slide my badge through the keycard reader installed next to an ivy-covered, wrought-iron gate. It's the second of January and Oxford's streets are barren of any signs of life.

"It's only eight o'clock at night, where is everyone?" I wonder as I let myself into the Barnard College grounds. Apparently, the city is still recovering from a long night of New Year celebrations. Two lone cars were the only sign of life I saw on my speed walk from my flat at St Margaret College, their headlights dazzling my vision for a few seconds each time.

When my fellow prefect Mathilde suggested we make a head start on our historical research into the origins of Oxford's magic, I didn't expect her to suggest we meet in the archives of the Barnard College library as soon as I got back from my holiday. Literally. After flying back from the ski resort, I caught a bus up from Heathrow, barely finding time to drop my luggage at my flat at St Margaret before dashing back into the centre.

As I stride across Barnard College's commons, the thick stone walls of the 15th century buildings blocking all moonlight, I wish I had my wyvern along to keep me company. I realise how weird that sounds as soon as the thought crosses my mind.

Three months ago, I arrived at the University of Oxford as the new Head of Ceremonies. I was excited to take on my first task, organising the annual gala at St Margaret College. I didn't expect to stumble over the dead body of St Margaret's famed chef, nor did I expect I'd end up identifying her murderer. I definitely was not prepared for the college cat to turn into a wyvern and announce I had the magic of Oxford running through my veins. Those childhood stories my grandfather used to tell were true. Oxford is full of magic, and as a prefect, I can see all of it.

But the magic of Oxford isn't working as it should, and it's up to me, Mathilde and Kate, the third prefect, to find out why - which is why I'm stumbling around in the dark instead of unpacking my suitcase.

"Where is that doorway?" I mutter to myself. Barnard College claims to be one of the oldest in Oxford, and looking around at its buildings, I can see why. The grey-stoned walls and narrow windows are a far cry from St Margaret's Edwardian facade.

I arranged a tour of the grounds before I left in December. Ms Evans, the college Master's young assistant, acted as my tour guide. Tottering around in a pair of expensive Louboutin heels, she showed me the ageing chapel with its bare wooden benches and the famous stained-glass windows in the dining hall.

As we wandered through Barnard's warren of walled court-yards and ivy-covered buildings, I could barely hide my disappointment in her attitude. Despite being several years younger than I am, she insisted I call her Ms Evans, acting more like the lady of the manor than the Master's assistant. I had hoped to find another friend like Harry, but Ms Evans showed zero interest in anything other than her own social standing.

I halt under the yellow glare of a pathway light to consult my notes. "The Old Library... where is it? I know I wrote it down... Here it is. Ugh, the library is back in the main building."

I spin around, retracing my steps until I find the sign for the Master's Garden. The main building forms one side of its walls. I quicken my pace, composing excuses since I'm later than expected.

I need not have bothered. Mathilde scoops me into a quick squeeze as soon as I come into the main building.

"Happy New Year, Nat, and welcome back to Oxford," she says.

"Happy New Year to you, as well, Mathilde. Did you have a pleasant holiday?" I ask. We exchange Christmas and Boxing Day stories as we climb the old wooden staircase to the next floor.

The main building is one of the oldest at Barnard, its front entrance guarded by massive wooden doors. At an imposing four meters tall, every centimetre of them is carved with scrollwork. I wonder when they were last opened. One of the doors features a lower panel that opens during the day to provide entrance for guests and visitors. At night they bolt it shut, which is why I came in through the garden gate instead.

The old library lays claim to most of the first floor, housing the college archives of historical manuscripts and ageing texts. You won't find any popular fiction novels gracing its shelves. Those are stored in the new library, a soaring glass building located outside of the old college grounds.

Mathilde strides down the hall, her steps confident. She waves us to a halt at a set of wooden doors, the top panels fitted with lead-lined glass. I can barely make out the shapes of the front desk through the light coming in through the library's outer windows. Mathilde slides her keycard through the reader, giving a small sigh of relief when the display light changes from red to green. With a sharp tug, we're inside.

"Hold on, let me find the lights..." Mathilde disappears behind the front desk. At the click of a switch, lights flicker to life, illuminating the towering stacks in pools of yellow glow. The only sign of human presence is a lone book lying haphazardly on the floor at the end of a row of shelves.

I glance at Mathilde, suddenly less certain of our plan to search through the Barnard archives after hours. "Are you sure it's okay for us to be here?"

Mathilde quirks an eyebrow, "I'm a librarian and you're on staff. We're hardly students sneaking in for illicit activities." She doesn't wait for any further comment, striding towards a bank of computers. "I'll fire up the online catalogue. Can you find us a comfortable alcove to set ourselves up?"

Nodding, I step into the aisle and pass the first row of shelves. They're over three meters tall. I have to crane my neck to see the top of them. Fortunately, there is a narrow ladder attached to the top of each bookcase, with wheels allowing it to glide to wherever it is needed.

The only sound I can hear is my breathing, occasionally interrupted by the click of Mathilde's fingers on the keyboard. I hate to admit it, but the place feels creepy. I give my head a firm shake, putting a stop to any further thoughts in that direction. I'm sharing a flat with a wyvern and I regularly chat with ghosts. How can an empty old room possibly scare me?

I look over my shoulder, calling out to Mathilde, "I see some sofas at the far end of the room. Unless you want to camp out at one of the tables, I think they're our best bet." She nods her agreement, still engrossed in her search through the online catalogue.

I step past the first row of shelves, a quick glance confirming their only occupants are leather-bound books. The spines face outwards, their titles barely legible.

Strangely, the one thing I don't see is any hint of an Eternal. You'd think in a building as historic as this one, at least a few ghosts would be walking along the hallways. Who knows? Maybe they take the holidays off.

I march onward, closer to the abandoned textbook lying on the ground. It's weird that it's lying there in the middle of the floor. Leaning over, I scoop it up, thinking to return it to its rightful home, but the leather spine, much abused by its fall, flakes off into my hand. Mathilde isn't going to be happy about this.

As I turn right into the nearest aisle, I spot a mountain of books on the floor. They lie in a tumble, pages open and spines cracked. A shelf lies bare, its empty space no doubt their rightful home.

"What the???" My eyes scan over the pile, trying to make sense of the scene: ivory pages, leather spines, a few scroll cases added to the mix. And at the very bottom is a pair of Louboutin heels, their cherry red soles a pop of colour against the dull background.

"EEEEeeeppppp!" The squeal slips out of my mouth when I realise the heels are attached to a deathly still pair of legs. Mathilde comes rushing over, passing by me as I stand frozen in place, and going straight into the aisle to unearth the person buried underneath.

"Quick, call an ambulance!" she implores, tossing the rare texts aside as though they were discards in a discount bin. I drop the book to the floor when a familiar face and body emerges, completely still and devoid of any signs of life.

This snaps me out of my numb state. I reach over and grab Mathilde's shoulder before she can do any further damage to the crime scene.

"I think it's too late for that, Mathilde."

She follows my finger past the still form to see a bloody brass candlestick rolled up against the base of the bookshelf.

Mathilde gasps as the implications set it. "Oh god, Nat, another murder!"

"That's not our only problem," I say, shaking my head. "I'd recognise that candlestick anywhere. I spent weeks looking at its matching partner at one end of High Table and wondering where this one had gone. Unless I'm mistaken, this candlestick is the one that went missing from St Margaret."

❖

My hand shakes as I dial the number for the college security office on the library desk phone. I suck in a deep breath and hold it for a second, releasing it in time with the double buzz of the ringing phone. By the time a gruff male voice answers, I'm back in control.

"Hello? This is Natalie Payne, from the Ceremonies office. I'm in the old library. You need to come straight away. There's been a terrible crime. It's Ms Evans. She's..." my voice trails off as I struggle to inhale. "She's dead."

The security guard assures me he will be right over, ordering me to stay put until he arrives. I don't need to convey the message to Mathilde; she's standing close enough beside me to have heard every word.

Within moments we hear hurried footsteps echoing down the hallway. A rotund face flushed red from the exertion peers through the glass window in the door. The face is recognisable, but it's not that of the security guard. Mathilde and I freeze like a deer in headlights.

The man shoves open the door and marches into the room, beady eyes glaring from underneath bushy eyebrows. His salt and pepper hair does not move, a glistening oil slicking it back from his forehead. He looms in both size and stature, his gaze scanning the space until it comes to rest on us.

"Master Finch-Byron, what are you doing here?" Shock makes my voice louder than I intend.

He looks down his beak nose at me as he buttons his blazer, the fabric straining to cover his pronounced paunch. His tie hangs in a loose knot below his jowls. "Ms Payne, I am the head of this college. The security team phoned me as soon as you disconnected the call. My apartments connect to the upper floor of this building. Now, tell me what has happened, starting with why you are in the library during the holiday closure."

Mathilde slides from behind the desk, stepping out into the aisle and capturing the Master's attention. "I'm Mathilde Seymour, a librarian at the Bodleian. It was my decision to come here tonight. I knew Nat was keen to begin her research into the college archives, so I suggested we meet this evening while it was quiet."

Master Finch-Byron harrumphs his response, his eyebrows arching. "What would our Head of Ceremonies need to research in the archives? Surely not party ideas."

Mathilde catches my eye, her gaze begging me to step in. Our first thought after finding the body was to phone the security team, not to coordinate a cover story for why we were here. Looking for information about magic is the truth, but not one which we can share, for obvious reasons. Thank goodness I'm quick on my feet.

"Every event I organise is unique to the college and requires me to have a keen understanding of the history. It's easier to read historical texts without other people milling about."

The Master opens his mouth, no doubt ready with another question. I jump in before he can speak. "But none of that matters now. It's Ms Evans. We found her lying in the floor between the shelves. She's dead."

Master Finch-Byron fishes a handkerchief from his pocket and wipes a line of sweat from his brow. His gaze is thunderous, his command sharp. "Ms Evans? Show me."

Mathilde gives me a nearly imperceptible nod before stepping backwards. "I'll wait here for the security team."

I steel myself before striding into the shelf-lined corridor, retracing my steps towards the abandoned book which marks the ill-fated row. I pause before we reach it, stepping to the side and waving a hand to indicate the Master should go ahead. He steps around me. Listening closely, his slowing footsteps are all the reminder I need of what lies before him. He stills for less time than I expect considering the body is that of his assistant.

His footfalls recommence but grow softer, as though he is moving further away. Before I can question what he is doing, his heated voice shatters the silence.

"What is this opening?"

My eyes widen in confusion as I slip down an empty row, emerging into the aisle on the far side of the room. The Master is standing in front of a small, open panel, a flickering light spilling out to illuminate his black leather shoes. I can see why he is perplexed as there is no door handle, nor a hinge to indicate that an opening would be there. I glance over my shoulder to see Mathilde following behind me, my questioning gaze echoed in her face.

"That's impossible," she blurts. "That should be a solid wall."

Impossible or not, Master Finch-Byron leans over, peering into the secret chamber which lies on the other side. "This is more than a murder. Someone has dared to burglarise our buildings. Ms Evans must have caught them in the act."

With his pronouncement, he rocks back on his heels before pivoting and returning to the front of the library, leaving Mathilde and me behind. Perplexed, we tiptoe over to the hidden doorway. I can see how it would blend seamlessly into the wainscotting along the wall. The opening is a little more than a meter tall and wide, barely large enough for an adult to slip inside.

Our bodies bent, Mathilde and I nearly bump heads as we rush to look into the narrow opening. A tapered candle sits abandoned in a puddle of wax on a shelf, illuminating a packed storage space, half full of wooden crates, towering stacks of books and artwork. Scattered books and papers cover the floor. The stacks of wrapped paintings lean against the crates, hastily torn shreds of cloth hanging down from them. The disarray testifies to the truth of the Master's statement. Someone was looking for something in a hurry, and poor Ms Evans was in the wrong place at the wrong time.

Leaning close, I whisper into Mathilde's ear. "A secret chamber in a centuries-old college is burglarised. Is there any chance that this doesn't have something to do with the problems with the magic?"

Mathilde's pale face shakes out a no as she rises back to standing. The scrape of the main library door opening signals the arrival of the security team and the end of any chance we have to continue investigating this line of thinking.

I sit alone, shivering, in the cold confines of a nearby conference room. I've pulled my chair up against the radiator in an attempt to absorb its warmth. The heating was off during the holiday closure, the library an exception due to the necessity of keeping a steady temperature within the space to protect the ageing books and manuscripts inside. In another day or two, this room will no doubt be roasting, but for right now, it is chilly.

The security team escorted Mathilde and me into separate rooms to await questioning by the police department. Although I can see the logic, I wish I had her or my wyvern H here with me.

My head is spinning as I attempt to make sense of the night's discoveries.

Am I doomed to start every term here at Oxford by discovering a body? When I found Chef Smythe lying dead in her kitchen, I had no idea I'd end up searching for suspects. This time around I know I'll have to step up. If the culprit's only connection to the college is the magic, how on earth will the police ever identify them?

Rustling through my handbag, I pull out a pen and notepad. I want to make notes now while the scene is still fresh in my memory. The scratching of my pen chases away the silence. I jot down Ms Evan's name, making a note of where and how we found her. Skipping a few lines, I write 'Secret Chamber' and list everything I can remember seeing inside.

A light tapping sound sends my pen skipping off the page, the only warning I receive before the Inspector steps into the room. Despite the late hour, his suit is unwrinkled, the crisp lines of the iron still sharp along the front of his trousers. His face tells a different story, worry lines carved into his black skin and heavy bags puffing under his eyes. His hair is close-cropped against his skin.

He looks up from his clipboard, his mouth dropping into a frown as he takes in my huddled form sitting across the room. "I was hoping the security team made a mistake when they told me your name. We've had two murders inside of Oxford colleges, and somehow you've managed to discover both of them. How is that possible, Ms Payne?"

I shouldn't be surprised to see the same Inspector who interviewed me and Dr Radcliffe at St Margaret. After all, Oxford is a relatively small town with a low crime rate. What use would they have for an entire department of murder investigators? I tuck my notepad and pen into my bag, my cheeks burning in embarrassment. "Poor luck, Inspector..." I lean forward to read his name from his badge. "Sorry, Detective Inspector Robinson. I'm sorry to meet you again in such terrible circumstances."

DI Robinson pulls out a chair on the other side of the table and drops into it. "I worked a twelve-hour shift yesterday, lending a hand to manage crowds in the centre. I was about to pour myself a gin and tonic when my mobile rang." Opening his blazer, he drags a pen from an inner pocket and settles into interview mode. "Let's start with why you were in the old Barnard library. I thought you worked at St Margaret College."

I straighten in my chair, crossing my legs and tucking them up against the radiator. "My role of Head of Ceremonies is at the University level; I rotate around the colleges as needed to organise major events. Last term I was at St Margaret, but this term I'm based here at Barnard."

Looking down at the form, he asks, "And yet your address is still listed as St Margaret College?"

"Yes, they offered housing for my first two terms."

He rattles through question after question. How do I know Mathilde? Why were we meeting up so late? Did we disturb the scene or touch the body? How long did we wait to call the security team?

I answer as truthfully as I can, given I can't mention anything about prefect roles or magical boundaries. The DI has me double and triple explain how I knew the candlestick belonged to St Margaret. Finally, he wraps up that line of questions, flipping over his page of notes before starting a new one.

"When did you notice the opening to the secret chamber?"

I open my mouth to answer but pause before any words come out. How did Master Finch-Byron spot it so quickly? He barely stopped at Ms Evan's side before continuing to exit the row. The candlelight from inside the space was invisible unless you were looking straight at the opening, the faint yellow flickers lost in the larger security lights Mathilde and I had turned on.

"The chamber, Ms Payne?" DI Robinson arches an eyebrow at my silence.

"Sorry, I was lost in thought," I explain. "Honestly, I didn't notice, or rather we didn't notice it until the Master called it to our attention. As soon as Mathilde and I saw Ms Evans and realised she was dead, we backtracked to the front desk to call security. The opening wasn't visible unless you crossed through the row and exited on the other side of the room."

Shifting in my seat, I scoot closer to the table, my voice lowering to a near whisper. "What you should be asking is how did the Master spot it straightaway? And why wasn't he more concerned about Ms Evans? She was his personal assistant; he must have known her relatively well."

Shaking his head, DI Robinson interrupts me before I can go any further. "Oh no, absolutely not, Ms Payne. You may have stumbled across the killer at St Margaret, but that could have just as easily gone wrong. Leave this crime to the professionals."

"But," I jump in, "it's weird, right? Why was Ms Evans in the old library in the first place? How did she even get in? Mathilde's keycard only worked because she's a librarian."

The sound of a clipboard slapping onto the table breaks my chain of thought, its echo rippling through the small room. "I said, that is enough. The Oxford Police Department does not need the help of an amateur sleuth. We will investigate all avenues. Not you, Ms Payne. The only thanks you will get from us is for staying out of it. You are, I assure you, far from qualified and are far more likely to hinder us than to lend a hand."

His words are still ringing as he pushes back his chair and rises to his feet. He spins and exits the room without a backward look, his dismissal clear.

"I'm far more qualified than you think, Detective Inspector Robinson," I mutter under my breath as I retrieve my notepad and pen. The bronze candlestick and secret chamber point towards the magic, but the Master's behaviour and Ms Evan's unexplained presence are ringing alarm bells in my head.

I step out of the meeting room to wait for Mathilde. I can hear the Detective Inspector's voice coming from the room she's sitting within. We have much to discuss. Was Master Finch-Byron correct when he pronounced the crime a burglary, or is something more afoot?

# Chapter Two

By the time I finish all the police interviews and have a lengthy chat with Mathilde, it is well after midnight. Part of me wants to ring Harry as soon as I get back to my flat at St Margaret, but the other part realises it will probably be her last night of calm for some time. Once I tell her about the murder, the reemergence of St Margaret's missing candlestick, and the secret room, I doubt she'll rest comfortably again until we've gotten to the bottom of what happened to Ms Evans. I know I won't.

After a night of tossing and turning, I text Harry bright and early in the morning, asking her to drop H by my flat before she heads into the office. I want to catch her before anyone else gives her the news, and there is too much to tell to do it in a quick call. I come flying out of the kitchen when I hear her car pull into the gravelled drive in front of my flat.

Flinging open my front door, I pull Harry inside before she has time to remove her finger from the doorbell.

"Thank goodness you're finally here!" I say as I give her shoulders a quick squeeze of hello.

"Oi, missie," cries out a gruff voice. "Wot am I, chopped liver?

A few weeks away and she's forgotten 'er best mate. Left me 'ere... all on me Jack Jones, she did. And then she can't even be bothered ta say 'ello to a bruv."

H flaps his way into the flat, slapping me in the head with his wing on his way inside. Guess I should I have grabbed him in a hug first. He swoops down to land on the back of the couch, his talons threatening the cushions, wings arched and smoke swirling out of his nostrils.

I step back from Harry and spin towards the window seat, picking up a colourfully wrapped package. "If I forgot my best wyvern, then whom could this present be for?"

As I lay the package in front of H, his eyes grow wide, the smoke trailing off.

"Ya brought me a pressie? A real pressie?" he asks, his voice trembling.

"Of course I brought you back a gift. It's just a little something, don't get too excited." I shrug, looking to Harry to see if she has any insights as to why H is so emotional, but she appears to be as confused as I am.

H stares down at the glittery red bow on the top of the package. His claw carefully pulls the taped edges. "Ya don't understand, Nat. No one 'as ever brought me a gift."

I'm gobsmacked. In four hundred years, H has never received a present? "How is that possible?" I ask.

"Dunno, missie," he replies, slowly sliding the inner box from the wrappings. "Yer grandda wasn't tha gifting type, and yer gran didn't know I existed. The ole bag Lillian, well, we didn't 'ave tha same sorta friendship. She thought of me more as a pet, iffen ya know wot I mean."

When the wrapping paper reveals a sealed carton, H's patience runs out, his claws shredding the cardboard as though it were tissue paper. Inside sits a black metal pot on a thin metal stand. H flips it around a few times before giving up. "Ehh, Nat. It's not that I'm not grateful. But wot is this?"

"Maybe it will help if I get the second part of your gift. Stay here." I leave H scratching his head while I dash into the kitchen and pull a plastic-wrapped tray from my refrigerator. Thankfully, the yellow cheese inside survived the journey back from Switzerland without any problems.

H's eyes light up when I place a giant wedge of wrapped Gruyere at his feet. "Cheese! It doesn't look like Lincolnshire Poacher, but I'll take it all tha same. But wot does it 'ave ta do wiff tha pot?"

"I decided it was high time to broaden your horizons," I explain. "This is a Swiss cheese called Gruyere. You use the pot to melt it and then you dip food into it. It's called fondue."

Patting me on the back, Harry compliments me on my choice. "Oh, that's brilliant, Nat! Just brilliant! But where's the little oil lamp that goes with it?"

"What does a wyvern need with an oil lamp, Harry?" I nudge her before crossing over to H. Picking up the metal pot, I demonstrate how it works. "When you're ready to try it, I'll slice the cheese into the pot for you and you can use your flames to heat it up. Then you use bread to scoop it out to eat."

His eyes jump between the pot and the cheese, his brain working hard to picture the final result. "Could I use a sausage roll instead of bread?"

Patting him on the head, I nod a yes. It won't be traditional, but does it matter if you're talking about a four-hundred-year-old wyvern?

I leave H to assess his present, waving Harry to follow me into the kitchen for a cup of coffee. Leaning against the countertop, I recount the tale from the previous evening, starting with my meeting with Mathilde and ending with my arrival back at the flat in the wee hours. Harry's coffee grows cold, forgotten as she listens to the story, interjecting here and there to ask questions.

"My word, Nat. Poor Ms Evans. And our candlestick? What on earth was it doing at Barnard? And a secret chamber? It sounds like a movie!"

"I know, Harry. If I hadn't lived it firsthand, I'd have trouble believing it myself." I pace around the kitchen, struggling to fit the picture together. "Mathilde and I are almost positive the secret chamber has something to do with the problems with the magic, but we can't figure out how Ms Evans fits in. Why was she in the library in the first place? Why did the culprit leave the candlestick from St Margaret behind, particularly after all this time?"

Before she can formulate a response, Harry's phone rings. She mouths Dr Radcliffe's name as she presses the button to answer the call. Although I can only hear half of the conversation, it's clear that Dr Radcliffe is already aware of the previous night's events.

Harry barely says hello before I hear a faint metallic voice coming from her phone. "Yes," Harry says, "I heard. I'm here with Nat... "

She listens, her expression changing from one of concern to the telltale flush of anger. "Master Finch-Byron phoned you? He said what? Well, yes, I know it is our missing candlestick, but that hardly means we're at fault for the murder... Edward? Why Edward?"

Harry motions for a pen and paper. Digging in a nearby draw, I thrust a shopping list notepad and a pencil into her hands. She balances her phone on her shoulder, scribbling a quick note for me to read.

*"Master Finch-Byron has demanded Dr Radcliffe send Edward Thomas to oversee the investigation. Apparently his reputation extends beyond St Margaret."*

My mind races through the implications of having Edward searching around Barnard, hunting for connections between the two colleges. I wave my hands, begging Harry to find an excuse to hang up straightaway.

When Harry catches sight of my frantic movements, she fakes the sound of static and gets off the call. "Talk fast, Nat. Dr Radcliffe will no doubt ring me back."

"We can't have Edward poking his nose into the connection between St Margaret and Barnard." I resume my pacing as I tick off the reasons why. "What if he somehow ends up uncovering the magic? Won't he wonder why Mathilde and I are so interested in the contents of the secret chamber? You all say he's brilliant. If anyone could figure it out, it's him!"

Shaking her head, Harry interjects, "It's no good, Nat. He's already at Barnard. That's what Dr Radcliffe was telling me."

My eyes dart around the room as I hunt for a solution to this new problem. "We need someone to run interference, someone Edward would naturally confide in, who can steer him in a different direction if it seems like he's getting too close to uncovering the existence of the magic."

My eyes land on Harry as her phone begins ringing again. "We need you, Harry. Quick, figure out a way to get yourself assigned to Barnard as well!"

With a grimace, Harry answers the call. "Sorry about that Dr Radcliffe, the connection dropped. You were saying something about Edward?"

I grab the notepad to jot a quick note underneath Harry's. *"Could you offer to fill in as the Master's Assistant? Temporarily?"*

I can see Harry running the calculations in her head as she skims my note. She nods before returning her attention to the call. "We can't leave Edward on his own at Barnard, particularly if Master Finch-Byron is trying to lay the blame on our doorstep since the candlestick came from our college. We don't have anything major in the diary, just your standard start of term meetings and a few welcome dinners in the dining hall. If you can spare me, I think I should go to Barnard to help Edward."

There's a pause and then Harry continues on, "The Master is without an assistant at the moment. I can offer to fill in temporarily while they interview for a replacement. If you insist on it, he can hardly say no..."

I cross my fingers as I wait to hear the response, and watch as the tension bleeds out of Harry's shoulders. She gives me a thumbs up.

"I'll pop by the office first, we can sort out coverage here at St Margaret before I go to Barnard. See you in a few minutes. I'm on my way."

❖

Harry and I agree to meet at lunch, by which time she hopes to be Barnard. After I lock my back door behind her, I turn to find H sitting on the kitchen table, a worried frown on his snout.

"Lor luv a duck, Nat. I can't believe thar's been another murder. Did ya talk ta any of the Barnard Eternals last night?"

I shrug, unable to explain their absence. "Neither Mathilde nor I saw any sign of them, and we were keeping our eyes peeled."

"Really? Then 'urry up, mate," H urges, flapping out of the kitchen into the front room. "We need ta get over thar. Iffen thar's a problem with tha magic, maybe something 'appened ta tha Eternals!"

H's words spur me to move even faster. I dial Mathilde's mobile as H and I make our way towards Barnard, launching into an update as soon as she answers.

"...So that's what's happened on my end. H and I are on our way, but I've got a full day of meetings with the Barnard staff and my assistants, Will and Jill. It's supposed to be our introduction day." I pause at a red light to catch my breath. "Is there any chance you can go back to Barnard today, maybe stake out the library and keep an eye on Edward?"

"I hope so," she replies. "I'm on my way into the Bodleian. I called an urgent meeting with the Head of the Library this morning. I'm hoping I can convince her to assign me to catalogue the contents of the secret chamber. With a little luck and a nudge from the magic, she should give her approval."

"That's fab news, Mathilde." My stomach unclenches for the first time this morning. "If you're stationed in the Barnard library, Harry's with the Master, and H and I are running around, we should be able to keep a close eye on Edward no matter where he goes. Not to mention, we can investigate the crime and learn more about the origins of the magic of Oxford."

"Fingers crossed, Nat. I'm at the door to the Bod, I better run. If all goes well, I'll join you, Harry and H for lunch."

Shoving my phone back into my handbag, I look up to see the stone walls of Barnard towering in front of us. H shoots a jet of flames in front of me, his not so subtle way of calling our walk to a sudden halt.

"Where did ya say ya found tha secret chamber?"

Together, our heads track the line of the masonry from bottom to top, left to right.

Pointing towards a set of stained glass windows, I say, "I remember those windows from last night, so that must be the room where the old library is located. But the secret chamber is on the other side of the building. I can't imagine how it remained hidden all this time."

H remains silent, deep in thought as we cross the street and enter the college through the main entrance. Although it is still early, the small door stands open, ready to welcome visitors and students inside. In a few hours, this entrance will be a mad house as the students return from the Christmas break and once again move their belongings into the college rooms.

The narrow entrance provides a shortcut from the front of the main building to the back; a glimpse of the perfectly groomed gardens is visible from the road. H is still fixated on the chamber, flying ahead of me into the gardens to see the far side of the library. Once again, I pick out a stained-glass window, my finger tracing the line of stone between it and another leaded window further along the façade.

"It must be there, in the gap where a window should be. There's a chimney further up, everyone must have assumed that the empty space was where the ground floor fireplace gradually narrowed as it climbed to the top. The room is in between the windows, maybe three meters wide and two meters long."

Letting out a smokey whistle, H mutters, "That's a penny-come-quick iffen I ever saw one. Right clever, whoever came up wiff that idea. No wonder it stayed 'idden for so long."

Satisfied with this information, H flaps back in the direction of the main hall. "Iffen we 'urry, can we stop by the library? We need ta check on the Eternals."

I check my watch, confirming we can spare some time before my first meeting of the day. "I don't know if it will be open, but it's worth a check."

I let H fly ahead of me as I climb the stone stairs to the next floor up. A bulky security guard stands outside the library, his back leaning against the door and his head focused on the mobile phone in his hands. Before I can call him back, H swoops through the stairwell doorway and along the hallway, coming to a hovering stop next to the security guard. He whispers something in his ear, and within seconds, the guard pockets his phone and marches off in the opposite direction. H waves me over, urging me to hurry as he holds the library door open.

As I slide inside the narrow opening, I ask, "What did you say to the guard? And how did he hear you?"

"I told 'im it was time for a loo break. I can make myself 'eard iffen I need ta be. But get moving. We won't 'ave long ta look around."

I guide H along the library corridor, recounting the story from when I first spotted the book lying abandoned in the floor until I came upon the pile of manuscripts covering Ms Evan's body. The aisle is easy to identify, a few strips of yellow police tape barring anyone from entering until the police finish collecting evidence.

I have little interest in staring at the now empty floor. I prod H to move on. "The secret chamber is further ahead. Follow me."

H takes one look into the little chamber before loosing a giant sneeze that sends him careening backwards and into the side of a bookshelf while a fireball rolls in the opposite direction. Thankfully, the magic extinguishes the flames and restores the carpet.

"Get a hold of yourself!" I chastise H. "You don't want to set fire to what might be our only set of clues about how Oxford's magic works, do you? We need to get out of here before your sniffles get the better of you again."

Before H can respond, the sound of the library door shutting echoes through the otherwise empty library. I freeze in place as heavy footsteps get louder, moving in our direction. My eyes widen when a shadow stretches from the end of the nearest aisle, looming larger and growing closer with every step. When a tall man appears, I can't help the small squeak which escapes from my lips.

"Nat? Is that you? What are you doing here?" Confusion colours Edward's gaze as he takes in my frozen state and H lying nearby. Once again, I'm grateful all Edward can see is a cat and not a small black wyvern huffing smoke from his nostrils.

Seeing H gives me an idea. "It's the cat's fault. I was on my way to a meeting when he darted off. The library door was cracked, he dashed inside before I could catch him."

Edward's face clears, seemingly buying into my excuse. "I don't understand why your cat follows you to work, but never mind that. I'm glad I caught you. I spoke with Master Finch-Byron this morning. He's asked me to oversee the investigation on behalf of the college. I can't say I relish the task, but he left me no room to decline."

Pointing at H, I reply, "Yes, I heard the news from Harry. Dr Radcliffe phoned her as she was dropping my cat by the flat. It appears we're right back into the deep end."

Edward grimaces. "Are you okay? The Master said you found Ms Evan's last night."

"I'd like to say I'm fine, but I'm not. I tossed and turned most of the night. I'll need lots of coffee today, but hopefully tonight I'll manage to get some rest." I lift my head to look Edward in the eye. "Thanks for asking."

Edward shrugs off my thanks, an apologetic frown replacing the friendly look on his face. "I wouldn't ask if I didn't have to, but can you tell me what happened?"

I close my eyes, casting my mind back. A shiver skims up my back as I remember my first glimpse of the expensive, red-soled high heel. Some part of me knew straight away that it had to be Ms Evans. Sensing my discomfort, H leaps over, leaning his scaly back against my leg and wrapping his spiky tail around my other ankle. Slowly, I recount the scene to Edward, pausing to allow him to make notes of my words. When I finish, my breath rushes out in a jagged huff.

Edward reaches towards me, but stops himself short, unsure of whether any contact would be appropriate. I give him a wobbly grin, trying desperately to reassure us both that I'm okay.

Running his fingers through his tousled hair, he rereads his notes, stopping to formulate his next question. "You were with Mathilde, right?"

I nod my confirmation.

"And she is employed by the Bodleian? That's how you two gained access out of hours?"

I nod again.

"This all seems straightforward, except for one element. Why did the two of you need to meet here at Barnard so late in the evening, particularly before term starts?" Edward waits, pen in hand, for my response. One more note to add to his paper.

I return to the excuse I provided to the Master and the Detective Inspector the night before. Consistency is key, any differences will no doubt catch Edward's interest. "As you know, I'm tasked with organising Barnard's women's celebration event. I wanted to spend time researching the college's history, and Mathilde suggested we start in the archives."

"But why yesterday? Why so late?" Edward asks.

"There was no specific reason or rationale behind it. Mathilde and I were both back from our holidays. She said the library would be empty..." My voice trails off as I shrug. "It seemed like a good idea at the time."

"And you didn't know anything about the secret chamber? You didn't see it until the Master pointed it out?"

I answer honestly, "No, it is safe to say that neither Mathilde nor I knew Barnard was hiding a secret chamber within its walls. When we realised Ms Evans wasn't breathing, we hightailed it back to the front desk and called security."

As Edward's pen traces my words into his notebook, I glance at my watch, looking for an excuse to call an end to his questioning. "Wow, will you look at that! The morning is running away from me." Scooping H into my arms, I ask Edward if he minds if we go.

My first meeting isn't for another twenty minutes, but we still need to find out if anything has happened to Barnard's Eternals.

❖

I whisper to H as we speed walk along the corridor, "Any clues where we might find an Eternal around here? With a building this old, I assumed they'd flood the hallways."

H skids to a stop in front of a door labelled 'Old Common Room', waiting for me to twist the handle to let us inside. "This used ta be for tha college Fellows, but now they've got a new space. One of the portraits in 'ere ought ta 'ave something ta say."

As we enter the room, my eye is immediately pulled towards a life-size painting of a medieval woman gracing the far wall. A nearby plaque lists her name as Lady Petronilla of Lewis, wife of Sir Osbert Barnard. Although the setting and clothing mark her as a woman of great standing, her face is young, her skin unlined. I'd guess her age to be no more than thirty.

She is seated in an ornate chair, a small book in her lap indicating her education and standing in society. Large curtains drape behind her, the rest of the painted room is simple wooden walls. The shape of her face and eyes seems almost modern, but the wimple framing them allows for no doubt as to the time period in which she lived.

H shouts over my shoulder, hovering high enough to look into the eyes of the woman in the portrait. "Oi, Petra, are ya there?"

"Thou needn't shout," chastises the woman as she rises from her chair and holds out a hand to let H help her descend from the painting onto the floor in before us. Her ruby-coloured dress looks simple, but the bejewelled neckline and the silk fabric of her billowing white wimple testify to her wealth.

I'm waiting until her feet are firmly on the ground before introducing myself, but H jumps in before I can say a word.

"Nat, meet Lady Petronilla of Lewis. Wife of Sir Osbert Barnard. Mother of a king. And the moneybags behind this 'ere institution. Petra, meet Nat, our newest prefect."

Lady Petronilla lowers her head in a quick nod of introduction. For some inexplicable reason, I find myself falling into a small curtsy, my head nodding hello in return. I rise to my feet, face flushed with colour, hoping I haven't embarrassed myself.

"It's my pleasure to meet you, Lady Petronilla. I'll be working here for the next term organising the celebration of the forty-fifth anniversary of the first female students at Barnard. As one of the most important women in the college's history, I hope to get the chance to get to know you better. But first, I cannot tell you how happy H and I are to see you are okay."

"Well met, Nat. I am also much relieved to see thee. There was much hue and cry in the eventide. Prithee, dost thou knoweth what happened?"

Once again, I launch into my story, but this time I explain why Mathilde and I were in the archives outside of hours, hoping Lady Petronilla may have some insights. When I finish, the expression on Lady Petronilla's face is grave.

"Yea, I know the woman of whom thou dost speak. She was beauteous on the outside, but her inner self was nay so comely. And yet, she dost not deserve such a terrible end. I shall pray for her soul."

After a moment of silence, Lady Petronilla continues, "I know of thine secret chamber. I remember well the eventide when the strapping young lads came up with the idea to hide away their work. They met in this room, asking my help with finding a suitable locale."

Gasping, I interrupt, "Do you remember who they were? Or what they hid away?" This could be just the clue we need to know whether we're looking in the right direction.

"I fear not. I have passed too many centuries within these walls, and many years have passed ere that day."

I look to H for guidance, but all he has to offer is a shrug. I'm sure he understands better than I can how easily the years can run together when you've seen so many of them.

Seeing my disappointment, Lady Petronilla offers up some good news. "Mayhap I can provide assistance with the events of yesterday? Permit me to call my lady's maid." Looking over her shoulder, Lady Petronilla calls into the painting. "Ada? Ada, I have need of thee."

A slim figure slips from behind the curtained wall which provided the backdrop of the image. Surprisingly, Ada appears older than Lady Petronilla, faint lines framing her eyes and mouth. Her dress is simpler, made of a coarse muslin with a woollen vest laced over the top. She takes a small leap from the painting frame, landing soundlessly behind her ladyship.

Once more focusing on us, Lady Petronilla provides the introductions. After nods of hello, she explains why she called Ada to join us. "We end each sabbath with a quiet meditation here. Attendance is nay mandatory, yet most Eternals choose to join us. Pray tell, Ada, doth thee remember if anyone failed to join yesterday?"

H and I watch with bated breath as Ada cocks her head to the side, her eyes cast to the ceiling while searching her memory. "Yea, my lady. There was one lad missing. Brother Simon."

Frowning, Lady Petronilla clasps her hands together, explaining, "I'm nay certain how much assistance Brother Simon will yield. However, it is worth the request. As thou shalt soon see, he is old-fashioned in his values, and only answers to me as I am the Lady of the house. Humphrey, pray seek him on our behalf."

With a salute, H soars across the room, flying into the fireplace. Seconds later, a young man floats through the nearby wall, his features hidden under the cowl of his deep brown robe. A rope belt marks his waist, a rosary hanging down from it proclaiming his status as a member of the church.

In a cloud of ash, H flaps out of the hearth. "I didn't 'ave ta look far. The bloke was eavesdropping in tha next room."

Lady Petronilla waves him closer. "Well met, Simon. Thou shalt have heard the hue and cry yesterday. A young woman has left the earth. Thou wert not here with us. Pray tell, didst thou see anything which may be of use in identifying her killer?"

Reaching up a hand, Simon slips the cowl from his forehead, his face emerging from the shadows. His sharp nose is flared, his eyebrows drawn into an angry spike. His disapproval of me is evident as his gaze travels down my body. I see now what her lady-ship meant. Simon's view of women has obviously not evolved since the fourteenth century.

When he finally responds, he sneers out his words. "Yea, I saw it all. Fie upon her head. She deserved her ending for what she did that eventide."

Our faces echo a look of surprise. H is the first to recover. "Wot is wrong wiff ya? Nobody deserves to die. Iffen ya know who did it, ya need to tell us. Now!" A jet of flame punctuates his last word.

Brother Simon's only response is to laugh in our faces as he floats out of the room. There's no point chasing him down; he isn't likely to go further than the college walls. Until he's ready to share what he knows, nothing we can do will convince him to speak sooner.

I survey the remaining group, shocked expressions colouring everyone's faces. "Well, that wasn't what I expected to hear, but at least he's given us a clue of sorts. Ms Evans was involved in something questionable. I guess it's up to us to figure out what he meant."

Ada pipes up from behind Lady Petronilla with a suggestion. "Mayhap thou shalt wish to speak with Lucy James. She was the Master's previous assistant. I saw her yesterday eventide with the Chaplain."

# Chapter Three

I think it is my frantic toe-tapping that finally wraps up my last morning meeting, but I'm in too much of a hurry to get to the dining hall to care. I speed walk across the college quadrangle until I spy its stained-glass windows looming in the distance.

The pale-yellow stone of the Hall, as it is known, seems nearly white under the overcast winter sky, the surrounding trees bare of leaves. The lawn must be lush in the spring and summer months, but for now the temperature is too low to think about relaxing on any of the wooden benches dotted around it.

The quadrangle gardens are full of people in marked contrast to the quiet of the night before. Students stumble along the pathways, their arms filled with boxes and bags as they move back into the dormitories. H takes particular glee in winding around their legs.

I notice he carefully selects his targets, picking the men who seem more interested in showing off their muscles than offering a hand to others. I swallow a laugh and let H carry on with his entertainment.

Following behind, I stride past the wide stone staircase which leads to the historic dining hall, carrying on towards the informal cafe housed underneath. I can barely wait to get inside to hear the latest news from Harry. As she hoped, Master Finch-Byron accepted Dr Radcliffe's suggestion that Harry fill in as his assistant for the next few weeks. Harry sent a text letting me know she'd arrived at Barnard and had another good news update. I've been desperate to catch her since my phone buzzed with her message.

The cafe is busy with students and staff, the delicious smells explaining why so many people have chosen to lunch here. Mathilde and Harry are tucked away at a round table in a corner, steaming bowls of soup at the ready. Harry slides one in my direction as soon as I get seated, while Mathilde passes a plate of sausage rolls over to H.

"You didn't have to buy me lunch, Harry," I say in between spoonfuls. "If anything, I owe you a meal in thanks for finding a way to come to Barnard with us."

Harry waves off my thanks. "Don't worry, you can pick up the next one. We're in a bit of a rush, which is why Mathilde and I decided to order for the two of you as well. We're meeting Kate in the secret chamber fifteen minutes from now."

"Kate!" I gasp. "How did you manage that? Is this your good news?"

Reaching for the butter, Mathilde jumps in, "Oh, it's better than that, Nat. Harry is practically a magician. You are not going to believe what she's arranged."

"Well stop chatterin' and let 'er get a word in, Tildy." H punctuates his words by shooting a jet of fire, melting the butter right off Mathilde's knife. I barely manage to hold back my snicker.

Harry finishes her bite of soup before offering an explanation. "The Master was fit to be tied when I arrived this morning. He's adamant that nothing about the death or the secret chamber get leaked outside of the college. That's why he asked Dr Radcliffe to send Edward over; he's all but barred the police department from setting foot back inside."

"So how did you convince him to let another person in?" I ask.

"I cornered him in his office, making him sit down with a cup of tea and a digestive biscuit. When his mouth was full of biscuit crumbs, I leapt in with the suggestion that he hand-select a small team of experts to catalogue the contents of the secret chamber. If there is something of real value, he could capitalise upon the announcement."

With a glance in Mathilde's direction, she continues, "Mathilde was the obvious choice from the Bod, particularly since she already knows the chamber exists. I told him he shouldn't settle for less than Kate, art historian and Director of the Ashmolean Museum, given the potential finds among the artwork. He took the bait and just like that, Kate had an invitation to join us."

I nudge Mathilde, murmuring, "Is it wrong that I want to take out my notebook and write all this down?"

Mathilde shakes her head. "Definitely not wrong. There's a lot we could learn from Harry if we could follow her around for a day or two."

After rolling her eyes, Harry waves us to hurry up with our lunch. I slurp down the final spoonfuls, tilting my bowl up to block the view of H demolishing his sausage rolls. He and I need to have a conversation about table etiquette if he's going to be a regular at our mealtimes.

Despite our rushed lunch, Kate is already inside the chamber when we arrive in the old library. After a round of hellos, we all climb into the chamber, crowding together in the tiny floor space. Someone has run an electric line inside and hung a couple of lights. They've pushed the crates aside, but there is barely room for the four of us to stand. H is forced to hover above our heads, his wings flapping gently as he floats from one side of the space to the other.

Kate's eyes shine as she takes in the stacks of covered paintings with their cloth and paper wrappers hiding their contents. "Harry, thank you so much for convincing Master Finch-Byron to invite me in. This could be the find of a career. I'd be devastated if I had to stand on the sidelines and let someone else discover what's hidden behind these wrappings. There could be unknown works by Renaissance masters or portraits of never before seen historical figures or..."

H interrupts her before she can go any further down that rabbit hole. "Lor luv, Kate. We get it. Old paintings. But that ain't all there is. Don't forget about the books, the antiques and whatever else is tucked away. 'Opefully there's also information about Oxford's magic somewhere in 'ere."

In silence, we each lean left and right, peering around our small group to take in the magnitude of the contents spread around us. Books and notebooks, covers tattered and frayed, are piled up around the edge. Old wooden crates dot the room, their contents a mystery. The wall farthest from the entrance is lined with shelves packed with oddly shaped, cloth-covered bundles.

"Kate, Mathilde... please tell me this isn't like an architectural site," I gulp. "You're not going to spend weeks diagramming the room before you move anything, are you?"

A booming male voice speaks up behind me. "Absolutely not. You've got two weeks at the maximum."

I nearly jump out of my skin when Master Finch-Byron's face appears in the chamber's entry. He nods his head in a silent instruction for all of us to climb out and join him in the library.

One by one, we pick our way back to the small opening, leaving H inside.

Harry oversees the introductions, trying and failing to wipe the glower off of the Master's face.

"I won't ask you to sign confidentiality agreements given you are all already bound by your contracts with the University." He looks us each in the eye, until we nod our understanding. "I do not want word of this discovery leaking out until I am ready to make a formal announcement. Given the police presence last night, it is only a matter of time before someone lets slip. Therefore, this project mustn't be your top priority. It is your *only* priority."

All business, Kate adopts a confident expression before replying. "I've cleared my diary. However, two weeks is not nearly enough time given a find of this magnitude. We need weeks, maybe even a month to prepare a catalogue. Only then can we start to look at each object in detail."

Mathilde adds her agreement. "The books and notebooks appear to be hundreds of years old. I'll have to use extreme care when handling them or we risk damaging them beyond repair."

Master Finch-Byron's face flushes with a florid red, his disagreement clear. "You have two weeks to find something of value so I can make a grand unveiling to our most important donors. Getting a first look and the chance to sponsor the public event could garner thousands of pounds in donations. The more I can keep attention focused on the good news, the higher the likelihood that Ms Evan's death stays out of the limelight. Is that clear? Or do I need to find someone who can work faster?"

I can tell that Kate wants to argue, but Harry squeezes her arm, reminding her of our own reasons for wanting to be involved. We can't afford to lose our chance to go through the materials looking for information on the origin of the magic.

Satisfied, the Master turns his attention in my direction. "I'm glad you're here, Ms Payne. I want you to organise the private reveal event, in addition to the celebration next month. Harry can assist you with the invitations and anything else you need."

I fight back a smile, hardly believing my good fortune. I'd been wondering how we'd justify my presence in the chamber, but the Master has handed me the perfect excuse. I copy Kate's professional stance, shoulders squared and back straight. I've got to play this just right. "I'll be very busy with the celebration planning, but I will do my best, Master Finch-Byron."

"I have high expectations, Ms Payne, particularly after hearing about the gala you organised at St Margaret last term. I'm sure you'll find a way to get everything done to an equivalent standard."

When his gaze moves onto Harry, I cast a worried glance at Mathilde. St Margaret's gala had indeed been a magical affair, particularly since I staffed it with a team of Eternals and got the college's famed dead chef to provide the catering. It's hardly a trick I could pull off again. I do my best to ignore the drip of sweat sliding down my back.

Two extremely high-profile events within a few weeks of one another, and the first has to be kept a secret. Harry and I are going to have our hands full.

❖

When Harry and Master Finch-Byron finally take their leave, I have to sprint across the college grounds to my office. It's hidden away in the back corner of one of the Victorian buildings, considered new only by comparison with the medieval main hall and old library. I flash my badge over the card reader, tugging open the building door when it flashes from red to green.

My office is the first door on the right. I quickly unlock the door and slip inside. Striding across the room, I reach my desk and pick up the phone to ring my assistants. Will answers on the second ring and promises to come straight over. As Will and Jill are only a few doors down, they appear at my desk before I can settle into my chair.

Having caught up with them this morning, I'm able to jump straight into a diary review. "Something rather unexpected has come up, which is going to require my attention for the next two weeks. Master Finch-Byron has asked for my help with a special project, and unfortunately I can't delegate any of the work."

Jill nods her head, replying, "As long as we don't have to do like we did last term at St Margaret and interview every chef within a fifty-mile radius, I'm happy to take on some extra work."

"No chef problems this time, Jill," I promise. "Since you two did such a phenomenal job organising all of the logistics behind St Margaret's autumn gala, I thought you could do the same again for the Barnard celebration."

Will scribbles some notes on his page before looking up. "That works for me. Jill and I can divvy up the event prep tasks as before." Will glances over at Jill. "That okay with you, Jill? You can handle the table, chair and marquee rental and I'll work on catering and entertainment."

Nodding, Jill agrees. "Hopefully we can use some of the same vendors again. That will save us some effort."

Smiling, I consult my own notebook. "Okay, so if you two have logistics, I'll focus my efforts on the theme and the finishing touches."

"Theme?" asks Jill. "I thought the theme was a celebration of the first female students. What's left to research?"

"We're honouring the first female students," I confirm. "However, how we choose to recognise them is up to us. I don't think a line of portraits and a few speakers is going to do it. We'll need something more if we want to make this a celebration worthy of the college archives."

On that note, I send the two of them off to our scheduled meeting with the Barnard College groundskeepers to discuss possible locations for a marquee. The problem with all of the older colleges is that other than the dining halls, none of them have an indoor space large enough to allow for a big event.

Celebration planning now in hand, I take a few minutes to catch up on my emails and to send my apologies for the rest of the day's meetings. I make sure to quote the Master's name liberally, knowing no one will question the last minute change in plans if they think I am acting at his orders.

In less than an hour, I'm back at the foot of the worn stone staircase that leads up to the old library. Shivering in the cold, I fly up the stairs and along the hallway until I reach the library doors. This time I don't need H to distract the guard; he waves me inside without any hesitation.

I can hear Mathilde and Kate chatting away as soon as I enter the room, their faint voices indicating they must be back inside the secret chamber. I should have guessed. With so little time, they've jumped right into the action.

"Oi, Nat! Watch this!" H calls out before swooping from the top of one of the nearby shelves. I stand aghast as he treats the shelving like a parkour course. He bounces off one shelf before flipping in mid-air. With a sharp talon, he grabs a hold of one of the leather-bound books, his claw ripping the binding in half. Thankfully, the magic repairs it before my eyes.

Before I can cry for him to stop, he hits the ground and immediately rebounds, leaping from book to book until he reaches the top again. From there, he wraps his legs around one of the shelf ladders. He tucks his head and wings in tight, spinning head over heels three times before making a perfect dismount.

Standing at my feet, he takes a bow and awaits a round of applause.

"Been a little bored without me?" I ask.

"I tried to 'elp but the two missies kicked me out of the chamber when I accidentally ashed one of the crates. It wasn't my fault, 'onest! There's so much dust in there. Plus, it reappeared right away," he harrumphs.

I give his forehead a quick stroke in sympathy. I can't imagine being willingly cooped up in there for days on end. After an hour, I'd probably end up turning the library into an obstacle course as well. There's a reason I chose events and not history as my specialism.

When I stick my head inside, I spot Kate first. Her perfectly coiffed hair is in sweaty disarray, her white collared shirt streaked with dust. I scan across the space to find Mathilde in a similar condition. Both are wearing plastic gloves and handling every item they touch with exquisite care. I call out a hello, startling both of them.

"How's it going? Any luck so far?" My hopeful smile fades when it is met with frowns.

"Two weeks, Nat, to go through all of these books and journals? It would be impossible under the best of circumstances. Once Master Finch-Byron reveals the discovery of the secret chamber, he'll have dozens of experts requesting access to the find. If that wasn't bad enough, look at this!" Mathilde crawls across the floor towards another towering stack of leather-bound tomes. With a halting precision, she lifts the top three books, exposing a stack of loose paper underneath. "There are dozens of sheets of paper, all handwritten, that appear to be torn from the notebooks. But which notebook? And who wrote them? How am I supposed to figure this out fast? Even if I could perfectly read olde English writing, it would still take ages."

Kate points to a pair of unwrapped sculptures standing on a

shelf. "I'm trying to be as methodical as I can; thus far I've only opened two items. Two, out of all of these!" She waves an arm at the packed shelf and scattered crates.

"Do you recognise the artist? Or the time period? Anything which might help us date the contents?" I ask.

"My best guess is late 17th century, but I'd need to get them to my lab to be sure." Kate pauses to pick one up. "There's something strange about them. They're heavy, heavier than they should be given the material used."

I look over at Mathilde, but she shrugs. "What does that mean?"

"Maybe something... maybe nothing. But it's weird. Everything about this chamber is weird. Hidden for years, discovered and potentially burglarised in the same night. Everywhere I look I find more questions than answers. I'm with Mathilde. There is no way we can catalogue all this in two weeks time without help."

Shaking my head, I mutter, "We already know what the Master will say to that request. If only there was a way to sneak some of your team in here..." I pause when a sharp talon pokes the back of my leg. "H? Did you need something?"

"Are ya forgettin' someone? Iffen ya need a team of specialists, you've got a whole group of Eternals sittin' around in the college 'alls. Who better ta read the writin' than someone who used ta do it everyday?"

I scoop H up into a big hug, taking care not to crush his wings despite his struggles to get free. "You're brilliant, H! Of course, the Eternals! Do you think they'd help?"

H shoots a narrow jet of flame, singing off the fine hairs on my arm. With a screech, I loosen my hold. Brushing himself off, he replies, "Will they 'elp? Of course they will, that's their main reason fer being. Let me go find Petra."

H dashes back into the library and out into the hallway, the sound of the library door closing echoing behind him. Within minutes he's back again, this time with Lady Petronilla and her lady's maid, Ada, behind him.

After a quick round of introductions, Mathilde explains the situation, showing Lady Petronilla the loose sheaves of torn paper and the still-wrapped paintings and objects.

Lady Petronilla surveys the scene before stepping away to confer with Ada. My shoulders tighten as their whispered conversation draws out, and I can see Mathilde and Kate react the same way.

Finally, the two women nod in agreement. Lady Petronilla takes a deep breath before gracing us with a smile. "Thou mustn't be overwrought or pitchkettled. By my troth, we shall provide all possible assistance. Mathilde, I can aid thee with the written word. Kate, Ada has a fine eye for art. Where needed, we may ask our other Eternals to lend a hand, drawing on their individual areas of expertise."

If Mathilde and Kate's answering grins are any indication, Lady Petronilla's offer is a godsend. That sorted, I turn my attention to my mobile, which is buzzing away in my pocket. I give the incoming message a quick read, pleased to see that Harry has once again come through.

"Come on, H. You and I have a meeting with the woman who used to be Master Finch-Byron's assistant before Ms Evans arrived. Harry tracked her down and now she's expecting to meet us in the middle common room for a coffee."

H perks up, his wings flapping as he flies ahead of me. "I remember the old bag. Sounds boring. But, if you promise I can get some chockie biscuits, I'll keep ya company."

# Chapter Four

The middle common room at Barnard is the space set aside for college staff who are not quite senior enough to enjoy membership in the senior common room, but equally have no desire to spend time with the undergraduate students in the junior common room. It is appropriately medium-sized, furnished with comfortable sofas and a few small tables with chairs. The one thing it doesn't have is a high-end latte machine like the one I enjoyed at St Margaret. I make a mental note to ask Harry to add this to her To Do list. If anyone can solve this problem, it's her.

I don't have any trouble identifying Lucy James, the woman who held the role of personal assistant to the college master prior to Ms Evan's arrival, because there are only two people in the common room - an older woman with fluffy white hair and a young man wearing a turban. After a quick process of elimination, I stride across the room, holding out my hand to introduce myself. H beelines for the cookie tin instead. No surprises there.

"Hello, you must be Mrs James. I'm Natalie Payne. Thanks so much for making time for me."

She returns my handshake with a firm grip, her eyes twinkling with delight. If you dressed her in red wool, you'd swear she was

Mrs Claus in the flesh. Her cheeks are rosy, and a friendly smile is spread across her face.

"You're welcome, but I profess I'm not entirely sure why you wanted to meet. Harry didn't explain much on the phone." She nudges a plate of cookies in my direction before passing me a cup of tea.

Thanks to my experiences interviewing potential suspects at St Margaret last term, I'm much better prepared this time around. You never know who the guilty party might be, so it is best to have a safe starting point for any conversations. In this case, Harry provided a few suggestions to help me on my way.

"I'm organising next month's celebration of the anniversary of Barnard's first female students, and I'm hoping to find a unique angle for the event," I explain as I add a spot of milk to my tea. "I understand you were here when they arrived."

"Yes, it was my first month at the college, if you can believe it. I was twenty years old, a newly recruited member of the typing pool. It was so exciting, watching those young women arrive."

I interrupt her with a question. "You must have been close in age to them, right?"

"One year older, but it felt like a lifetime. There they were, starting at the uni, their futures still a blank canvas. And here I was, in my professional dress, sitting behind a desk worrying whether I'd make enough to pay the rent on my flat." Mrs James chuckles to herself, lost in the memory. "On that first day, I think most all of us would have given anything to be standing in their shoes. By the second day, we were glad we weren't."

Taking in her wry smile, I wonder what she's not saying. "What do you mean? What happened?"

She waves off my question, "Oh nothing big. More of a series of small things. The men harassed them; the professors gave them extra tough exams. It was death by a thousand cuts, but I have to give those women credit. They stuck in there and made it out to the other side, rewriting the history books with their every success."

On that thought, we pause to sip our tea and nibble on a biscuit. In between bites, I ask, "Forty-five years later, you're still here. Has Barnard changed much?"

Mrs James glances around the room, reassuring herself that no one else is within listening distance. The man who was here earlier left shortly after I arrived, and H has curled up to sleep in a sunny patch on the hardwood floor. Leaning in closer, she murmurs, "Institutions like Barnard don't change. The old stone walls are resistant to all efforts to the contrary. Take Lady Petronilla for example. I assume you've heard of her? Hundreds of years ago she ensured the college would live on, providing funding and support, but it's her husband's name on the front of the building. Men still rule the roost here and we women will always remain hidden away in the background. Don't let the male to female student ratios fool you. I played the game for as long as I could. Longer than I ever thought I would, if I'm honest."

"I take it you're referring to stepping down as assistant to the Master?" I confirm.

"Shoved down would be more accurate," she replies. "Less than six months from my retirement, after twenty-five years in the role, in walks Ms Evans in her towering high heels, and the next thing I know I'm put out to pasture."

I shake my head at the situation, the injustice clear as day. "I take it you weren't a fan of hers, then?"

Mrs James huffs in response, folding her arms across her chest. Her cheeks flame again, this time in anger. "Master Finch-Byron claimed he wanted to make my last few months easier, relieving me of the stress of managing his affairs. It would have been nice if he'd at least thought to ask me for my thoughts before presenting the situation as a fait accompli. Ms Evans made it clear from day one that she had no need of my help or my friendship. She only had time for the Master and the men who buzzed around her."

Nodding, I say, "I only met her the once, but my experience was much the same."

A small smile ghosts across Mrs James face. "Thanks, that makes an old biddy like me feel somewhat better..." Her voice trails off for a moment before she continues, "Nonetheless, it's a terrible thing what happened to her. To think, I was a few buildings away, having my monthly dinner with the Chaplain, and she was lying dead in the old library. We didn't hear a sound, not even a hint of something being awry."

"Yes," I agree. "It's strange that she was in the library after hours, particularly given it was closed during the holidays. I certainly didn't expect to find anyone else there. I wonder what she was doing..." I let my voice trail off, hoping Mrs James will fill in the gap.

Mrs James shakes her head. "I can't think of a single valid reason for her to be there on her own. She must have been meeting someone. I had heard she was seeing someone... you know, romantically. Maybe they met up there looking for a private spot."

Aha! Exactly the type of information I need. "Do you know who she was seeing?"

When Mrs James looks unsure, I add, "I happen to know Professor Edward Thomas. Master Finch-Byron sent an all-staff announcement yesterday explaining that Edward is leading on the investigation now. You must have seen it. Edward asked me to keep my ear to the ground and pass along anything I hear. I'm sure he'd appreciate any leads you can offer." I leave unspoken the fact that I'm more likely to check them out than pass them on. If something pans out, I'll make sure Edward is the first to know.

"Let me think..." Mrs James drums her fingers on the table, her eyes cast towards the ceiling. "There was one young man who

I spotted with her a few times. Charles Graves, one of our graduate researchers. You might try him."

My mission accomplished, I refresh our teas and spend the next twenty minutes asking her questions about the recent history of the college. Her earlier story about the first class of female students has given me an idea for the celebration theme. By the time my phone pings with a reminder for my meeting with Harry, I've got pages of notes I can use in my celebration planning.

Harry and I spend the rest of the afternoon in my office reviewing the college's donor archives, getting an idea of whom we may need to invite to the private unveiling of the contents of the secret chamber. The attendees will have first rights to sponsor a public unveiling and to potentially purchase any items the college chooses to sell.

Unsurprisingly, there is a mix of Lords and Dames, a Saudi prince, and a shortlist of the nouveau riche whose net worth might allow them to make the cut. We agree to cap the number of invitations at ten, ensuring both the exclusivity and intimacy of the event.

After Harry promises to send a tray of sandwiches to Mathilde and Kate to tide them over while they work long into the night, I head off to track H down in the college gardens. He promised he'd stay within the walls of the Master's Garden, so he shouldn't be too hard to find.

The door to the college chapel stands ajar, warm light spilling out onto the stone pavement. I give a quick glance inside, but it is empty. No doubt, the chaplain has left it open in case any students need a quiet haven from the busy dormitories. Beyond it, the Master's Garden lies in shadows, the faint moonlight providing little illumination. It's only six pm, but it feels like midnight.

I stand on my tiptoes, peering around the shrubs and whisper-shouting H's name. A soft scuff sounds from behind me; I spin to see who is there. "H, is that you? I'm ready to go home now. Come on!"

The back of my neck itches with the feeling of being watched, but no matter where I look, I can't find anyone. Up ahead, the rattle of branches signals H's arrival, his scaly hide backing out from underneath one of the evergreen shrubs. When he sees me standing there, he drops something out of his mouth and quickly kicks it out of sight.

"What was... wait, never mind. I don't want to know. Are you ready to go now?" I ask.

"I'm starvin' over here," mutters H while rubbing his stomach. "Those chockie biscuits didn't last very long. It's about time you and 'Arry finished yer yappin'. What's fer supper?"

"I'm feeling pretty peckish myself. Let's see, the last time I went to the market was back in December... so takeout? Curry or Chinese?"

We spend most of the walk planning our takeout order. H's appetite is bottomless; I'm already dreading the number of poppadoms I'll have to pay for, not to mention his request for a mango lassie. When we wait for a light, once again the feeling of eyes on my back sends chills down my spine. I surreptitiously look around, but the people nearest us are lost in their own conversations. No one seems to be interested in me or H, not even in the slightest.

H huffs a scorching breath on the backs of my legs when I fail to notice the cross walk sign illuminate. "Wot's wrong wiff ya, Nat? Why do ya keep lookin' around everywhere? Are ya expecting someone?"

"I'm not expecting anyone, but I can't help feeling like someone is watching me."

H flaps into the air, spinning around to look me in the eye. "Watchin' ya? 'Ave ya lost yer loaf? Why would anybody be spyin' on ya?"

Unable to explain it myself, I shrug. "It started outside the Barnard chapel. I could swear I heard a noise behind me, but then no one was there. Maybe I'm being silly, but after what happened to Ms Evans, I can't help but worry. What if her death is related to the magic?"

H mulls over my words as we pick up our pace. We're only a block from our flat and we're both eager to get inside its warm interior. "I was 'alf-snoozin' in the sunlight during tha meetin' this afternoon, but I thought the old Mrs James said Ms Evans must 'ave met someone in the library. Doesn't sound like she was caught unawares by a stranger or a stalker."

"I guess..." my voice trails off as I hunt for my house key in my handbag. "But who was she meeting? And why? What if she was somehow part of the burglary of the secret chamber? Maybe she met someone and let them inside... and then they offed her when she asked for too much?"

"Fer god's sake, Nat. Keep yer 'air on! That's a lot of conjecture yer doin' there. Maybe it was like old Mrs James said? Ms Evans met a man in the library and 'e offed 'er in a fit of passion."

I lock the door behind us, leaning against it as I let H's words set in. I'm sure he's right. I'm letting my imagination get carried away.

Before I can step away from my flat door, I hear the sound of the main entrance door squeak open. Heavy footsteps echo in the hallway, pausing outside of my door. I hold my breath, frozen in place. After a second, they continue, growing softer as they climb the stairs.

It's Edward. Not a stalker. Not a spy... right? Although he must have been coming back from Barnard, as I heard his voice in the hallway as I said goodnight to Harry. Did he follow me home from the college, maybe checking to see where I was going? He must have left just moments after me to arrive so quickly behind me.

And yet... he never called out to me, asking me to slow down and wait for him to catch up. Surely we're friendly enough by now to justify walking together if we're going the same way. Right? He seemed to accept my explanation for why Mathilde and I were in the library after hours, but what if he didn't? What if he thinks we're somehow involved in the discovery of the secret chamber... or with the burglary?

H fans my face with a wing, the blast of cool air calling a halt to my wandering mind. "Oi, Nat? Get yer loaf outta space. 'Urry up and order those poppadoms, will ya?"

I shove the last of my doubts into the back of my mind. I'll deal with them later. "Alright, H. I'm dialling the number. But three orders of poppadoms is the max I'm willing to request. Deal with it."

When our stomachs are full to bursting, H curls up on the window seat, leaving my mind once again free to wander. Almost on autopilot, I click, skim, file or delete messages until my inbox once again reads zero. My brain is occupied trying to piece together the puzzle pieces, but no matter how hard I try, I still have giant gaps in my understanding. How did the candlestick get to Barnard? How did the burglar or burglars know about the existence of the secret chamber? And what was the Master's Assistant doing there?

Until Mathilde and Kate make some headway on understanding the origin of Oxford's magic, we're unlikely to solve the magical elements of the current mystery. Ms Evans is my best avenue for investigation. I look at my notebook, reminding myself of my final task for the evening: search for information on

Charles Graves. If he was Ms Evans' paramour, maybe he was the person she went to meet.

Since he is a graduate student, I start my hunt by rationalising that he is more likely to be on Facebook than TikTok. Sure enough, a quick search within the Oxford area reveals his profile. His privacy settings are woeful, likely because he posts so little. The only consistent activity is his daily check-ins. A few scrolls of the page and I've got a good idea of where I might bump into him the next day.

# Chapter Five

The next morning, I wake to the sound of raindrops dripping down my windows. The curtains reveal a classic British rainy day, with the spitting wetness every British citizen comes to hate. Not wet enough to warrant a brolly and wellies, yet just enough moisture to ensure your hair is a soggy mess by the time you arrive at your destination.

"Morning, H," I call across the flat. "What do you say to giving my new bicycle a try? It will turn our twenty-five-minute walk into a ten-minute ride?"

I've been desperate to use the bicycle since I bought it off a departing student at the end of last term. The bright blue frame makes it easy to find within a crowded cycle rack, and the wicker basket on the front is big enough to hold a handbag... or, in my case, a wyvern. Or at least I think it is, since thus far H has been unwilling to give it a try.

Today's the day, though. I can feel it.

In the end, I have to promise H a full English breakfast with extra sausage links in order to get him into the basket. I roll to a stop at the entrance to our carpark, waiting for a break in the road traffic.

H's eyes are wide as he ducks into the basket, hiding from a spray of water a passing bus throws in our direction. "Are ya sure ya know wot yer doin', Nat? I can fly, ya know."

"Live a little, H! You're four hundred years old and you've never been on a bicycle. You're an Eternal! What's the worst that could happen?"

His response is lost to the wind as I put my feet to the pedals, dart into the road and pick up speed. From my perch on the bicycle seat, I watch as his shoulders loosen, his head sliding up to look over the basket's edge. Within two blocks, his tongue is lolling out of his snout as he tastes the air like a dog at an open car window. I can't control my laughter. I slip my phone out of my pocket with one hand, snapping a quick photo to share with Mathilde, Kate and Harry later.

We arrive at Barnard to find the grounds quiet this early in the morning. The students must be sleeping in after a long night of welcome back parties. H walks alongside me as we cross the quadrangle lawn and climb the stone steps which lead into the dining hall.

"Food first, missie," H demands. "I'm starvin' after our cycle ride."

"How can you be starving?" I ask. "I did all the pedalling."

He harrumphs in response before marching towards the open food windows.

True to my word, I load my tray with a full English, adding a bowl of porridge to the side. The cashier, a dour-faced man, avoids eye contact as he swipes my card through the payment machine.

I don't have to look hard to find my target. Charles Graves sits alone at one of the long tables stretching along the length of the room. He looks like his Facebook profile photo, his telltale brown hair flapping over his forehead and black-framed glasses perched on his nose. Unlike his confident profile photo, his thin shoulders are slumped, and the swollen eyes and red nose are definitely new. Nudging H with my toe, I nod towards Charles before heading over.

Charles looks up when my tray clatters onto the table, his surprise at seeing a stranger before him evident on his face.

"Mind if I sit here?" I inquire. "I hate to sit alone in these big rooms, and you look like you could use some company."

I can see that Charles is tempted to say no, so I quickly take the plate, bowl and cup from my tray, setting them onto the table. H jumps into the chair next to mine, and then uses a claw to slide the plate of eggs and sausages in front of himself. Thanks to the power of the magic, Charles is unfazed by the sight of a cat joining us for breakfast.

When I introduce myself, however, Charles' eyes grow wide, tears threatening to spill out of them.

"You're the..." His voice trails off until he coughs and regains control. "Sorry, you're one of the women who found her. Victoria. Ms Evans, I mean. Is that right?"

This time it's my turn to be caught off-guard. "How did you know that?"

"One of the porters told me yesterday," Charles explains. "He caught me as I arrived in the morning. He knew that I liked Victoria, and he wanted to make sure I didn't hear the news of her death through the rumour mill."

I give him a sympathetic smile as I stir a packet of sugar into my rapidly cooling porridge. Silence falls over our trio while we concentrate on our food. I'm desperate to ask more questions, but the poor young man looks like he might break if he gets hit with a gust of wind. It will be better for both of us if I give him a chance to carry on the conversation in his own way.

He waits until I'm finishing my last sip of coffee to clear his throat and speak again. "I know I shouldn't ask... maybe you don't want to remember... but I need to know." Leaning forward, he stammers, "Did she suffer? I mean, do you think she did? The porter couldn't tell me anything about what happened to her, and my mind keeps running towards the worst."

I shake my head in an automatic response while my brain processes his question. I had wondered if Charles might be the killer, but nothing about his demeanour suggests he is play-acting the role of an innocent. He also seems too broken up to have been nothing more than Ms Evan's distant admirer.

"No, it seemed like whatever happened, it was sudden. Mathilde and I were shocked to find her there in the library. The lights were off and there was no sign anyone had entered before us." I pause, watching Charles closely. "Did you know her well?"

Charles nods, then shakes his head. "I met her here at Barnard. My advisor's office isn't far from the Master's office, so I often passed her in the hallway. She let me take her out to dinner several times, but we hadn't gotten more serious than that. I had hoped that would change this term."

"Was she seeing someone else? Or simply busy?" I ask, trying to be casual.

"She said she wasn't seeing anyone else, but I always had the feeling that she wasn't being entirely truthful when she answered. I suspected..." He stops himself before he can finish.

"Suspected what?" I ask.

I watch as he fights an internal battle, various emotions criss-crossing his face. Sadness, but also anger. When he finally comes to a decision to speak, his voice is barely louder than a whisper. "I saw them together once. Embracing. On the sofa in his office. They didn't know. He still doesn't know."

"He? He who?" I whisper back.

"The Master."

I rock back in my seat. "The Master? Finch-Byron? But he's married."

Charles doesn't bother to hide the grimace on his face. "He has money and power, and that's enough to buy anything, or anyone he wants."

Charles picks up his napkin, crumpling it into a ball. His fist squeezes it tight until his knuckles turn white. "I'm not naive. I know... I knew what type of woman Victoria was. Her ambitions included marrying someone rich. Someone who could open doors for her into high society. That's why I was away. I interviewed for a finance job in London. Six-figure plus to start. The recruiter called me Sunday afternoon to make me the offer."

I mull over his description of Ms Evans and his stunning accusation. I only met her once, but that's enough to know that it is possible she'd use the oldest trick in the book to get ahead. Plus, it would explain Lucy James's abrupt reassignment from Master's Assistant to general office aide. The porridge turns over in my stomach.

Charles rises from his chair, getting in one last word before he goes. "I spent Sunday evening booking dinner reservations at La Maison and thinking of how to tell her my news. She was probably already dead. Gone. Forever." Choking back a small sob, he rushes off, leaving his tray of empty dishes lying on the table.

H and I are subdued on our walk from the dining hall to the old library. Neither of us expected Charles Graves to reveal that Ms Evans was having an affair with Master Finch-Byron. Every time my mind's eye tries to picture the two of them embracing, I shudder and rush to block it out.

I trudge into the library to find the aisles in disarray. Books are stacked into piles lining the walls, open crates and artwork interspersed between them. It appears that Kate and Mathilde have pulled everything out of the secret chamber and spread it across the open spaces in the library. After carefully picking my way through, I find the two of them sitting on a sofa in the back corner sipping coffees while planning their day.

Mathilde is wearing her normal uniform of jeans and a t-shirt, but I'm surprised to see Kate dressed in something other than business attire. "Is that loungewear you're wearing, Kate?"

"I do own something other than a business suit, you know?" she replies. "What do you think I wear on the weekends?"

"I've never thought about it, if I'm honest. Every time I see you, you're dressed impeccably." I pause when I notice the glare on Kate's face. "Not that you don't look great. You do. Just relaxed... Is that cashmere?"

Fortunately, Mathilde chooses that moment to jump in and save me. "We abandoned all thoughts of both business dress and working within the secret chamber when we realised how much dust there was. I got permission to close the old library so we could pull all of the contents out and organise it around the room, grouping by time period. Since no one will be coming in here, I convinced Kate to dress a bit more casually."

H chimes in from his perch atop one of the nearby bookshelves. "That explains tha mess we saw on our way in. Where's Petra? 'Ave ya managed ta find any books or notes about tha magic?"

I drop down onto the nearby sofa as Mathilde shakes her head. "We spent all day yesterday taking photos of the room and all of the contents, and we worked late into the evening pulling everything out into here. Lady Petronilla and Ada offered to work through the night, but we haven't seen them yet this morning. We did find one thing though."

"Oh?" I ask. "What's that?"

Leaning over, Kate unearths a wrinkled piece of bright blue

paper from beneath a stack of notebooks. H swoops through the air and plucks it out of her hand before she can pass it over to me. When he is once again perched up high, he carefully unfolds the paper, licking his snout as his eyes skim the page. "Mmmm, fish 'n chips. I could go fer a takeaway right now."

"We literally just ate breakfast. Give me that," I call out to him, catching the paper as he lets it flutter to the ground. "What was a London fish n' chips flyer doing in a sealed secret chamber?"

Kate looks smug as she explains, "I found it on the floor in between two of the opened crates. It was folded into a tiny square, so our best guess is that it fell out of the intruder's pocket while he or she was bending down and digging through the crate. They probably kicked it with their shoe without even realising it."

"That's amazing!" I exclaim. "So where is this place? Is it near anything?"

Mathilde grimaces, "It's near everything. Practically in the heart of central London. There are seven museums near it, Shakespeare's Globe Theatre, the HMS Belfast, the Millennium Bridge, office buildings, shops... the list goes on and on. But, if you run an imaginary line from Oxford to the National Gallery, this takeaway would sit on it. So at least we can narrow down to a neighbourhood, even if it is chocked full of places where our stolen items could be hidden away."

"That's sort of positive, I guess?" I shrug my shoulders, unconvinced. "Hopefully something else useful will emerge from the books and papers. I could really use some good news after the morning I've had."

"What do you mean 'morning you've had'?" asks Kate. "The photo of H in the bicycle basket had us laughing for a good few minutes. Surely the live view must have been hilarious."

"Was that this morning?" I sit back, somewhat stunned. "My conversation with Charles Graves completely wiped that whole adventure from my mind. Wow."

Kate looks over at Mathilde before remarking, "This doesn't sound like it will be good news. He's the boyfriend, right? Do you think he did it?"

"He wanted to be the boyfriend," I clarify, "but Ms Evans, or Victoria as he called her, was reluctant to make things official. And no, I don't think he did it, although he would have had a good reason. He has an alibi for the night of the murder."

"That's somewhat disappointing. It would have been nice to narrow down our suspect pool and confirm her death was not related to the problems with the magic." Mathilde muses. "Why did you say your morning was terrible?"

I rise from the sofa, doing a quick look around to make sure no one else is in the library. Mathilde and Kate watch wide-eyed, wondering what possible news could warrant my behaviour.

"Charles Graves suspected that Victoria, Ms Evans I mean, was having an affair with the Master."

Kate blinks and then asks, "What master?" Her confusion is mirrored on Mathilde's face.

"Finch-Byron!" I whisper harshly, barely able to force out his name.

Before Kate and Mathilde can react, we hear the sound of the library door opening and Harry's voice calling out a hello.

I let the women take in my news while I update Harry on my morning activities. Her face pales as I tell her about Charles Graves' suspicions.

"It's not unheard of, but inter-office affairs are certainly frowned upon here at Oxford," Harry remarks. "And he was her manager... he would lose his job if it came out."

"That sounds like a pretty strong motive to me," I murmur.

Mathilde speaks up, interrupting me before I can go any further. "Yes, but motive for whom? The Master... or the Master's wife? What if his wife found out about the affair and killed Ms Evans out of jealousy?"

"Ugh," I groan. "This keeps getting worse. All we know for certain is that Ms Evans was up to something. Simon, Barnard's Eternal monk, said as much. But it could be anything. Maybe she was having an affair as a means of getting access to the college so she could let the burglars inside? Or maybe she had nothing to do with the burglary and either the Master or his wife killed her?"

"Or..." Kate adds, "maybe she was supposed to meet the Master here in the library for a private moment and happened to be in the wrong place at the wrong time. The burglar could have knocked her out with the candlestick just as easily as the Master or his wife."

Silence blankets the room as we run the scenarios through our minds. Every possible direction is fraught with potential pitfalls.

Harry is the one to eventually break the quiet. "I think we need to be pragmatic. What is our number one priority here at Barnard? Is it finding Ms Evan's killer or is it learning everything we can about the magic from this newly discovered treasure trove of documents?"

Frowning, Mathilde replies, "The magic. It has to be. The sooner we can get the magical boundaries back in place, the better off everyone will be. If they were working properly, Ms Evans would still be alive. The magic would have found a way preventing it. If we don't solve the problem with the magic, someone else is at risk of getting hurt or killed."

"There's our answer, then," Harry observes. "If we confront the Master or his wife, he'll lock us out of the college. So, we set aside the question of Ms Evans until either you've gotten what we need from these books and journals, or until we have incontrovertible proof that one of them committed the crime."

I look around, relieved to see Kate, Mathilde and H all nodding their agreement. This isn't the ideal way forward, but it is our only option for the time being.

Rising to her feet, Harry waves for me to join her. "On that note, we should let these two get back to work sorting through the contents of the secret chamber, while you and I focus on our own tasks. Who knows, maybe we'll get lucky? Maybe Edward will uncover the same information and take care of the accusations for us."

# Chapter Six

After I say my goodbyes to the group and exit out of the main building, I realise I'm too wound up to concentrate on event planning.

Sensing my mood, H flaps in front of me, causing me to grind to a halt. "Lor luv, missie. Look at ya! Yer trudging along, acting like the world is crumblin' in front of yer eyes."

He herds me to one of the stone benches in the Master's garden, glaring at me until I sit on it.

"Sorry, H. I know it's the right thing to do, but I hate the thought of letting a murderer run free because we need to read some old books. And my job seems so unimportant. Even though I know in my head that our events and ceremonies play a role in strengthening the connection to the magic, right now planning a couple of parties feels inconsequential."

Having said the words out loud, I slump on the bench, letting my handbag fall from my shoulder to rest beside me. I stare down at my shoes and force my mind to go blank.

"Ya know wot ya need?" asks H, poking my arm with a talon.

"A dummy's guide to Oxford's magic? A set of identifiable fingerprints on the murder weapon?" I mutter.

"No, that's not wot ya need," H growls. "All of that is some-body else's job ta do. Wot ya need is a reminder of why yer here."

"I know why I'm here, H. I'm the ceremonial prefect. I plan events. I just said I don't feel like doing that this morning."

H bats the back of my head with his wing. "That's not what I meant. Ya need to remember wot tha magic does, what Oxford gets from havin' all us Eternals here ta help them. Lucky fer you, I know just tha place. Iffen ya can spare a few more minutes, it's right 'ere on Broad Street."

Part of me wants to stay on the bench and mope for the rest of the morning, but the other part is freezing in the January cold. "I don't have any meetings before lunch, so I guess I can get away for an hour or two."

I grab my handbag and follow H back through the main building and out the front doorway onto Broad Street. The name of the street is accurate, sprawling wide enough to allow a small carpark in the middle of the two traffic lanes. At the top end sits the Weston Library and the cobblestone square which is home to the Bodleian Libraries and the Sheldonian Theatre. The other end opens into Oxford's central business district, whose high street shops offer everything a tourist could want to buy.

I expect H to turn towards the shopping district or cross over to one of the Bodleian buildings or the History of Science Museum. However, he stays on our side of the street, clearing a path through the tourists waiting at the Oxford Tour Bus stop. With a flap of his wings, he darts inside a narrow open doorway. I barely have time to glance at the name above the door before following inside.

"Blackwell's? A bookshop? Thanks, H, but I've had enough of books to last me for a while."

But H ignores me, motioning for me to follow him. Without saying a word, he leads me past general fiction and into the colourful children's section. He finally waves us to a stop in front of a large table display decorated with Alice in Wonderland memorabilia.

"How many kids around the world 'ave read this 'ere book, Nat? Thousands? Millions?" he asks.

"Alice in Wonderland? The number must be in the millions, plus there's the Disney movie. Why are you asking?"

"Old Lew wrote tha book 'ere in Oxford. Tha magic 'elped open 'is mind up to tha possibilities of an alternate world. Didn't ya feel like ya fell down a rabbit 'ole the first time ya 'eard me talkin' to ya? Now look over there."

Eyes wide, I slide over to the next display. The rich colours of Philip Pullman's illustrated covers capture my attention. H perches on the top of a display rack, using his wings to balance on the narrow edge. "'Ow do ya think Pullman 'ere came up wiff the idea of people 'avin' daemons by their sides? Or C.S. Lewis sending them kids through the wardrobe inta Narnia?"

"Magic?" I ask, already knowing the answer.

"Magic," H confirms. "But it's not only tha made up stuff tha we 'elped wiff. Come on!"

Once again H takes flight, dragging me back through the store to a wide wooden staircase. We wind our way down, squeezing past a group of shoppers, before coming to a stop at the edge of a small balcony. Below us, books stretch as far as the eye can see. Tall stacks, book-lined walls, tables covered in piles of books.

"Thar's more than 150,000 books in this room. Not all of them come from Oxford, but some of them do. Books on maths and science. Medicine and 'istory. Many of them buildin' on ideas we Eternals 'elped shape."

I walk down a small set of stairs to stand on the basement floor. Thanks to the high ceiling, the room feels spacious and open despite having no natural light. I head over to a small seating area I'd spied from the balcony and sit on an empty sofa.

My gaze skips from one side of the room to the other, my mind absorbing H's words. So much knowledge and information. I wonder, how much creativity have our Eternals inspired? H was right. This is exactly what I needed: a reminder of why I am here and what Mathilde, Kate and I are working to protect.

H gives me a moment to enjoy the dual feeling of empower- ment and responsibility this trip has inspired. When my expres- sion shifts from stressed to determined, he passes me my handbag and motions to the balcony where we arrived. "Now that yer feeling more yer normal self, can we go upstairs and get a chockie biscuit from tha café before we go back ta Barnard? All this inspirin' I've 'ad ta do 'as left me starvin'."

The café is overflowing with people, a mix of students, tourists and locals unique to Oxford. The students are easily recognisable with their college jumpers and textbooks. The tourists crowd around the windows, their eyes leaping from their guidebooks to the Oxford skyline stretched before them. The locals are mostly women - young mothers begging their toddlers to sit still for a moment so they can enjoy a sip of coffee.

On any other day, I'd avoid the chaos. But today, the crowd's energy is reinvigorating me even more than my caramel latte. There's just one thing wrong though.

"Why do ya keep lookin' over yer shoulder, Nat?" H asks in between bites of a double chocolate biscuit. Crumbs cover the table and floor around him, but I'm not sure whether to blame him or the little boy who sat at the table before us.

"I've got that itch again, H. Like someone is watching me." I peek over my shoulder, but the only thing there is a sea of strangers.

"Of course somebody's lookin' at ya," H laughs. "Yer sittin' at a table with a cat. The magic makes them accept what they see as normal, but they're going ta take a gander at ya first."

Shaking my head, I brush off his answer. "No, it's more than that. I would swear that someone is standing over there." I spin in my chair and point to the next room. "What section is that? Can you see the name?"

Despite leaning left and right, the signage is angled in a way that makes it impossible to read from our seats. Seeing that H has finished his biscuit, I propose, "Why don't you fly close to the ceiling and see if you can get a bird's eye view. At minimum, you should be able to see what the sign says and that could be a good clue. Even better, you might spot someone we know. Go on. Go check for me. This is driving me crazy."

H huffs black smoke from his nose but does as I ask. Barely a second later he is barrelling back, his wings flapping furiously. "It's Edward. He's two aisles over."

Leaping from my chair, I squeak, "Edward Thomas? I knew it! Remember when I said someone was watching me on our walk last night? I heard him come into our building mere moments after we got home."

H shoots out a talon, catching the edge of waistband before I can go running off. "Come on, missie. Why would Edward be followin' ya around? 'E knows ya well. Iffen 'e wanted ta ask ya somethin', 'e could pop downstairs and knock on yer door."

I untangle my trousers from H's claw, giving him a dirty look. With a hoarse whisper, I point out, "But he hasn't popped down, has he? In fact, he's not spoken to me other than when we ran into him in the old library. Yet both times I've had this creepy feeling, there he is. And if he's not following me, why would he be on this floor in Blackwell's, in the middle of the morning, when he's supposed to be investigating a murder?"

"I don't know, Nat. Maybe 'e needed to buy a book? Don't rush over there wavin' yer finger at 'im. I know ya two had a rough start, but Edward's a good chap. And it's clear ta everyone that you two half-fancy each other. Give 'im a chance ta explain."

Could H be right? If I'm honest with myself, Edward and I did have a moment at the St Margaret Christmas party. It seemed like we were heading towards... I don't know, something? But since our chance encounter in Barnard's old library, we've gone right back to our awkward dance. Is that Edward's fault? Or could it be mine?

There's only one way to find out.

Squaring my shoulders, I trek over to chat with Edward. Sure enough, he's exactly where H said he was, two aisles over, leaning against the wall with his nose shoved in a book.

"Hello, Edward Thomas. Fancy meeting you here," I purr.

Edward jumps sideways, bumping into the shelf beside him before looking in my direction. "My word, Nat. You startled me."

Startled him? Did I, or is he faking his surprise?

"Yes, it's weird running into you here in Blackwell's, before noon. Strange that we'd both be away from Barnard and end up on the same floor in the same shop at the same time..." I let my voice trail off.

Looking perplexed, Edward replies, "Yes, that is a coincidence. Oxford is not exactly a metropolis, but it does have more than one bookshop."

"Hmm, yes." This approach isn't getting anywhere. I try again. "How's the investigation going? Have you uncovered anything?"

"Mostly more questions than answers," Edward groans. "Master Finch-Byron strongly believes Ms Evan's death is tied to the break-in, so I'm focusing my attention on the burglary."

"Is he suggesting she opened the door for the intruders? Or that she was somehow involved?" I ask.

Edward shakes his head. "At this point, anything is possible. The police are investigating her background and activities prior to arriving at Barnard. I'm looking for any clue to how someone could have uncovered the existence of the secret chamber. I came to Blackwell's to see if any of the old college floor plans or histories might offer up a hint." He points to the sign hanging above our heads. "Their History department has an entire section dedicated to the Oxford colleges."

I don't know whether to sigh in relief at this reasonable explanation for Edward's presence here at Blackwell's, or to be nervous that he's investigating the secret chamber. I need him to look into Ms Evans' time at Barnard, not her background, and not old college floor plans. I need him to uncover her relationship with the Master. I'm sure once he knows about it, his investigative plans will change dramatically.

"Yes, the secret chamber is mind-boggling. But I still think it is strange that Ms Evans was in the library at that time of night. Surely if there was something in her background, it would have come out during the hiring process, right? Maybe she was there for something unrelated to the burglary. Something more recent? Is anyone looking into that side of things?"

Edward runs his hand through his hair, frustration evident on his face. "The Master's demand for secrecy is limiting how many avenues of investigation I can pursue at one time. Not to mention his insistence that the burglary be top of the list. He's forcing me to run this line of questions to ground before I can do anything else. And to make matters worse, the head of the Oxford police force has washed his hands of the whole thing. I had to call in favours to get the London police to check Ms Evans' history."

I stand in a stunned silence. Could the Master's interference be proof of his own guilt? Is that the reason he's preventing Edward from uncovering his relationship with Ms Evans? And what will Edward find in his search into the history of the secret chamber?

"Listen, Edward... If you need any help, you know you can

knock on my flat door, right? Anytime, day or night. Well, maybe not the middle of the night. Oh, you know what I mean."

I barely manage to put a halt to my babbling as Edward raises an eyebrow. "Thanks, Nat, but it would hardly be appropriate for me to pull you deeper into the situation. It's bad enough you discovered the body. Anyway, you must have your hands full as well, planning the great reveal event."

Raising my hand, I wave away his objection. "Oh, that's nothing special. All in a day's work, you know. If you need help, I'm sure I can find time."

"I'll keep that in mind," he says and then looks at the book in his hand. "I should get back to my research. It's lovely to see you." His eyes crinkle as a smile ghosts across his face. "Maybe we could do it again sometime? On purpose?"

"You mean, like a date?" I blurt stupidly. Of course, he means a date. "Yes, sure. I'd like that."

"Great. Unfortunately, it will have to wait until I make progress on the investigation. But as soon as I can get clear, we could go for a drink? The Ashmolean Museum has a roof top bar."

"The Ashmolean? Yes, that sounds nice. I'm in... you know, whenever you're free. And I'm free. When we're both available." I clamp my mouth shut when the nervous babbling takes over again. Blushing, I say an abrupt goodbye and dash off.

What is wrong with me?

Surprisingly, H is sitting exactly where I left him at the café table, sipping what was left of my caramel latte. He makes a slurping sound as he sucks up the last few drops through his straw. "Did 'e confess?"

"Not exactly. You were right, it was a coincidence. But, Edward did give me some bad news. Master Finch-Byron has Edward focusing his investigation on the one place we don't want it."

"The secret chamber?" H asks, his expression grim.

"Exactly. I need you to do me a favour, H."

H straightens in his chair. "Sure, Nat. Wot do ya need me ta do fer ya?"

I lean in close, my voice barely audible above the buzz of the busy café. "I want you to follow Edward around for the rest of the day. See if you can find out what he knows and which questions he's asking."

H takes one final slurp of my drink before passing me the empty cup. "Aye, Captain!" he calls, and with a last puff of smoke, he salutes me and heads on his way.

# Chapter Seven

With a clearer head and a sense of purpose, I leave Blackwell's for my office. I've got at least an hour of free time before lunch and I want to start sketching out my ideas for the celebration theme. Deep in thought, I enter Barnard's front doors and make my way to the office building in the back of one of the smaller quadrangles. For once I'm happy to be tucked away on my own, far from any distractions.

Birds chirp. Evergreen leaves rustle in the wind. Students call to one another from across the lawn. I soak in the sounds of an Oxford college. Everything is exactly as it should be, until a scuffing noise breaks through my reverie.

I tune the noise out. There is no sense in me spinning in place or looking behind every bush and branch. If someone really is following me, I'll catch them sooner or later.

Once inside my office, I grab my door before it swings shut behind me. I'm curious to see whether leaving it open might entice whoever is following me to try to peer inside. Given I'm the last door before the exit, there's no logical reason why someone would be milling in the hallway. I drop my handbag to the ground, positioning it just right to keep the door from closing on its own.

Ignoring my laptop, I pull out giant sheets of paper and my favourite coloured markers from my desk drawer. Within minutes, I'm lost in my lists and sketches. Whatever plans I had to keep an eye on the door disappear as I fall into a chart and list-filled trance.

As I put the final flourish on my theme planning worksheet, my back screeches in agony. I've been bent over my desk for who knows how long, my muscles locked into the same position. With a groan, I roll my head from side-to-side, loosening my neck muscles. I open my eyes to see a face peeking around the edge of my open doorway.

Freezing in place, my heart races when our gazes meet. The head disappears, jostling me out of my frozen state.

"Wait, stop!" I shout from my chair. My voice catches in my throat. I have to squeeze the next word out.

"Grandfather?"

A second passes and then another. I don't move, listening desperately for another one of those scuffing sounds that has been following me around.

Can it really be him? I'm sure I was mistaken, or it is simply a case of wishful thinking. It must be the result of one too many shocks to my system. Too much stress. But what if?

"Grandfather, is that you? Please, don't hide from me." My voice is thick with unshed tears.

My grandfather, gone for nearly twenty years, emerges. It is as though he just stepped out of my childhood memories and into my doorway.

His white hair is slicked back with Brylcreem. All the years of broad smiles and happy memories are etched into the deep creases of his face. His clothing is rumpled, pens tucked in his shirt pocket, exactly as I remember them. His brown eyes shimmer, tears spilling from the edges.

I leap from my chair, dashing across the room to throw myself into his open arms. Despite being an Eternal, he smells like toffee and feels exactly the same as he always did. I want to tuck myself under his arm and fall asleep like I used to do as a child.

He pulls me close, whispering in a soothing voice, "Don't cry, my darling girl. I'm here now."

I say a silent prayer of thanks that the magic at Barnard is strong enough to make my grandfather feel as solid as any living being. With a last squeeze to reassure myself that it is really him, I step back and take a deep breath to calm my emotions.

"But how?" I falter and start again. "Why didn't H tell me you were here? And why haven't you shown yourself sooner?"

"So many questions! You always were an inquisitive child. Sit, sit. There's plenty of time to tell you everything you want to know."

Using my foot, I nudge my handbag over and kick the door closed. As far as the rest of the world is concerned, I'm not available. All of my attention is focused on my grandfather.

We settle into the pair of chairs in front of my desk, angling them so we can look at one another. My grandfather reaches across the space to pat my hand. "I can't tell you how happy it makes an old man to see you here. My legacy - not just carried on, but surpassed. I always hoped you would find your way to Oxford. And now look at you! You've been here a short while and look how much you've accomplished."

I nod, a watery smile the closest I can come to saying thanks for his words.

"And you've found H, or should I say that he found you? Did you remember the stories I used to tell you when you were a wee one?"

A snort slips out before I can stop it. "Yes, the adventures of the mischievous Humphrey. I'll be having words with him later for not telling me you've been here all this time."

"None of that now," my grandfather interrupts. "H isn't to blame. He didn't know I had returned as an Eternal. I knew he needed to bond with the next prefect, so I stayed hidden from him. Anytime he came near, I moved to another college. Then you arrived to replace Lillian just as I had hoped you would."

"And? Why weren't you there to greet me, Grandfather?" I ask, sniffling. "Did you think I wouldn't want to see you?"

"You needed to find your feet. You didn't need an old Eternal coming in and telling you how to do things. You are the prefect now; you make the rules."

When I look unconvinced, he carries on. "Think of everything that happened last term at St Margaret. Using the Eternals at your gala. Having dead Chef Smythe cater the event. None of us would have ever imagined it possible, but you did. I had to be patient and let you figure it all out, although my impatience nearly killed me all over again."

I can't help myself. I tear up when I see his face brimming with pride. There were some nights last term when I worried he'd think I was a failure. Or that I lacked respect for tradition by continually tossing the old ways of doing things out the proverbial window. Yet here he is now, sitting before me, looking prouder than he did on the day I told him I wanted to grow up and be just like him. I guess, in my own way, I did just that.

With a gentle smile, he says, "You're the one in charge now. I'm here to lend my support however I can. I adore you, my darling child. I always have and always will. So, tell me, what on earth is going on at Barnard?"

The rest of the morning and the afternoon flew by as I spent time catching my grandfather up on the last twenty years of my life. I told him about the rest of my childhood and recounted funny stories about my parents. For his part, he shared his experiences as an Oxford Eternal. He always believed I'd find my way back to him, but he had to be patient and wait until the time was right.

My grandfather had explained, "As an Eternal, I couldn't travel beyond the borders of Oxford's magic. When I realised Lillian was sick and would need to retire, I knew the magic in your veins would find a way to nudge you into applying for her role. All I had to do was move your application to the top of her pile. The magic took care of the rest."

It's only when Mathilde texts, threatening to send out a search party to look for me, that we emerge from my office.

As we walk through the college gardens, I feel like a weight has been lifted off my shoulders. "Those scuffing noises I heard and the times I thought someone was watching me, it was you, right?"

He has the grace to look abashed. "I'm sorry if I worried you. I have to admit that my patience ran out. I was looking for the right opportunity to present myself, but you were always with other people. I didn't know how you would react, so I waited and waited, looking for a time when you were alone."

I give his arm a squeeze of reassurance. "I'm glad it turned out to be you, Grandfather. Speaking of alone time, I wonder what happened to H... EEP!"

Before I can finish my sentence, a scaly black wyvern leaps from the branch of a leafy evergreen tree, diving straight towards us. It lands on my grandfather's shoulders, wings flapping madly, and its smoky snout moving a mile a minute.

"Alfie? Alfie Payne! I thought ya were lost ta me, and 'ere ya are." H flies around to face my grandfather, his eyes gleaming with happiness. "And yer an Eternal, like me. A wispie! Where 'ave ya been all this time?"

I motion everyone over to a nearby bench, sitting to watch H and my grandfather's big reunion. Much like them, I'm smiling ear to ear, pure joy bubbling out like laughter. It takes the buzz of another text message to break up the scene, Mathilde wanting to know why I am taking so long to make my way to the old library. She has no idea of the surprise I have in store for her.

Mathilde, in fact, is the first person to spot us when our unlikely group enters the old library. One woman, one wyvern and a ghost. It sounds like it should be the opening line to a weird joke, I chuckle to myself.

Mathilde's gaze skips from me to my grandfather, her eyes narrowing as she tries to figure out why he looks familiar. "Nat, is that your...?"

"Mathilde, meet my grandfather, Alfred Payne, former bibliothecae praefectus and now an Eternal."

Shocked, Mathilde carefully sets her notebook aside, rising from her crouched position in front of a pile of old journals. After dusting her hands on her trousers, she crosses to us, her face solemn. Carefully, she reaches out a hand. "It is my honour to meet you, sir."

I watch her exhale when he grasps her hand in a firm shake, clearly as relieved as I was to find him solid. She calls for Kate to detach herself from a stack of paintings, and I repeat the introduction once again.

"Well," says Kate, "I believe this calls for a coffee break. I don't know about you, Mathilde, but I have a million and one questions to ask. Shall I call Harry to join us before I launch in?"

"You'd better," I reply. "Otherwise we'll have to repeat everything we learn... and that's assuming she doesn't gripe at us for leaving her out. I'll get a round of coffees from the machine in the corridor. Want to ask her to meet me there so she can help carry them?"

In less than ten minutes we're all comfortably ensconced on the library sofas, coffees in hand and curious expressions on our faces. My grandfather starts by explaining the rules which govern the Eternals' activities.

"All of us Eternals fall into one of two groups: university-bound or college-bound. H and I both fit into the first group. We can go anywhere we want within Oxford because we don't have any affiliation with a specific college. The second group is the opposite. Eternals like Lady Petronilla here, and Bartie at St Margaret, are limited in where they can go. They have full run of their respective college grounds, but they cannot enter any other college."

"But they can go outside their colleges," Kate interjects.

I cast a side-eye in her direction. "How would you know that, Kate? Have you had experience with any particular Eternal?"

Kate fails to respond, but her blush gives her away.

"Where can the college Eternals go, Grandfather? Say, someone like Bartie, for example. Could he visit the Ashmolean Museum?"

Chuckling, he replies, "Yes, a college Eternal can go into any building in Oxford as long as it isn't owned by one of the other colleges. They have some freedom, but it's why Bartie can't lend a hand to your group here at Barnard." After a moment's pause, he adds, "It seems silly to block someone from entering for all eternity. However, the rule, which has been in place for its entire existence, reflects how fiercely independent each college remains despite all falling under the umbrella of the University of Oxford."

Harry nods in agreement, understanding better than all of us how competitive the colleges are with one another. "How did you end up back here, Alfred? Are there more Eternal prefects hidden around?"

"Aahhh, that's a good question, Harry. As you know, only a small group of families have the ability to become a prefect. In most families, like Kate and Mathilde's, it will take several genera-tions before another prefect emerges."

He reaches over, wrapping an arm around my shoulders. "Nat was barely out of nappies when she demanded to plan her own birthday party. Nothing made her happier than organising events. I knew she was destined to become the ceremonial prefect. When my time came, I struggled desperately to stay behind so I could see her again at Oxford."

He places a gentle kiss on the top of my head, as though I were still his little girl, explaining, "I was a rare lucky one to be able to meet the family member who would follow in my foot-steps. I think it gave me the strength and will to change into an Oxford Eternal."

We sip our coffees in silence, absorbing my grandfather's words and their implications.

He coughs suddenly to get our attention. "Let me be clear about one thing. You three ladies are the prefects. I'm not here to take over. I am here to help. What's the best way an old Eternal librarian can lend a hand?"

Mathilde leaps at the chance to have an extra set of hands helping her sort through the stacks of books, journals and loose papers discovered in the secret chamber. For his part, my grandfa-ther promises to work through the night alongside Lady Petron-illa and Ada. While the two women can read the books and identify the artwork faster than he can, his knowledge of how to catalogue will make the whole process move more quickly.

Although I'm loathe to let my grandfather out of sight for even a moment, I know it's the right thing to do. After all, it isn't as though he is going anywhere. He's an Oxford Eternal. He'll be here anytime I need him. My heart is bursting over this unexpected, incredible gift.

As Kate and Mathilde return to their work and Harry takes her leave to go home, I look up to see H sitting on the coffee table in front of me. The sight jogs a recent memory from my brain. "Wait, aren't you supposed to be following Edward around? Did you learn anything?"

Before he can form a reply, H lets loose one of his classic sneezes, setting our discarded biscuit and tea napkins alight. That's never a good sign; he only sneezes when he's nervous about something.

Together we stamp out the smouldering flames until nothing is left but his telltale pile of ashes. Given they were used napkins, I wish the magic didn't immediately replace them. That could have been an easy clean-up.

H swats a few fluttering ashes out of his face and finally launches into his report. "I followed Edward around fer most of tha day like ya asked. Yer lucky he stopped in tha Dining Hall fer lunch or else we'd be havin' words now, missie."

I wave away his complaint knowing full well H is at no risk of starvation. "So, where did he go? What did he do?"

"I'm gettin' ta that iffen ya'll stop interruptin' me. He spent ages at Blackwell's lookin' at tha books. Then he came back ta Barnard and stopped fer lunch. After lunch it looked like he was goin' ta go to the Middle Common Room. I flew up ahead and spotted Master Finch-Byron's old assistant, Lucy James, sittin' inside sippin' a cuppa."

"Oooh," I interrupt, "that sounds positive. Did he speak with her?"

"No such luck, Nat. It was a coincidence that she happened ta be there. He skipped right past tha door and continued along the hallway until he came ta another office. I stuck around fer a while, waitin' ta see if he would say somethin' useful, but after a while I got so bored that I gave up."

"And that's why you were up in the tree in the gardens when my grandfather and I walked past?" I ask.

H nods in confirmation, his snout in a proud grin. "I bet ya couldn't see me at all, could ya? I was tucked away in an upper branch, waitin' fer Edward ta come back out again. There's no way 'e could 'ave slipped past me."

I mull over H's words, confused about one thing. "None of that sounds too bad... and certainly not bad enough to warrant one of your nervous sneezes. What aren't you telling me? Who was in the office Edward visited?"

"It was tha security office. Edward was askin' ta see the security films."

"From the night of the murder?" I clarify. "That could be a big help! What did he see?"

Shaking his head, H replies, "The police already looked at tha footage from that night. That was one of tha first things they did. Ms Evans arrived on her own that night, then nothing else until you and Mathilde showed up."

"Hmm, still doesn't rule out someone or something related to the magic coming inside. The cameras wouldn't pick them up." My mind is spinning. "If the police already viewed that footage, why did Edward stay so long, and why did you get bored enough to leave?"

H coughs, motioning with his talons for me to lean in close. He whispers, "Edward asked tha guard to show him footage from tha last month showin' Ms Evans, Mathilde, Kate or yerself."

My mouth drops open. Footage of me, Mathilde and Kate? Why would he need to see that? If he suspected me or one of my friends, surely, he wouldn't have asked me to get a drink?

I raise my finger to my mouth, "Sshh. Don't tell anyone else what you just told me. None of us were involved in the murder or the burglary, so there's nothing for us to fear. Unless it seems like he is close to discovering the existence of the magic, we're better off leaving him to his investigation. There might be something more to this story, but I don't want to worry anyone until we can get to the bottom of it."

H's face is the picture of seriousness as he agrees.

On that somber note, we call our goodbyes to the group and make our way towards the stand where we left my bicycle. Hopefully seeing H riding in my basket will be enough to wipe all worries away from my head for the rest of the evening.

# Chapter Eight

H begs me to cycle to Barnard again in the morning, thanks to his newfound love for my bicycle basket. As I pedal along the busy streets, H practices acrobatic moves. When he attempts to do a handstand on my handlebars and nearly causes us to fall, I threaten to tie him to the basket if he doesn't settle down.

I give a small prayer of thanks when we arrive at Barnard before I rush off to the old library to see my grandfather. As soon as I walk into the door, he comes over and envelops me in a big hug, matching smiles shining from our faces.

"How did the work go overnight?" I ask, looking around in amazement at the ever-growing number of piles of books and artwork.

"I think Mathilde will be pleased this morning. Lady Petronilla, Ada and I managed to organise all of the books, notebooks and artwork by decade. We still need to read through everything, but hopefully now it should be easier to see how things connect with one another."

"That sounds promising. I hate to pull you away from this important task, but I wondered if you might be due for a coffee break?" I glance over at my grandfather, wondering aloud, "Do Eternals get to sit down and prop their feet up? Or go out for some fresh air?"

H interjects before my grandfather can answer. "Course we do, Nat. After listenin' ta ya toss and turn all night, I'm guessin' ya want ta chat with Alfie here. I'll give Petra a 'and so ya two can go fer a walk, iffen ya want."

"Thanks, H. That would be amazing." I turn to my grandfather, "Is that okay? H is right, I could use some advice on something, and you might be the only person who can give it to me."

"Well now, that does sound important. Of course, I can, my dear. Let's go." With that, my grandfather leads me out of the old library and down the stairs towards the building entrance. We exit through Barnard's main doorway, putting us on Broad Street.

"Have you been to the Christ Church Meadow yet?" my grandfather asks.

"No, or at least I don't think so. Lead the way." I link my arm through his, revelling in the joy of being able to do so again after twenty years without him in my life. As much as I had suffered his absence all of those years, it has made this reunion that much sweeter.

Together we cross Broad Street and walk deeper into the centre of Oxford. We make a quick stop at a local coffee shop so I can get a steaming latte before we wind our way through more narrow streets.

We finally arrive at an imposing metal gate, complete with an iron turnstile. That's one way to keep bicycles out of the grounds. I push my way through, envious of my grandfather's ability to simple disappear and reappear on the opposite side.

Despite the winter cold, the grass is a vibrant green. On one side, the college cricket grounds are match-ready. On the other, an imposing red brick wall blocks our view into the enclosed gardens and halls which make up the college proper.

"Now then," my grandfather says, "there's no one here except a scattering of winter birds perched in the trees. What's on your mind, my girl?"

"It's a question about my grandmother," I confess. "I'm guessing you never told her about the existence of magic here in Oxford."

He chuckles in response. "No, I never told her. I always thought she'd catch on. After all, having the same 'cat' for thirty years should have been a giveaway, but it was as H had promised on my first day. Your grandmother accepted it as normal, no questions asked."

"How did you juggle it? Magic, work, having a family... how did you keep from slipping up, like maybe telling her about your day and accidentally mentioning an Eternal?"

Shrugging, he answers, "What can I say, Nat? It sounds trite to say it was a simpler time... but it was. I didn't have murders to solve or mysterious problems with the magic to keep me up at night. I took care of the library books and I let the Eternals get on with their side of things. Your grandmother never had cause for concern because I was always home on time for supper."

"Oh." I let my heels scuff the dirt pathway, watching as small puffs of dust fly up into the air. When we pass a bin, I get rid of my empty takeaway cup.

"Is this about Edward Thomas?"

My head jerks up, my eyes flying over to my grandfather's face. "Why would you ask me about him?"

"I was also in Blackwell's, one aisle over from you two. It was my eyes you felt on the back of your neck, although poor Edward took the blame." He winces in a silent apology. "I couldn't help but overhear him ask you to join him for a drink one evening. I take it you've taken a shine to him?"

"I guess. Maybe I have, but I'm worried." My voice wavers. "How can I think of getting close to someone if half of my life has to be kept a secret? He's a criminologist, for goodness' sake. If he has even an inkling that I'm keeping something from him, his brilliant mind will spur him to investigate until he gets to the bottom of it."

"But you do like the fellow? You must or you wouldn't be worrying about all of this." My grandfather's gaze is piercing. It reminds me of when I was little and he'd find a discarded candy wrapper on the floor. He'd track me down, asking if I knew anything about it. I always crumbled and confessed.

"I don't know him well enough yet to say for sure, but..." my breath comes out in a huff. "There is something that keeps pulling us together. He shouldn't have anything to do with Barnard College. And what are the odds he'd live in the flat above my own? When we do chat, he just... well, he seems to know where I'm coming from."

"And when you need him?" my grandfather interrupts.

"He's always there," I say, marvelling at the truth of my statement. "What do I do, grandfather? Am I inviting trouble if I go out with him, even for a night? Is it better for everyone if I walk away now?"

My grandfather doesn't rush to respond. Although part of me wants him to reassure me straightaway that all will be fine, the other appreciates his thoughtful approach. We walk in silence, following a tree-lined path until we arrive at the banks of the Cherwell River. A few ducks and geese are the only things floating on the surface, no doubt enjoying the absence of tourist-filled boats.

When he speaks, his voice startles the ducks into flight. "The prefectus magic in our veins requires much from us, Nat. Even though you've only been here a few months, I am sure you realise you will spend the rest of your career in this place. You probably didn't show up expecting Oxford to be your forever home, but that's exactly what it is."

"Am I courting trouble by thinking about having a relationship now? Is that what you're saying?" I mumble, my vision firmly fixed on the water flowing past.

My grandfather reaches out a hand, nudging my chin up until my eyes meet his. "No, Nat. I think we give so much of our lives to Oxford, I can't imagine the magic would let you two grow close only to demand you stay apart. My best advice is to take things slowly. Let him in a little at a time. Give the magic time to do its part, to make him accept all of the oddities as perfectly acceptable norms."

I try to remain serious, but I can't stop a small smile from forming on my face. "Thanks, grandfather."

He wraps an arm around my shoulders, pulling me in close like he used to do when I was a child. "I'll always be here for you, to answer questions, lend a hand or to give you a sympathetic ear when H drives you mad."

My answering bark of laughter sends the rest of the ducks and geese scattering away.

❖

"Looks like ya worked a miracle, Alfie!" H exclaims when we get back to the old library.

Mathilde and Kate arrived while I was out walking, both already hard at work examining materials. Kate moves to stand but I shake my head, cutting off her approach. My grandfather has made me feel better, but I'm not yet ready to talk about Edward with Mathilde and Kate.

"I hate to say this, but I need to steal another one of your helpers, Mathilde." I give her a cheeky grin, crossing my fingers that she won't complain too much.

Rolling her eyes, Mathilde smirks, "Fine, but only if you promise to take H with you when you go. He's been playing parkour again. Even if the magic repairs everything he destroys, my nerves can't handle the sound of tearing leather book spines any longer."

This time it's H's turn to give a cheeky grin as he leaps between bookshelves until he lands at my feet. "Wot's our plan, Nat? Where are we goin'? Iffen it's ta tha Dining 'All, I won't say no."

"Sorry, H. Nothing quite so exciting for you. I'm hoping to spend some time with Lady Petronilla learning about the history of Barnard College," I explain. Turning in her direction, I ask, "Lady Petronilla, would you do me the honour of giving me a few hours of your time?"

Lady Petronilla rises from her seat in the corner where she is reading through old journals. As she makes her way over, H mimes dying of starvation, swooning and collapsing to the floor.

"Oh well," I call out, "since H has passed out, I guess I'll have to eat this chocolate muffin I bought for him while I was out."

"Chockie muffin?" he asks, cracking one eyelid open. I open my handbag, pulling out a small paper bag.

"It's a shame that he's gone. I guess I'll have to eat this so it doesn't go to waste."

"I'm back, Nat. No need ta be 'asty." He tries to grab the bag from my hand, but I jerk it away from his grasp.

"Come along like a good little wyvern and I'll let you have the biscotti I bought as well," I say to H before nodding my hello at Lady Petronilla. "Shall we look for a quiet space to sit where we won't be interrupted?"

"Come hither, Natalie and H. We can retire to the Old Common Room," Lady Petronilla proposes, gathering her skirts before moving towards the doorway.

Together, we walk the hallways, although my footsteps are the only ones which echo on the wooden flooring. With her straight back and head held high, her gait is so smooth that I can't help but wonder whether, unlike the other Eternals, she is floating. Somehow, though, I suspect she walked the same way when she was alive. Probably while balancing a book on her head.

When we get inside the room in question, door closed securely behind us, Lady Petronilla sits herself at the head of the table, her skirt carefully spread to prevent wrinkles. I pass H the muffin and biscotti packages and then launch into my thoughts.

"As I'm sure you know, Master Finch-Byron has asked me to organise a celebration of the 45th anniversary of the first class of female students here at Barnard College." I pause for her confirmation and Lady Petronilla nods regally.

"I know exactly what he expects me to do - hang up pictures of the women and little signs below them highlighting their accomplishments in the last forty-five years. I might even go so far as to select a few other women who have since graduated, perhaps inviting them in to give a short speech." I pause to lean back in my chair, crossing my arms. "However, the more I think about it, the more that strikes me as somehow insufficient."

"In what manner?" asks the Lady.

"The history of women at Barnard didn't start forty-five years ago when the college accepted its first female students. It began more than five hundred years in the past, when you, Lady Petronilla, provided the funding and the charter allowing the college to live on past your husband's death. But I bet if we went out into the street and took a poll of passers-by, few would know your name. Most would know your husband's. I think it is high time we corrected that." I hold my breath for a second, waiting for her reaction.

"Thou makest a valid argument, however I cannot foresee our Master Finch-Byron providing his seal of approval. It would be a red-letter day for all of us, but I see not how thou might avoid his ire."

Good, she didn't immediately dismiss the idea. There's hope. I explain, "The Master can't get angry about something he doesn't know."

This time Lady Petronilla arches an eyebrow, intrigued.

"With everything else going on right now, the women's celebration is the least of his worries. He hasn't brought it up at all, not with me or with Harry. He's focusing all of his attention on Edward's investigation and the contents of the secret room. I suspect that even if I did try to bring it up with him, he'd simply brush me off. This may be our only chance to properly honour all of the women who helped build Barnard College into the success that it is."

When the Lady smiles with a glint in her eye, I know I've got her. "Very well, Natalie. Thou hast proven thy point well." She turns her attention to the other side of the table. "H, be a yon fellow and seek out our other lady Eternals. Tell them we have need of their assistance."

Somehow in my head, I assumed that Barnard College would have a similar number of Eternals to St Margaret. When H returns with dozens of Eternal women in tow, I nearly fall out of my chair. Their lives span hundreds of years, starting with cooks, cleaners and laundresses, carrying on to the wives and children of masters and fellows and finally staff roles. All of these women share the same Eternal dedication to Barnard's success.

Lady Petronilla asks them to group themselves by half century and to appoint someone to act as a liaison between myself and all of them. I marvel at her foresight as I hadn't given any thought to the monumental task of trying to capture so many stories, each one as important as the next.

Together, we all agree on meeting times and locations when I can interview them, getting the details I need to make the women's celebration a success. As the morning goes on, Lady Petronilla's eyes sparkle with delight. I insist on making sure every group is represented, allowing no contribution to fade away into obscurity. When the last meeting is arranged, I once again thank Lady Petronilla for her help before letting her return to Mathilde's side.

H and I grab a sandwich from the dining hall cafe, opting to eat at my desk instead of trying to cram ourselves into the space which is overflowing with boisterous students.

In between bites of cheese and onion crisps, H looks over at me with a gentle gaze. "Nat, do ya want to tell me why ya were turning somersaults in yer bed last night? I know ya talked to yer grandda, but ya know ya can talk ta me, too. Iffen ya want..."

I try to stop the blush creeping up my neck, but it's no use. "It was about Edward," I mumble, half-hoping he'll let it drop.

Confused, H asks, "Was 'e walkin' around upstairs and makin' noise or somethin'?"

"No," I mumble. "He asked me out for a drink. When we saw him in Blackwell's. I said yes, but I don't know..."

We sit in silence for a moment, each of us gathering our thoughts.

"H?" my voice wavers. I take a sip of cola and try again. "Did you ever get the feeling that Edward thought you were something more than a cat? Or maybe he acted like he saw Bartie or one of the St Margaret Eternals wandering the hallways?"

H shakes his head fiercely, crumbs falling from his snout. "No, no way, no 'ow. Edward never even gave me a look before ya got 'ere. I've seen Bartie walk beside 'im, whispering in 'is ears, and 'e didn't have a clue."

The last bit of tension falls from my shoulders. "Believe it or not, H, that was exactly what I hoped you'd say. I guess Grandfather was right. I need to put my faith in the magic, let it sort everything out."

"Alfie's always been bright. Iffen that's what 'e told ya, then ya should listen." Problem solved. H shakes the crumbs from the bottom of his crisp packet into his mouth. I pass him a napkin to clean up the resulting cloud of cheese and onion dust.

H chooses to curl up in the cat bed and snooze in a puddle of sunlight while I forge on with my afternoon meeting. I'm due for a catch-up with my assistants Will and Jill.

Right on schedule, I hear a brisk knock on my door at exactly one in the afternoon. After I call out, the pair come inside. "Make yourselves comfortable," I say as I wave them towards my two visitor chairs. "How are you both getting on with your celebration assignments?"

Will jumps in first, passing around catering offers and sample menus. We spend half an hour debating the merits of brunch versus lunch versus high tea, weighing up the cost implications against guest expectations. Next, I use my large wall-mounted whiteboard to sketch out table arrangements, erasing and redrawing over and over again until we finally all three agree on a solution.

For her part, Jill has brought along fabric samples for chair covers and tablecloths, paper and envelope samples for invitations and brochures of the latest marquee models. The shades of cream, ivory and white stand in stark contrast to Jill's colourful African head wrap. I stare at it until I get lost in my own thoughts, trying to envision a way to bring Jill's vibrancy into the event. As a start, I make her promise to source a brightly coloured floral arrangement for the centrepieces.

Every once in a while, I glance down to reassure myself that H is still asleep. These conversation topics would leave him bored out of his mind. Only someone as passionate about events as myself and my assistants are could find our technical discussions on party planning minutiae interesting.

When I catch sight of H stretching out his back legs, I realise a quick change of scenery is in order. "Team, what do you say to a little field trip? How about we stop by the Middle Common Room for a cuppa and a biscuit and then head over to look at the shortlist of marquee locations?"

I don't have to ask anyone twice. H nearly trips Will in their haste to get out of the door. It's all I can do to hold back my giggle of laughter. If only Will knew it was a wyvern wrapping around his legs, he might not be so quick to nudge H aside.

The Middle Common Room has a stack of takeaway cups next to a brand new coffee machine. It is suspiciously similar to the one at St Margaret, leaving me no doubts that Harry is responsible for the unexpected upgrade to my daily latte. I pass a stack of chocolate digestives to H when no one is looking, hardly believing my eyes when he shoves the towering stack into his mouth in one go.

"Does everyone have a coffee?" I ask. "Great! Jill, want to lead the way to the right area of the gardens?"

Jill nods her assent, guiding us through the warren of brick and stone buildings until we finally emerge on a sprawling grassy lawn. An expanse of bright green, unbroken by trees or pathways, sits waiting like a blank canvas. It is impossible to believe that something this large sits in the middle of Oxford, one of the most expensive real estate markets in the UK. The land value alone must be in the millions.

Jill nudges me with her elbow, "I know I said I'd find a few options for the marquee, but once I saw this, I stopped looking."

"Fair enough," I reply, my approval evident in my broad smile. We meander around the green, letting our mind's eye fill in coat check tents, welcome desks, and happy guests sipping bubbly prosecco. We huddle together in the middle of the lawn, our backs to the wind as I explain exactly how I intend to execute the theme.

"We'll have the main entrance over here, a long and narrow tent with some hightop tables scattered around to hold discarded glasses. Beyond will be the entrance to the dining area, but I want us to have doors closing it off until it is time to eat."

"I don't know," interrupts Will. "I don't think we can fit the expected number of attendees into the front room for any extended period, Nat."

"Ahh, but wait, Will. There's more to the plan," I reply with a wink, before twisting on my heels and walking off. "I want us to create four long galleries, two on either end of the entrance hall."

Will and Jill wear matching confused expressions, but follow along, curious to see what I mean.

"Think of it like a museum gallery." I use my hands to trace a square shape around us. "You come into the main foyer, and then work your way in and out of the exhibition galleries that branch off it."

I point to either side of us, indicating where the galleries would be, explaining, "That's what we're going to do here. We can have a gallery branching off from each corner. In each of the four galleries, we'll display roughly one century worth of women's stories."

"Century?" asks Will.

"Four galleries?" adds Jill.

I motion them to step in closer as I let them in on the rest of the plan. Their eyes grow wide, excitement shining out of them. "... We can have a mix of paintings and portraits, maybe a few sketches and relevant antiques. Different items to use as anchor points as our guests make their way through the story of the history of women at Barnard College."

"That sounds amazing, Nat," Jill gushes, "I wonder if we can find some costumes as well."

"Costumes? Do you want to dress us the wait staff again?

Because that was kind of a one-time deal for the St Margaret gala," I explain.

"No," Jill waves away my argument. "I was thinking of statues or mannequins."

"Mannequins? Jill, you're brilliant! Absolutely brilliant! I know just the place to get a set of perfectly authentic period statues."

Jill beams with pride while H taps my leg with a talon and makes a fake coughing noise. I guess he's figured out where I plan to find my 'mannequins'.

I glare down at him, holding a finger to my lips to shush him. He quiets down, but not without making his opinion clear. If his eyes roll any harder, they're likely to fall out of his head.

Let's hope Barnard's Eternals are more enthusiastic about the idea than H is.

# Chapter Nine

T he next morning, I bypass my standard work wardrobe, opting for a pair of comfortable black leggings and an oversized jumper instead. I've got a long day of work in the old library marked in my diary and I'm really looking forward to the chance to spend time alongside Mathilde and Kate.

Although I haven't admitted it to anyone, I've been a little jealous of their together-time over the last several days. Who knows what kind of lost treasures they've uncovered from the crates, shelves and stacks inside the secret chamber? Now it's my turn to find out.

H and I take a meandering walk, detouring to pass through the university parks on our way from St Margaret to Barnard. Since we'll be spending most of the day locked inside, we both thought it best to get some fresh air and exercise first thing in the morning.

Nonetheless, we're the first to arrive in the library. I brew a pot of fresh coffee and set out a tray of breakfast pastries and fresh fruit I picked up at a nearby bakery. When everything is perfectly positioned, I give Harry a quick buzz to invite her to join me.

"I cannot tell you how happy I am to be away from that over-bearing man for a day!" she exclaims as she walks into the library.

"I assume you mean Master Finch-Byron and not your husband Rob? What's the Master done this time and where is he today?" I'm curious to know how Harry is getting along in her temporary role.

"He's off in London today for some society meeting. Good riddance! I don't know how Lucy managed to work for him all these years. He never says please or thank you, just drops a load of papers on my desks and orders me to 'deal with them' - as though I have a clue! He expects me to be at his beck and call, heaven forbid I step out for a loo break." She falls onto the sofa beside me. "Look at this spread, luv! You've outdone yourself!"

"Who's outdone themselves?" Mathilde calls, the library door swinging shut behind her. She follows the sound of our voices until she reaches our seating area. "Oh, are those pain au choco-lat? Please say they're for me!"

"Help yourself," I say, waving my arm over the tray. "I thought you and Kate might need a break from cold sandwiches and crisp packets."

Mathilde swoons as she bites into her pastry, golden brown crumbs sticking to her mouth. I love how down to earth she is, always wearing printed t-shirts and jeans. She is dead serious about her work, but for everything else she's relaxed. She's the perfect escape for those moments when I'm stressed out.

"Don't fill up too much," I caution her. "We've got lunch coming as well. One of the potential celebration caterers is drop-ping off samples of their cream tea offering."

Kate arrives moments later, joining us in the back. She perches on the sofa near Mathilde before filling a plate with fruit and a pastry. On the surface, she is Mathilde's total opposite. Her sleek bob, tasteful jewellery and cashmere jumper stand in stark contrast. However, her sharp wit and seemingly endless knowledge of art history allowed her to forge a fast friendship with Mathilde. Left alone, those two could talk English history for hours.

Harry has us in stitches, recounting stories of H's misadventures while he stayed with her over the Christmas holidays. I take a moment to look around at our little group, amazed at how well we fit together. It doesn't matter that we're different ages and come from different backgrounds. The experience of discovering magic exists created an unbreakable bond.

When we manage to stop laughing, Mathilde asks, "Okay, now that we've had breakfast, what are your plans here today, Nat?"

"Master Finch-Byron has signed off on the invitation list for the reveal of the contents of the secret chamber. Harry and I now need to prepare an invitation," I explain, "and we thought it would be a good idea to include a mini-catalogue with photos and descriptions of some of the items they'll see."

Nodding, Harry adds, "We'll need someone to help us with the descriptions, but we'll do our best to stay out of your way while we stage our photoshoots. Is there a place we can set ourselves up?"

Kate leads us to the other side of the room and before long we're all hard at work on our respective tasks. Between Harry's eye for photography and above-average amateur skills, and my wizardry with the layout software, we make steady progress on our catalogue. Mathilde and Kate take turns selecting items for our use, and then hand us over to either Lady Petronilla or Ada for an explanation of the significance of each one.

The old library is the perfect backdrop for our photos, with its aged wooden shelves and rich velvety fabrics. Before long, Harry and I are chatting away as we position and reposition old books and bronze statues, trying to capture the best lighting.

It takes me half an hour to work up the courage to tell Harry about Edward. In my heart, I know my fear is rooted in the fact that I actually like him. Even though I know Harry likes Edward, what if she doesn't approve of the idea of us being together? I shove my worries down, blurting it out in a rush before I can stop myself.

"Edward invited me to the Ashmolean rooftop bar for a drink."

When Harry doesn't immediately respond, I raise my gaze from the book in my hand, looking over to see her reaction. The grin on her face stretches from ear to ear.

"Oh, Nat, that's wonderful. Two of my favourite people, finding their way to one another..."

I can't stop myself from snorting. "Finding our way? You practically shoved us together, moving me in downstairs from him and talking about him all the time."

"Well," she huffs, but a laugh softens her tone, "I hardly knew anything about you when we offered to put you up in college housing. But I will admit that the idea crossed my mind on the very first day, when you asked who lived in the upstairs flat. But I can't take credit for anything else. That was the two of you... and a murder investigation."

"Ha! I can picture us now, telling our children how we met. 'There was a dead chef and then we had a flat tyre.' Sounds like a love story for the ages."

Harry and I dissolve into a fit of laughter, loud enough to attract Kate and Mathilde's attention.

"What has gotten into you two?" asks Kate, her brow furrowed in annoyance.

Mathilde, however, casts a curious gaze in our direction, clearly happy to have an excuse for a break.

I nod my head at Harry, giving her permission to let the others know my news.

"Our Nat is going to have drinks with Edward."

Rolling her eyes, Kate scoffs, "That's hardly news. We all saw the two of you at St Margaret's autumn gala and at the children's Christmas party. It's about time you finally admit you've got a crush."

Mathilde rubs her hands together with glee, "What I wouldn't give to be a fly on the wall for that tête-à-tête. Do you know where you're going yet?"

"The Ash," I mumble, hoping they won't hear me.

"The Ash? My Ash? The museum?" Kate clarifies. "Is he taking you to the rooftop bar? If so, you're in luck. It's gorgeous up there."

We spend the next ten minutes discussing the Ashmolean's cocktail menu. After a while I fall silent, letting the other three women carry on their debate over whether I should get a sophisticated cocktail, a girly drink or a simple glass of wine. Not one of them seems bothered by his lack of knowledge of Oxford's magic, or what that means for all of us.

When their debate grows heated, I wave my hands and call them to a stop. "If you three are done arguing over my drink order, I've got a more important question."

All three of them turn their heads in my direction.

"Let's say my drinks date goes well. We move on to a dinner date and before you know it, we're a couple. Since you all are my best friends here in Oxford, we'll inevitably end up spending time with you..."

I glance around to make sure they're paying attention. "When Edward is around, H is a cat, Bartie doesn't exist, my grandfather is dead, and there is NO MAGIC AT ALL. Now, do you think we're capable of keeping this secret from him?"

Kate and Mathilde are thunderstruck, but Harry taps her finger against her lips with a thoughtful gaze in her eyes. "I worked with your predecessor Lillian for years and she never let on about the existence of magic. Never hinted at it, and we were the best of friends. So, it is possible."

Kate nods in agreement, but Mathilde still shows signs of concern. "Maybe we should give it a test run, Nat. You know, before you go out for drinks. In fact..." Mathilde checks her watch before continuing. "Didn't you say we're having catered lunch today? Why don't you give Edward a ring and see if he wants to join us?"

"I don't know..." I say while shaking my head.

"That's a great idea!" Kate exclaims. "Harry, why don't you call him instead of Nat? That way there's no pressure at all." She reaches over and gives my arm a quick squeeze. "You'll see, Nat. I'm sure it will go smoothly. Then you'll be able to set this worry aside and focus on more important things."

I arch an eyebrow. "Such as?"

"Such as - what are you going to wear for your date?" Kate replies before laughing at the look of terror on my face.

Harry doesn't wait for me to answer. She grabs her phone off a nearby table and finds Edward's number in her contact list. I forget to breathe as we stand huddled around her, listening to the phone ring. Harry makes quick work of the invitation, and Edward accepts, none the wiser of the bigger question at hand.

*Can Mathilde, Kate and I get through an entire lunch without ever mentioning the words 'magic' or 'Eternals' or 'H'?*

That question runs through my head for the next hour as we wait for our lunch delivery. My nerves stretch, my shoulders creeping up as the tension sets in around my neck. I keep telling myself that it is a simple lunch with friends, but I'm not sure I believe it.

When the library desk phone rings, its loud tone trilling through the library, I nearly leap out of my skin.

"Sorry," Mathilde calls out as she dashes over to answer it. "I turned the volume up to the max so we could hear the phone from anywhere."

It's the security guard at the front entrance letting us know the catered lunch has arrived and is waiting for us to collect it. Kate and Harry offer to walk downstairs, both voicing a desire to stretch their legs. I make a quick escape to the loo, using water from the taps to tidy my curls. I swipe on a coat of lip gloss and smooth the wrinkles in my jumper before going back to the library.

Kate and Harry are inside with the food and already busy laying out a spread of mini-quiches, bitesize sandwiches and an array of desserts.

"Come on, Mathilde," I call, "Edward will be here any minute now. Don't you want to wash some of the dust off before we eat?"

"Ugh, I know you're right, but I've only got two pages left in this old journal and I was hoping to finish it. The handwriting is so crabby and faded, it is taking forever," Mathilde complains as she hunts around for a bookmark.

"Here, Mathilde. Pass it over to me," my grandfather offers. "I'll finish it up while you're eating lunch. Whose journal is it?"

"Sir Christopher Wren, if you can believe it," she replies, handing the journal over to my grandfather. "Thus far he's only talked about his failed studies into the earth's magnetic field. I can't figure out why anyone would hide it away in the secret chamber."

My grandfather carefully opens the journal, his hands cradling the ageing leather spine. As he begins turning the pages, the rest of us get back to tidying up and setting lunch out. I glance back to see him fully engrossed in the book, the old handwriting obviously not as much a problem for an Eternal as it was for Mathilde.

Mathilde walks back in, drying her hands on her trousers. She halts when my grandfather calls out, pointing at the journal excitedly.

"My word, I can't believe it. You found it, Mathilde. The last experiment Sir Christopher Wren documented in the journal went awry. This journal documents the very day when he and his fellow researchers uncovered the existence of the magic."

We all stand agape, hardly able to believe our luck. But before any of us can snap out of our stupor and ask a single question, the library door swings open.

"Oh, hello everyone," Edward calls out, "I wasn't expecting a group here. Is it still okay for me to join you? If you don't have enough, I can eat in the dining hall."

Harry elbows me in my side, jolting me into action. "Don't be silly, we've got plenty. Come on in," I say as I move to intercept him on his way towards us, buying Kate and Mathilde time to get themselves back in the present moment. I wave Edward on in Harry's direction, pausing to whisper at my fellow prefects, "Pull yourselves together! We can find out what the journal says after Edward leaves."

Kate nods her understanding, but I can see that Mathilde is torn. If given a choice, she'd pick the journal over a plate of iced petit fours. I wrap my arm around her own and manoeuvre her to the sofas where we've laid out lunch.

When everyone is seated and enjoying the tiny sandwiches, I finally release the breath I'd been holding. Having Edward here in this very moment is far from ideal, but we've got the worst part behind us. If we can all hold back our curiosity for another hour, it should all be fine.

I begin to settle back into the sofa cushions. Just as my back relaxes, I hear the telltale screech of one of the library exterior windows sliding open.

"Oi, bruvs, why didn't ya tell me it was lunch time! Is that a pot of clotted cream I see? And wot's Edward doin' 'ere?" H bellows as he somersaults through the window and into the room.

I leap from the sofa, crossing the room to swoop H into my

arms. "Hahaha, there you are, you bad kitty. I was wondering where you were hiding away."

H takes one look at my glowing red face and immediately settles into my arms, tucking his wings and claws in tight so he doesn't injure me.

"Did your cat fly in through that window?" Edward asks, peering at the stained-glass object in question. "How did it get up that high?"

I force out another nervous laugh before depositing H onto the rug near our feet. "Of course, he didn't fly in through the window. That's ridiculous. He must have spotted a bug flying around and leapt off one of the bookshelves trying to catch it."

I give Harry a pointed look, my eyes begging her to help me out with this situation. It is rapidly getting out of control and I need someone to step in and distract Edward while I get H settled.

"So, Edward," Harry jumps in, "how is the investigation coming along? Is there anything you can tell us?"

I shove a bowl of clotted cream in H's direction before reclaiming my seat on the sofa.

"I've hit a bit of a wall, if I'm honest, Harry," Edward replies in between bites. "I've looked at the security feed; the London police have investigated Ms Evans' background. There simply isn't anything there which would provide a clue as to what happened."

I give Edward a reassuring smile when he glances in my direction. His stalled-out investigation is a good thing, at least in my mind. If he's managed to rule out Ms Evans' as a suspect in the burglary, hopefully he'll start to look into her interactions here at Barnard. Just in case, I decide to give him a gentle nudge in that direction.

"You know, I heard someone talking the other day in the dining hall. It was a young man, he seemed quite fraught. I'm sure

I heard him mention Ms Evans' name. Her first name was Victoria, right?"

Edward raises an eyebrow. "Yes, that was her name. A young man... a student perhaps? You didn't happen to hear his name?"

"He looked older than the undergrads," I explain, "more like a graduate student. When he ran out, one of his friends called out his name. Charles something? Gibbs? Gravesend?"

I cast an eye at Harry, silently urging her to fill in the rest. No need for Edward to know I've been running my own investigation into Ms Evans' death.

"Graves? Could that be it?" Harry asks, guilelessly. "There's a masters student named Charles Graves who works in one of the offices close to Finch-Byron's. He'd certainly have had ample opportunity to interact with Ms Evans."

Edward fishes a notebook out of his pocket. "Charles Graves. Right, I've written his name on my follow-up list. I've got a few final lines of inquiry to wrap up today, but if nothing pans out, I'll look him up tomorrow. The coroner is due to send the autopsy results to the Oxford police department first thing in the morning and I'll need to check in with them first."

"Autopsy results?" Mathilde interrupts. "Surely the cause of death was obvious? Are you expecting to find something?"

Shrugging, Edward admits, "I'm not too hopeful, but the police conduct an autopsy and toxicology screen in all suspected murder cases. If they've managed to identify any findings outside of the expected, I'll take whatever assistance they can give me."

The rest of lunch passes uneventfully, and thank goodness for that. Mathilde and Kate take turns peppering Edward with questions in an attempt to get to know him. Before I know it, everyone stands up, calling an end to our lunch break.

Edward eyes me hopefully. "Nat, would you walk with me to the door?"

"Um, sure, of course." I drop my stack of paper plates onto the table and dust my hands with a napkin.

His face softens into a boyish grin as he reaches out a hand. Without thinking, I slip my hand into his. Together we make our way through the library, exiting the room into the outer hallway.

Edward turns, putting us face-to-face, but he doesn't let go of my hand. "Thanks for inviting me to join you and your friends."

"Oh, it wasn't me, it was Harry. She phoned you." I murmur. Heat flushes up my neck.

"I know she phoned, but I suspected you were somehow involved in the invitation." He winks at me as he confesses, "I actually had a lunch engagement, but I postponed my meeting so I could be here instead."

"Oh."

"Yes, oh. About my invitation to get a drink..." he starts.

"Yes?" I ask.

"I know I said we should wait until I wrap up this investigation, but I don't know if I want to hold off that long. What would you say to next week? Maybe Thursday night?" His eyes twinkle as he waits for my response.

"Yea. Sure. That should be... I mean, I'll need to check my diary to be sure, but I guess I could move something around if I have a conflict, as long as it isn't anything time-sensitive..." I hear myself babbling but can't seem to stop myself.

Does it sound like I'm saying no? I try again. "Of course, I'm sure it will be fine, I don't do anything important. Um, wait, that didn't come out right. Of course, my job is important, but, ugh, you know what I mean."

Chuckling, Edward gives my arm a squeeze. "Why don't you check your diary? If I don't hear anything from you today, I'll assume that Thursday is a yes."

I nod my agreement, not trusting my mouth.

Edward gives me a gentle smile and a final arm squeeze. Then he spins on his heel and makes his way along the corridor in the direction of the staircase.

For my part, I lean against the wall, a giant smile blossoming on my face. An hour ago, I'd have sworn that the lunch was a total disaster. But if H's awkward arrival and Kate and Mathilde's interrogation didn't put Edward off, maybe he has more patience than I thought.

Any further daydreaming screeches to a halt when Mathilde opens the library door and says, "Will you stop mooning around and get in here? Alfred won't read us anything from Wren's journal until we're all inside to hear it."

# Chapter Ten

I follow Mathilde back inside the old library, trailing behind her as she bustles over to one of the large study tables. Kate, Harry and H are already seated with Lady Petronilla and Ada standing behind. I slide into the remaining seat, looking up at my grandfather. Journal in hand, he is sitting at the head of the table.

His face is serious as he begins. "As Mathilde said earlier, there are only two pages of specific interest to us in this journal. If we want to know more, we'll have to hope we find the next one in the series. It might yet be hidden away in one of the remaining piles of materials left for us to review."

Kate and I grimace, but Mathilde looks gleeful at the thought of rifling through more ancient journals.

"Rather than give you a summary, I think it's best if I read this entry out loud, letting you all hear it firsthand. Is that okay with everyone?"

I glance around the table. We're all leaning forward, keen to hear whatever details my grandfather is about to reveal from Sir Christopher Wren's journal.

"Sir Christopher, as you may recall from your primary school days, was a famous architect in the late seventeenth century. He is credited with redesigning much of London following the Great Fire," my grandfather explains. "However, before he took up his position in London, Sir Christopher was a student here at Oxford. One of some renown, I might add. He was part of the inner circle of natural philosophers who later formed the Royal Society. Some of the greatest scientific discoveries of the seventeenth century came out of the work of this group of men."

"Apparently, more discoveries than anyone was aware, if what you are about to read us is true," Kate murmurs.

"What does it say, Alfred?" Harry urges, "Go on and read it to us."

"Very well, but I wanted to make sure you appreciated the time period before I started. Now, where is the page?" He flips a page over, scanning down the lines with his finger and finally starting to read.

*"Somerset College, Oxford, 7 July 1655 -*

*My hand shakes even now as I reflect back on the activities and events of this momentous day. But I am rushing to the end without explaining the beginning. My day started as so many others. I encountered Wilkins in his study and invited him to accompany me to a larger chamber where I intended to conduct a study into terrestrial magnetism. I laid out rods of copper and bronze in a semi-circle. When I fell short of one, Wilkins flung me a bronze candlestick from the mantlepiece. I moved to cross to his side, brushing a curtain in my haste. A single ray of sunlight landed on the candlestick, setting forth a glow much like a small flame. In the next instance, a vision of Lady Somerset herself leaned out from her portrait, berating us for our carelessness with her family possessions. What had been a likeness in a painting was now flesh and bone. It took Wilkins and I some moments to believe our eyes, sure we were hallucinating. Eventually, Lady Somerset asked for a hand. With my help, she stepped out of her portrait, guiding us around the college to see sights never before seen. Scholars long lost to time. Statues which speak. She called them 'Eternals'. In time we began to see the veracity of this alternate version of Oxford. Tomorrow night we shall share this news with the rest of the club and determine what steps to take next. One thing is apparent - this mystical realm could have grave implications if made public for all to see and know."*

"There you have it. Wren and Wilkins meant to study the earth's magnetic properties. They found the magical ones instead." With that final pronouncement, my grandfather closes the journal and carefully lays it on the table. "It is a fascinating tale. The power of sunlight together with a highly ductile metal like bronze..."

"Forget the science for a moment. Does it say what happened next? Anything at all?" Mathilde asks as she reaches for the leather-bound book.

"No," he shakes his head. "It was as you said earlier. Those were the last two pages in this volume. To learn more, we must search for the next and hope it was stored away in the chamber as well."

I can feel my eyes beginning to cross at the thought of looking through any old books filled with faded handwriting. Surely there must be a quicker way... I run the story back through my mind, searching for any clue. "Wait, right at the end. He mentioned their club. You said it turned into the Royal Society, right?"

My grandfather arches an eyebrow, "Yes, that's right, Nat. The roots of the Royal Society are well documented."

"In that case," I say, "couldn't some of us start from the other direction? I'm sure a roster of Wilkins' club members exists on the internet."

Mathilde leans back in her chair, looking thoughtful. "That might work. It would give us a place to start, although I'd still want the next journal for confirmation. We need to know exactly who was at that meeting, what they were told and what they did next. But if you can give us some additional ideas of other journals we could search, that would be helpful."

I glance at Harry, smiling as she nods her agreement. "Okay, that's the plan. Mathilde and Kate, you'll obviously need to keep your focus on the contents of the secret chamber. Harry and I will see what we can uncover through the more modern route."

Kate pushes back her chair, prodding the rest of us into action. "Let's all put our noses to the grindstones for two hours, and then regroup for a coffee."

❖

A hush falls over the library as our group disperses, each of us heading off into a different part of the large room. The only sounds are the clacking of computer keyboards and rustling of papers. Even H is silent, having curled up on the sofa for an afternoon nap after gorging himself at lunch on cheese soufflés and clotted cream.

Harry moves deeper into the library, chasing the afternoon sunlight for the final photos we need. I'm left alone at the front desk with my head full of fast-moving thoughts. It doesn't take me long to update the chamber reveal catalogue; once that is done, I turn my attention to researching Wilkins' philosophical club. As expected, the internet is rife with information and I quickly jot down the names of the other members I can find. There are quite a few who appear to have been in Oxford in the 1650s, but I don't have any luck finding meeting minutes or other detailed records.

With my tasks complete, I let my mind wander. When I have this many priorities fighting for my attention, I find it best to let my subconscious determine how to tackle them. It's hardly a surprise that my thoughts head straight to Edward. It's been three months since I arrived in Oxford last October and I've been doing a careful dance around Edward since the day we got a flat tyre on our way back from interviewing a potential suspect out in the Cotswolds.

I wish there was a way to tell him about Oxford's magic and to explain why he needs to turn his investigation in a different direction. The Eternals barely agreed to bring Harry into the fold, and that was an act of desperation. There is no way they'll ever agree to let me tell Edward about their existence. Saying 'I might somewhat fancy him' isn't exactly a convincing argument for breaking four hundred plus years of protocol.

No, it's up to me to figure out how to juggle the various aspects of my life. Lillian managed it, as did my grandfather before her, so I know it is possible. "You haven't even been on the first date, yet!" I remind myself. I reel my mind back in before it goes any further down that path.

My thoughts drift, but not far. Edward's investigation. His offhand remark about the autopsy results has me wondering what they might reveal. Edward may not know it yet, but I've narrowed the suspect pool down to either Master Finch-Byron or his wife. If the autopsy showed evidence of a recent romantic encounter, that might take the Master's wife out of the running.

If only there was some way to get my hands on a copy of the report. My mind spins in circles, but nothing reasonable pops out. I'm hardly going to break into the police station and there is no way Edward would share the information with me. How would I even justify asking?

Shutting off my thoughts for a moment, I let my gaze wander the room. Harry is busy snapping photos. Mathilde and my grandfather are fully engrossed, working their way through a stack of dusty books and loose papers. Kate, however, sits with a perplexed look on her face and a matching pair of wooden carvings in each hand.

Happy for an excuse to take a break, I rise from my chair and cross the room to see what is going on. "Hiya, Kate. It looks like you're getting ready to do bicep curls with those carvings, but I'm guessing that isn't correct. What's up?"

"Either I'm going crazy, or there is something really weird about these wooden statuettes. Here, you hold them and tell me what you feel." Kate passes them into my outstretched hands. I raise and lower my hands, weighing the two items.

"One of these is heavier than the other one. Not by much, but enough that I can tell," I reply.

"Yes! That's exactly what I thought. But why would a matching pair weigh different amounts? I've been looking over the craftsmanship, comparing what I can see of the wood, and they seem identical. But yet, they aren't." She shrugs, confusion writ across her face.

I stare at the carvings, thinking over everything we've learned so far. A thought niggles in the back of my mind. I close my eyes for a second, stilling my movements to give it a chance to work its way to the forefront.

What would someone hide in a carving? The statuettes are glued tightly to their wooden bases, so whatever it is wasn't meant to be accessible. The items aren't useful; they're designed to sit on a shelf somewhere and look nice.

Wait a minute. Something designed to sit around in an Oxford college?

"Kate, this may sound crazy, but do you think one of these carvings might have a piece of bronze inside of it?" I ask.

"Bronze? Why would someone..." Kate's brow furrows in concentration. "Oh. Oh yes. You're a genius, Nat. Could that be how the magic works? With a bunch of bronze rods hidden around Oxford?" Kate takes the statuettes from my outstretched hands, once again eyeballing them. "I am loathe to do anything which might damage them. But maybe we could x-ray them? I've got an x-ray machine in the basement of the Ashmolean. We use it to check on our mummies."

"That's brilliant!" I exclaim. "But you'll have to sneak them out of here in your handbag. Finch-Byron will never give you permission, and how would you explain what you want to do with them?"

Kate grabs a nearby pile of cloths and carefully wraps each carving, tying them closed with string. She places them into her handbag as though she were laying a baby down in a bed. "The Ashmolean may only be two blocks from here, but I am going to be a nervous wreck transporting potentially priceless antique carved statuettes in my handbag."

Before I can respond, we're interrupted by the sound of a loud growl coming from Mathilde's direction.

"Ugh! I can't believe it!" she groans, looking down at the loose papers scattered around her.

"No luck finding the next journal?" I query, mostly to distract her from glaring at the offending pages.

"No, it's the opposite problem." Mathilde picks up a leather-bound tome. "I found the journal, but half of the pages have been ripped out."

She waves her hand over the papers lying in disarray. "As best as I can tell, these are some of them, but look," she cries, picking up a torn sheet. "This is only half of a page. Where is the rest of it?"

Kate and I climb to our feet, moving closer so we can see first-hand the damage. Mathilde is right, most of the papers have jagged edges, their different lengths testifying to the missing elements.

Mathilde opens the journal to the first page. "Wren picks up his next entry on the evening of the Philosophical Club meeting. The entry spans two pages and finishes with a list of the atten-dees. But someone has torn off the bottom of the page. Why would they do that?"

"Can you see any of the names?" Kate interjects.

"Yes, some of them are still here. There's Wren himself and Wilkins, no surprises there. I can make out the names of Robert Hooke, Seth Ward and Robert Wood, but then the list ends abruptly there. I've been looking for the missing scrap."

"Some of those names sound familiar. Hold on." I stride across the room and reach over the front desk to get my notepad. Skimming the list, I mentally check off the names. "I found all of those in my quick internet research, and I've also got three others. But, I couldn't find any confirmation of whether these men were active in the club in 1655."

Mathilde takes the list, lining it up side by side with the journal. "Wren wrote each name on its own line, see?" She points to her page. "The missing part would be large enough to hold up to four more names, or it might have one more and the rest blank. UGH!" she groans again.

My grandfather steps in to tidy up the papers and journal before Mathilde can take out her frustration on them. "Don't stress, dear, we'll find the information somewhere. As a fellow librarian, you know as well as I do that things are rarely written down only once. It's simply a matter of continuing to look."

Huffing out a breath, Mathilde wonders aloud, "But why would someone tear off that particular scrap? Why would they damage this journal?"

As we ponder the question, the sound of ripping leather breaks the silence. H, apparently awoken by Mathilde's groans, is using his talons to slow his slide down the front of a nearby shelf.

"Lor luv, missies. A bruv can't get a nap with all yer natterin'. I've been listenin' for a while and I can see ya need some new ideas, so I'll tell ya wot I think. Whoever did this 'as ta be related ta tha magic. 'Ow else would they know where ta find tha journal?"

We stare openmouthed at H's pronouncement. Why didn't we think of this before?

"There have always been three prefects, right?" When everyone nods, I continue, "But it takes more than descending from the right bloodline to land a job here. Look at the three of us, we all have relevant degrees and at least several years of experience."

I pause, carrying on when no one interrupts. "And we know that being a prefect can skip generations, usually more than one. That suggests that there is a larger pool of potential prefects wandering around, right?"

Nodding, Kate replies, "Of course, that makes perfect sense. We know for sure that there were at least five men in the original group. Nearly four hundred years of descendants... that could mean there are hundreds of people walking around now with the right bloodline."

As the implications set in, Mathilde looks stunned. "What if..." her voice trails off. "What if one of them found out about the magic? What would someone do to get access to all of the magical advantages we have here in Oxford?"

Kate whispers, barely loud enough for us to hear, "If that's true, the break-ins and thefts would make a lot more sense. We've been thinking that a person is behind all of this, but what if it is someone guided by an Eternal instead?"

My stomach roils at the thought.

# Chapter Eleven

The next morning, the buzz of an incoming text wakes me from my slumber. I feel around my bedside table until I find the offending object, barely managing to read the message with only one eye open.

"Do you want to meet for an early morning run?" I read aloud.

H grumbles from his nearby cat bed, "Iffen yer asking me, tha answer is a definite no. Go back ta bed, Nat."

"I wish," I mumble back, my voice heavy with sleep. "I knew I'd regret telling Kate that I sometimes like to go for a jog."

I pull the covers over my head but it's no use. I'm awake and I might as well get up and join Kate in her morning sweat. With that decided, I throw my covers back and crawl out of bed.

I'm somewhat more alert by the time I reach the pavement in front of my flat. As I jog through the quiet streets, I give myself a figurative pat on the back for making it out so early.

The outdoor air is crisp and cold, but the sky is clear of even a hint of a cloud. My breath fogs in time with my steps. I pick up my speed in an effort to warm myself.

I'm looking forward to catching up with Kate. Mathilde and I have regular TV nights in our diaries, but Kate's schedule is too erratic to allow her to commit to a standing date. There is always some gallery opening, art auction or cocktail event, and as the Director of the Ashmolean Museum, she is expected to attend. This will be our first chance in a while to have a conversation that doesn't centre around the burglary or the problems with the magic.

Kate had suggested we go directly to Port Meadow, setting a meeting point at the bottom of the bridge in the nearby neighbourhood of Jericho. Since I'm a couple of minutes late, I arrive to find Kate warming up while she waits. She waves me on, falling into place by my side, jogging at a leisurely pace.

"Morning, Nat! I thought for sure you'd ignore my text, but I'm glad to see you made it out. I have to ask, are those pineapples on your leggings?"

My mind instantly flashes back to that fateful evening last term when I went for an evening run, got caught in a downpour and ended up unmasking a murder. I haven't worn these leggings since then, which is weird since they are one of my favourite pairs. Maybe having them on again will lead to another epiphany.

I skim my eyes over Kate's slender form, starting with the steel grey runner's jacket to her black t-shirt and finally down her black leggings. Even her trainers are black. "Ha, yes. I've also got leggings decorated with flying cats. Maybe I should loan you a pair? We need to get you out of your basic black running uniform." I pretend to seriously consider the situation. "On second thought, I'm not sure you're ready for something that bold. Maybe we should start you off on a basic blue or red?"

"You know us artsy types, Nat. We have to dress all in black and pretend to be suffering," Kate says, laughing. "But on to more important matters. I can't get my mind off yesterday's discovery. Sir Christopher Wren, of all people! I hope Mathilde and Alfred can piece together more of the story. If an Eternal is behind all of this... I still can't wrap my head around it."

Grimacing, I reply, "Me either. Even H was shocked at the idea. He moped around all evening, distraught at the idea that an Eternal could be working against us."

Kate gives a knowing shake of her head. "I know exactly what you mean. Bartie didn't believe me at first; I had to phone Mathilde last night and get her to confirm everything I told him."

I let our conversation lapse into silence for a moment as I debate whether to ask my next question. Is it considered rude to pry into someone else's relationship? Or is that what friends do? It's not like Kate held back on her thoughts about Edward.

Eventually, curiosity gets the better of me. "So... what is going on with you and Bartie?"

I glance to the side in time to see a broad grin break out across Kate's face.

"He's wonderful," she says, dreamily. When I arch an eyebrow, she continues, "Oh, I know it's all rather unorthodox, but as long as we're within the magic's boundaries, Bartie is as solid and real to me as any man I'd meet on a night out."

"But what about date nights? Meeting your family?" I pause to leap over a puddle. "You know, down the line. How will you manage that?"

Kate remains quiet, waiting until we stop beside the River Thames to catch our breath. Right as I begin to worry I've been too nosy, she breaks the silence.

"We haven't known each other very long, Nat, but you've seen what my working life is like. I'm always off at some event or another. The last thing I need is a partner who wants to go out on the rare night I'm at home."

I search her face, taking a measure of the truth of her statement. Reassured by what I see, I say, "Bartie certainly fits that requirement. You don't have to justify why you won't bring him to a work event, and he's not going to complain about missing a night at the pub with his mates."

"Exactly!" Kate exclaims. "I remember the first time I used my key to unlock the magic. I felt the zing all the way up my arm. When he kisses me, I feel that all over again. But it isn't just physical. In some ways Bartie is old-fashioned, always holding the door open for me or waiting for me to sit down first. But he isn't staid or stodgy. He has seen how the world has changed over the years; he knows how hard I had to work to get where I am. He cares for me, but, more importantly, he also respects me."

I pick up a stone and skip it across the placid surface of the river. "Here I was worrying I was going to be the prefect who breaks all of the traditions!"

Kate laughs while giving me a gentle nudge with her elbow. "You've broken your fair share, and something tells me you aren't done yet. Where we see a rule to obey, you see a challenge to overcome. I envy you that, Nat. It's an exciting way to view the world."

"Sometimes too exciting," I mumble, scuffing up a small cloud of dust with my foot. "It seems like we're constantly rushing around, barely able to put one fire out before another one starts."

"On that note, we'd better head back." Kate does a final stretch before setting off towards Jericho. "What's on your agenda for today, Nat?"

"I need to work on the plans for the secret chamber reveal event, and I really should check in with Will and Jill on their progress on the Barnard Women celebration. Plus, I should keep half an eye on Edward, to make sure he follows up with Charles Graves. I wish there was some way I could get my hands on a copy of the autopsy results."

"Good luck with that," Kate says wryly. "Maybe Edward will leave them lying around somewhere."

I pick up the pace as we get closer to home. "I'll never be that lucky. I'd have better luck snooping around the central police station. Too bad the magic can't make us prefects invisible. That would certainly come in handy."

As soon as the words are out of my mouth, Kate comes to a screeching halt. "Wait, Nat, we can be invisible!"

"Huh?" I blurt.

"Not us," Kate clarifies, "but the Eternals. Bartie, Lady Petronilla... your own grandfather! Any of them could get in and out of the police station without anyone being the wiser."

"Of course! Why didn't I think of that? Do you think one of them would do it?" I ask.

Kate nods, "I'm sure Bartie would do it if I asked him."

Glancing at my watch, I grab Kate's arm and pull her into motion. "Well, then, what are we waiting for? From what I remember, shouldn't he be in the Fellows Garden at this hour doing his morning meditation? Let's ask him straightaway. We need him to get to the station before Edward picks up the report and puts it into his bag. He keeps that thing with him all day, we won't get another chance anytime soon."

Kate splutters, "But my hair! I'm so sweaty. Can't I shower first?"

"Your boyfriend is a ghost, Kate. I hardly think he's in a position to complain if you smell a little bit. Now come on!" I dash off before she can offer up another excuse to delay.

Bartie had practically glowed with delight when Kate and I turned up in the Fellows Garden. It was clear as day that he couldn't have cared less that she was hot and sweaty from our sprint back from Port Meadows.

It took no convincing to get Bartie to go to the police station. Kate barely had the words out of her mouth before he was spinning off. I called after his departing form to let him know we'd await his return at my flat at St Margaret.

"You know Bartie is head over heels for you, Kate?" I ask as we walk up the back stairs into my flat.

"I still wish you'd have let me shower, Nat," Kate mutters as she slides into one of my kitchen chairs. "But yes, I'm starting to get the hint that he's serious about seeing where this all goes. It took me ages to convince him that I really don't mind him being an Eternal."

"Watching you two together gives me hope. If you can find a way to date an Eternal, surely I can make a relationship work with a wily professor. Right?" The last part comes out as more of a question than I intended.

"Of course, you can, Nat! Set your worries aside, go on your date and have fun. We'll be there to help you deal with any problems or roadblocks that turn up down the line."

I busy myself with my cafetière, pointing Kate towards my refrigerator to scavenge around for breakfast ingredients. H comes out of the bedroom, rubbing his eyes and dragging the bottoms of his wings on the ground.

"Oi, Kate! Wot are ya doin' 'ere so early?" He slides up next to Kate, peering into the refrigerator with her. After a moment, he flaps his wings, flying up to open one of my cupboards. "Nat 'asn't been ta tha market yet. We'll 'ave ta make do with some old cereal, iffen yer hungry."

Kate takes one look at H eating directly from the box of half-empty Weetabix before saying, "I think I'll stick with coffee, thanks."

Shrugging, I place two steaming cups of fresh coffee on the table. "I have to go to the market this weekend. This week has flown by. Has it only been five days since Mathilde and I discovered Ms Evans' body in the library?"

"Five endless days, if you ask me. Even by my normal crazy

standards, I've been working longer hours this week than ever before," Kate mutters.

H crunches another bite of cereal, showering the countertop with crumbs when he asks, "Back ta my question, Kate. Given our food shortage, thar's no way Nat invited ya 'ere for brunch. Wot's up?"

Kate and I take turns bringing H up to speed on Bartie's errand. H looks impressed that we came up with the idea but seems somewhat put out that we didn't think to ask him first. I have to think quick on my feet to keep him from feeling insulted.

"I knew you were tired from playing in the Barnard gardens most of yesterday. I didn't want to wake you up. Kate was sure Bartie would be wide awake, having his meditation time in the Fellows Garden," I explain.

"Yes, definitely," Kate adds, nodding. "If we'd known you were awake, you would have been the first person... er, Eternal we asked."

When H sticks his head into the cereal box, chasing the last crumbs, I give Kate a wink of thanks.

A sharp knock on my back door startles all three of us. I look through the window to see Bartie standing outside.

Opening the door, I ask, "Why did you knock on the door, Bartie? You can appear anywhere you want."

Bartie steps inside, doffing his cap and nodding a hello at H. When his eyes land on Kate, a gentle smile blossoms on his face. "Passing on cannot erase a lifetime of good manners, Nat. It isn't polite to barge into someone's home uninvited."

I wave him towards the table, inviting him to take a seat. He pulls a chair close to Kate, resting an arm on the back of her seat. If he's put off by her sweaty state, he doesn't show any sign of it.

"So?" I prompt him. "Did you have any luck trying to find the autopsy report?"

"It was fortunate you sent me when you did," Bartie replies.

"Edward arrived to collect the file while I was there. I had to whisper in the Detective Inspector's ear the suggestion to offer Edward a coffee. I barely had time to skim the folder while they were off in the break room."

"That was clever of you, darling. Was there anything of note in the results?" Kate asks.

"The good news is that it doesn't appear that Ms Evans suffered. The bad news is that she was pregnant at the time of her death."

"Pregnant?" I gasp. "Oh, that's even more awful. I wonder... did the file mention how far along she was?"

"About eight weeks, according to what I saw." Bartie frowns. "I didn't have time to read the other pages within the report, hopefully I haven't let you down."

I wave away his apology, my mind stuck on the news of Ms Evans' pregnancy. Depending on how quickly she took up with Master Finch-Byron, the child could have been his.

"What's going through your head, Nat?" Kate asks.

"What if she met with the Master to tell him about she was pregnant. Would Finch-Byron kill the woman carrying his child? It seems so callous, inhuman even. He isn't exactly the welcoming, friendly type, but still. I can't believe it."

"Especially since tha Master 'asn't got any other children. At least, as far as I know," H adds.

I rise from my chair and cross the room to collect a notepad and pencil. "Okay, what do we know so far? Evans was pregnant. We suspect Finch-Byron could be the father. If that is correct, who would feel threatened enough by the situation to kill her?"

"What about the potential boyfriend? Graves?" Kate looks to me for confirmation. "Maybe he found out and hit her in a fit of anger?"

I shake my head, saying, "Good theory, but I know for sure he was away the night of the murder, remember? And even though I only spoke with him for a short time, I have the feeling he'd be the type to offer to marry Ms Evans and raise the child as his own. He was completely in love with her, faults and all."

I stare at my notepad. "It must be the Master's wife, then. She's the only suspect left. What if she was worried that Finch-Byron would leave her? Do any of you know her at all?"

Kate's face is the picture of distaste when she answers. "I've met her. The best way I can describe her is as Cruella de Vil. I presume you know the movie, Nat, given your time at Disney."

I arch an eyebrow. "That is not a flattering comparison. Is she really that bad?"

"Worse." Kate gives me a frank look. "I've seen her a couple of times, swanning around events at the Ashmolean. She's always dressed extravagantly, jewels and fur at a minimum. Her voice can cut through the noise of any crowd, and she always has a gin and tonic in hand. She is titled - a Lady if you can believe it. I once saw her cut down a staff member who failed to use her title when speaking to her. The poor girl left in tears, and Lady Finch-Byron actually smiled as she watched her rush off."

"That does sound like Cruella," I mutter. "So, I guess it isn't too much of a stretch to think she'd off her husband's mistress?"

With a wry frown, Kate replies, "If Lady Finch-Byron felt threatened, I wouldn't put anything past her."

I pause to collect my thoughts, but as far as I can see there is only one logical next step. "I have to find a way to meet with her... see if I can get her to say or do anything which might incriminate her in Ms Evans' death."

H, Kate and Bartie begin shaking their heads furiously, somehow in perfect unison.

"No way. No!" Kate wags her finger at me.

"Uh huh, missie. Ya can't do that." H punctuates his sentence with a jet of flames.

"There must be some other option, Nat," Bartie implores,

ever the level-headed one in the group. "Perhaps you could go to Edward?"

"And say what, Bartie?" I throw my hands in the air. "That I sent a ghost to look at the autopsy results and know that Evans was pregnant? And it might be Finch-Byron's baby?"

Bartie's shoulders drop. Chagrinned, he replies, "When you put it that way..."

"Exactly. If I can get any evidence, any hint at all, I'll go straight to Edward. But until then, we're on our own." I pick up my pencil and tuck it behind my ear.

"Ya can't go on yer own, Nat. It isn't safe," H implores.

"Ok," I agree, seeing where they are coming from. "What if I take Harry with me? I'll probably need her help arranging the meeting anyway."

"'Arry?" H scoffs, "She can be fierce iffen ya get on 'er bad side, but I think ya need someone who can do more than scream for 'elp. Wot about..." H pauses for thought. "'Ow about ya take Petra along?"

"Lady Petronilla?" I lean forward to make sure I've heard him correctly. "How is she going to be more helpful than Harry?"

"Well," H explains, ticking his reasons off with his talons. "For one, iffen ya get into trouble, Lady Petra can get ta any of us right quick. Second, she's a Lady, just like Lady Finch-Byron. She'll know 'ow ta see through any high fallutin' airs the Master's wife might put on. Third, she's an Eternal. She can use tha magic to protect iffen she needs ta do so."

Kate and Bartie nod their agreement. It looks like we've got a plan.

❖

I make a quick call to Harry before I go to shower and get dressed. She promises to do her best to arrange a meeting with the Master's wife. After mulling over ideas, we agree that the secret chamber reveal event is probably our best excuse for why I need to speak with her urgently. There's no doubt that she'll be expected to attend, and asking for her approval of the plans and invitation list are a good way to curry her favour.

I get a text from Harry as I arrive at Barnard, letting me know she's arranged a late afternoon meeting on my behalf. Lady Finch-Byron is expecting me at her home at 4pm. I send H off to track down Lady Petronilla, so he can explain the situation and ask for her help. In the meantime, I've got a day full of interviews with Barnard's other female Eternals. I am already falling behind in my To Do list for the Women of Barnard celebration.

Some of the more famous residents have been honoured with portraits and books about their lives. One Eternal tells me of a family portrait which hangs in the Ashmolean, commemorating the first time a married man was elected Master of Barnard. His wife and four daughters charmed both Fellows and students alike, bringing warmth and laughter into the previously male-dominated environment. I make a note to ask Kate if she can loan me the painting for the celebration.

After a quick lunch, I meet with Barnard's first female Domestic Bursar, the college equivalent of a housekeeper. After spending her life overseeing Barnard's housemaids, cleaners, cooks and domestic staff, she remained on as the Head of Eternal Affairs. She is a plain woman, her gown in a dull brown colour designed to blend into the background. A hefty ring of master keys hangs from a leather belt around her waist.

Her initial expression is so dour that I'm almost afraid to open my mouth, but before long she is regaling me of tales of Bartie and her other counterparts around the rest of Oxford's thirty-eight colleges. Apparently, the Eternals hold monthly gatherings in the old lecture hall at the Bodleian Library, having drinks, exchanging information and sharing updates. As our conversation continues, I realise just how little I've learned about Oxford's magic and how the Eternals work, and I make a note to learn more.

My mobile buzzes with an alarm at a quarter to four, my reminder that I need to get ready to leave for the Master's apartments if I want to make it on time to my meeting with his wife. I gather all of my notes and laptop, thrusting them into my handbag before I lock up to leave. I don't think I've ever been so happy to reach the end of the work week. Has it only been five days since I arrived back in Oxford and met Mathilde at the old library? I still haven't unpacked my suitcase from my holiday ski trip, although it feels like it happened five lifetimes ago.

Lady Petronilla is waiting for me in the Master's Garden. "Well met, Miss Natalie," she says with a smile as she sees me approaching. She looked resplendent in the sun, her jewels sparkling.

"Thank you for agreeing to accompany me, Lady Petronilla. I hope that H has explained everything." I pause to let the Lady gather her skirts and join me on my walk.

"Yes," she reassures me, "H hath explained all, it is my pleasure to aid thee in this venture. The Master's lodging is one floor above the old library, where Mathilde, Kate and your grandfather Alfred are toiling diligently. Should we have any need of their assistance, they can be upstairs within moments."

The spot of tension sitting in between my shoulders loosens at her words. "I will tread carefully in my conversations. Hopefully we won't need anyone to ride to my rescue. However, should you see anything concerning, or read a deeper meaning into her words, please speak up. I'll be the only one able to hear you, so we should use that to our advantage."

Lady Petronilla nods her agreement as we climb the last flight of stairs and arrive at the Master's front door. Although the building is centuries-old, a modern doorbell sits waiting for our use. I give a gentle press, listening to hear the pealing tones from inside signalling our arrival. My eyes grow wide when a woman wearing a maid's outfit opens the door.

"Please, come in," she says, standing back to allow me to enter. "Her Ladyship is waiting for you in the Drawing room."

*Ladyship? The Drawing room?* I think it, but manage to stop myself before I say it out loud. I can tell already that this visit is going to test the limits of my patience with pretentiousness.

I step into the foyer, a mid-sized antechamber decorated with a muted rose Persian carpet and polished wooden furniture. A gilt-framed mirror hangs on the wall, reflecting the oversized floral arrangement which sits atop an oak entry table. I pass my coat to the maid who hangs it on a coatrack before leading me into the next room.

The Master's Lodging claims the top three floors of the main building. Barnard's Eternals had told me that the first floor is laid out in a long row of rooms for public use, starting from the entry foyer past a pair of receiving rooms, a dining room and finally the Master's study and kitchen. The second floor holds the bed and bathrooms, while the top floor is the servant's domain.

The maid leads me through a small reception room and into the larger Drawing room. Framed artwork covers most of the papered walls and an ostentatious crystal chandelier sends facets of light raining around the space. A grand piano claims one corner of the room, its top propped open and sheet music sitting at the ready.

Lady Finch-Byron is indeed waiting, her back to me as she fixes herself a fresh gin and tonic. She looks like a strong wind would blow her away, her spare frame swathed in expensive clothing. I recognise her scarf from the latest Prada collection, its bright colours had caught my eye in the shop window of the Prada boutique in the French Alps.

She takes a quick sip from her drink before spinning around

to face me. "Hullo, Miss Payne. I am Lady Frances, as I'm sure you know. Shall we have a seat and perhaps you could explain the reason for your visit?" As she sips her drink, she scans me from head to toe, and there is no question she disapproves of my shoes.

I meet her in the middle of the room, perching uncomfortably on the seat of an antique armchair. While I get settled, Lady Petronilla walks around the room before coming to stop behind the sofa where Lady Frances is seated.

Kate's description of Lady Frances is accurate to a T. Her forehead and eyebrows are frozen in place, no doubt thanks to a heavy dose of botox. There isn't even a hint of wrinkles on her forehead, although I know she must be in her fifties. Her thin nose and slight overbite are classic features of the British aristocracy. At the rate she gulps down her G&T, I suspect she'll need a refresh before we are done.

I notice that she doesn't offer me a cup of tea or plate of biscuits, sure indications that she expects me to keep our conversation short and sweet. The hired help are not invited to linger, apparently.

I launch into an overview of the plans for the invitation-only event where the Master will reveal the contents of the secret chamber. As I flip through the catalogue Harry and I put together, she shows little interest in the books and journals, but does take a close look at the art finds. I can see her mentally calculating the values of each one in her head, no doubt wondering whether she can add them to her own walls.

The last thing I cover is the invitation list. "Harry and I went through the college's major donor list and hand-selected those individuals we thought most likely to be generous. Master Finch-Byron was clear that he wanted to use the event to encourage the donors to sponsor the public unveiling. Is there anyone missing?" I ask.

Lady Frances views the list carefully before she hands it back over. "You've surprised me, Miss Payne. You and Harry have done a thorough job. I do say, that Harry is a darling. If only there was a way to convince her to remain here at Barnard with us. She is much of an improvement on Ms Evans." Her face turns down when she utters the name.

Seeing my opportunity, I leap in with a question. "I take it you weren't a fan, then?"

Lady Frances' vicious laugh sends chills down my spine. "Hardly, my dear. I know a social climber when I see one. She was determined to get her claws in here. I won't spill a tear for her loss."

My head snaps up to Lady Petronilla, who is still standing behind Lady Frances. Disapproval is written on her face, but she nods at me to continue.

I decide to take the conversation a step further. "I hate to be indiscreet, Lady Frances, but I feel I should tell you a rumour I heard about Ms Evans... I'm sure it isn't true, but..." I pause, struggling with indecision about whether or not to say any more.

Lady Frances stares at me over the rim of her cocktail. "What have you heard?"

I cough delicately, unsure how to best frame my next statement.

Her face hardens, her gaze steely. "The rumour about Ms Evans and my husband? Is that the one you mean?"

Apparently she isn't in the dark about his activities. I nod my confirmation.

Her eyes spark like lightning bolts. "Barnard is my domain. Nothing happens here without my knowledge, no matter what the likes of Ms Evans might think. If my husband wanted to have a spot of fun with the help, I would hardly begrudge him that. All I ask is that he keep his ridiculous dallying quiet."

My eyebrows shoot up my forehead. I've heard rumours of the

upper class, but I assumed they were an exaggeration. Apparently, I was wrong.

Lady Frances rises from her seat to return to her cocktail bar. I wait until her back is to me before I wave Lady Petronilla to get closer. She glides over, leaning against the far wall so that she can see Lady Frances' face, even if I cannot.

I speak up to make my question heard over the clinking of fresh ice falling into her glass. "What if there was a child?"

Lady Frances' shoulders stiffen for a moment but relax again as she reaches for the tonic water. "You are rather impertinent, Ms Payne. You are fortunate I am in a forgiving mood today, or you might find yourself in a very precarious position."

She finishes topping up her glass and then spins back to face me. "I will tell you this only so that you may put a stop to any other gossiping voices. I am the Lady here - which in the event you are unaware - is a position of tremendous power and authority. I have never, nor will I ever, fear any social climber who dares set foot in my domain." She pauses to sip from her cocktail. "My husband may be the Master, but it is my family name and my inheritance which sustain our lifestyle."

Her hand tightens around the glass. "No one, and I do mean no one, could ever threaten my position. My husband knows that better than anyone else. Now if you've nothing else to discuss, I'd suggest you take your leave."

I gather up my handbag and notes and rush out of the lodge as quickly as I can.

I fly down two flights of stairs before I hear Lady Petronilla's voice calling me to stop. My eyes are as round as saucers when I turn to face her on the landing.

"Cometh with me," she insists, her tone allowing no room for argument. Together, we walk along the hall and into the room where her portrait is hung.

I flop into one of the chairs, leaning forward to rest my head in my hands. "What have I done, Lady Petronilla? I knew I was going too far, but I couldn't stop myself. What if she tells the Master about my visit?"

"There, there," Lady Petronilla says as she rubs a cool hand across the top of my head. "Thou mayhap disagree, but I have little fear that Lady Frances shall repeat the tale to anyone. It wouldst embarrass her to do so."

"Really?" I lift my head from my hands to read the truth on Lady Petronilla's face. Her gentle smile gives me a ray of hope that I haven't ruined my career trying to run an unsanctioned murder investigation.

"Really," she replies, perfectly matching my accent.

"Okay, I will set that worry aside for the moment. However, I'm not any closer to determining her guilt. Even reading between the lines - it could go either way. What was your view, Lady Petronilla?"

The Lady slips into a nearby chair, her expression serious. "When thou first raised the discussion, I sensed no animosity towards you. However, the question about a child..."

My gut tightens. "I saw her freeze, but you could see her face. What did you notice?"

Lady Petronilla's eyes look to the side as she relives the moment. "I saw pain. Great pain. But no fear. Only pain and anger. I daresay the decision to remain without children mayhap 'twas not a conscious one on her part."

I cock my head to the side, considering the situation. "Do you think she would kill someone for giving her husband something she couldn't give him herself?"

"Nay, Natalie. I watched her closely, seeking the unspoken

truth. At no point did I see fear or surprise. Lady Frances spoketh verily."

I reflect back on the visit. "Yes, you're right. She wasn't at all surprised when I brought up the rumour. If anything, she was annoyed that I knew... but also curious as to why I would dare to bring it up with her."

With a sigh, Lady Petronilla murmurs, "I know well what it means to be the Mistress of the house. There is no means to hide a secret from she who overseeth all. Her Ladyship hath no reason to resort to murder. A quiet word in the right ear to order Ms Evans gone, and her problem wouldst be solved."

I raise my head, my gaze steely with determination. "Then there is only one suspect left: the Master himself. Now we have to find a way to prove it."

# Chapter Twelve

Saturday passes by in a flurry of food shopping and seemingly endless loads of laundry. H joins me for a quick dinner before darting off for a date night with Princess Fluffy, the neighbourhood white Persian cat. I wonder what Fluffy would think if she knew her boyfriend was a wyvern.

Left alone, I turn on a Downton Abbey marathon, losing myself in someone else's drama for a night. It's nice to get a break from my own worries, even though I know they'll be waiting for me in the morning.

I sleep in on Sunday, barely rising in time to make a morning train to London. I had promised my parents I'd join them for a traditional roast dinner, but I wanted to do a little reconnaissance before I did.

As I'd hoped, Barnard's Eternals had agreed enthusiastically to act as mannequins for the women's celebration. The stumbling block wasn't getting them to say yes, it was convincing them I could help them come up with interesting ways for them to sit and stand. Much like Bartie at the St Margaret gala, they were worried about getting stage fright at the last minute.

I had solved Bartie's last minute melt down by pulling out

what I call my devil voice, issuing a booming command to shake him out of his last-minute nervousness. This time around, I had decided to be more proactive in searching out a solution. I tried looking for mannequin poses, but everything I found looked closer to a clothes hanger than a person.

But the answer to my problems had popped up in the form of an ad on the train ticket website. I was in the middle of booking my weekend travel ticket when I saw an ad for 2-for-1 entry at Madame Tussauds. One look at their waxen displays and I knew I needed to drop in for a visit.

My London-bound train arrives at Marylebone Station on time. The first item on my itinerary is nearby, only four blocks away. I make quick work of the distance, arriving to find a minimal queue waiting outside. A dreary Sunday in early January is one of the only times of year when Madame Tussauds famous waxworks doesn't have a crowd waiting out front.

Once inside, I sidestep tourists, dodging their camera flashes in my haste to skip past the modern celebrities and superheroes who make up the front displays. Deeper in, I locate the older displays, the waxed versions of Britain's kings and queens standing in a row for the masses to behold. I slip into the role of tourist, taking photo after photo of the various scenes.

I half hope that one of the waxworks will come alive. It might be possible. After all, last term Kate told us that a statue of Queen Victoria had come to life in a London museum, letting her know that Oxford's magic was reaching far beyond the city borders. Madame Tussauds isn't too far away from the museum. I'd like to ask Vincent Van Gogh why he cut off his ear, or chat with Dickens about British literature.

However, no matter how hard I look, their empty wax gazes give no hint of an Eternal harboured inside. No amount of winking, nudging, whispering or straight out asking results in any reply.

In the end, I decide that they must be too recently made to be susceptible to the power of the magic.

I make it out of Madame Tussauds with still two hours to go before I have to be at my parents' home. I retrace my steps, stopping at Baker Street Station, where I catch a Jubilee Line train to London's centre. I emerge again at the London Bridge Station, near the address for the fish and chip shop whose flyer Kate found in the secret chamber.

The Shard, one of London's most famous landmarks, towers over the neighbourhood, its glass exterior reflecting the weak January sun. I must have walked past the building dozens of times when I worked in London, growing immune to its incredible architecture. It's nice to be able to take a moment to appreciate it, instead of having to run from one meeting to another.

Grabbing a latte at a nearby cafe, I pause to reflect on how much my life has changed in such a short amount of time. Was it really only four months ago that I was finishing up my last project here in London? I try to imagine what my reaction would have been if someone had stopped me on that final day, and said, "Nat, in your next job you'll have a talking wyvern for a sidekick, you'll staff your events with ghosts and you'll get to hang out with your dead grandfather."

Yet here I am, back in London, with a fish and chip shop address in my hand and an assignment to look for talking statues. As bizarre as all of that sounds, now that this is my life, I wouldn't change it for anything else in the world.

I gulp down the last few sips of my latte and get moving again. It doesn't take me long to find the chip shop with the smell of fried fish wafting along the pavement. Kate was convinced that the burglar who uncovered Barnard's secret chamber must live or work nearby. Why else would they carry around a random chip shop flyer in their pocket? I had volunteered to check the area out during my trip down this weekend, to see if I could spot anything out of the ordinary.

I start at the shopfront and then work my way out in ever-growing circles. However, nothing stands out as unusual. There are no wayward Eternals wandering the streets, no statues come to life. None of the pigeons strike up a conversation. When the cold begins to seep into my bones, I abandon my quest and return to the warmth of the underground station. It takes me half an hour and two metro lines to arrive at my parents' home in Kensington - plenty of time to imagine a dozen crazy antics H might get up to if given the chance to ride the London underground.

Over dinner, my parents chatter away, full of gossip and news learned in their first week back at work. I let them talk without interruption, simply enjoying the chance to sit back and listen for a change.

When dinner and dessert are done, my mother disappears off into the kitchen, dishes rattling over the sound of running water. My father and I are left alone, sipping the last of our cups of coffee. His greying temples remind me of my grandfather, sending a wave of melancholy washing over me.

"Dad?" I wait until he looks up at me. "Do you ever think about grandfather?"

My father arches an eyebrow in my direction. "What brought that question on?"

I squirm in my seat, as I can hardly tell him it's because I saw my grandfather yesterday. "Oh, I don't know. I guess being in Oxford makes me think about him."

"I'm not surprised to hear you say that," he says, chuckling. "Your grandfather spent hours telling you his fairytale stories about Oxford and its crew of eternal mischief makers."

I smile, wondering what my dad would think if he knew the stories had all been true. "He told the best bedtime stories, that's for sure. But you didn't answer my question."

My father places his coffee cup on the table, resting an elbow beside it. "Of course, I think about your grandfather. He was my dad! I hope you'll think about me when I'm long gone."

"What are you talking about, dad? You're going to live forever. You promised me that you would when I was six." I give him a wink. "But seriously, if you could see grandfather one more time, what would you say to him? What would you want him to know?"

"Hmmm," my father leans back in his chair, his look pensive. "That's a good question, Nat. There have been so many moments in my life where I wished I could pick up the phone and give him a ring... like when you graduated from uni or when you came back from France and settled closer to home. He was always so proud of you; I hate that he's missed seeing you grow into an accomplished young woman."

I grab my napkin to blot the tears that threaten to spill from my eyes. "Oh, Dad, that's lovely. But what about you? You must have some message of your own."

My dad shifts uncomfortably in his chair, gazing off into the distance. He sits silent for so long, I begin to wonder if he's going to answer. Right as I'm about to say his name, he turns his head and locks eyes with me.

"You may not believe this, Nat, but it's true. If I could go back in time and have more time with my father, I'd settle onto the sofa beside the two of you and listen to him tell you his stories."

When I shake my head, my dad stops me from interrupting. "No, really, Nat. He tried to tell me those same stories when I was younger, but I was more interested in playing sports and running around with my friends. Then when you came along, I was so busy with work..." his voice trails off, his gaze a million miles away. "I thought I'd have more time."

His face softens, a ghost of a smile slipping across his face. "When you talk about Oxford, you get that same faraway look in your eyes as he used to have. I swear, it's like looking at him. Seeing how much you have blossomed and come into your own, how quickly you've settled in at Oxford and made friends, you remind me of how happy he was there. It makes me wish I'd given him more time to tell me about himself."

I reach over, sliding my hand over his and giving it a quick squeeze. "Thanks, Dad. That means a lot, really."

Casting my mind back, I think about the day when I discovered my grandfather was an Eternal. We spent hours catching up, with him asking as many questions about me as he did about my parents. I don't have to guess as to what he would say if he were sitting here with us.

"If Grandfather were here, I know he'd be proud of you, too, Dad. Look at all you've accomplished - having a good job, a warm home, a solid marriage. You chased after your dreams, and from what I can see, you achieved them."

I give him a light punch in the arm. "And let's not forget about your magnificent child! She just might be your greatest accomplishment."

My father pulls me into a bear hug, squeezing me so tight I can hardly breathe. I squeeze him back, imagining my grandfather's arms laying on top of my own, holding all three of us together.

The sound of the kitchen door swinging open breaks up our moment. My mum's head pokes around the door, calling out, "If you two are done, I could use an extra pair of hands in the kitchen to help dry and put away the dishes."

I wave my dad towards the reception room, knowing he'd much prefer to turn on the BBC than hold a dishtowel. I step into the kitchen, falling into place beside my mother.

"Mum, would you and dad like to come visit me in Oxford one weekend?"

My dad and grandfather may not be able to speak to one another, but there's no reason I can't act as a go between. My grandfather has given so much of his life and afterlife to the uni, maybe it is time for the magic of Oxford to give him something back in return.

I get to work drying while we discuss potential visit dates. It turns out my parents have been waiting on an invite.

"We've got a charity event next weekend, but what about the one after that?" my mum asks as she passes me another wet plate.

I mentally run through my plans for the rest of the month. "That could work! I know it's only an hour train ride, but why don't you stay overnight? We could make a weekend of it? Maybe visit Blenheim Palace?"

"Are you sure, honey? We don't want to take up too much of your time. I know you're busy planning the women's celebration at Barnard."

Although my mother is right, there's no shortage of work on my plate, I'm too excited about the idea of having my whole family - parents and grandfather - together. "I'm positive, Mum. I haven't done any of the touristy things yet; this will be a good excuse to get out a bit. Dad can show us all of his old haunts and maybe Kate can give us a special tour of the Ashmolean..."

When the kitchen is clean, my mother and I head off to share our plans with my dad before I have to rush off to catch my train back to Oxford.

All I have to do is identify a murderer, pull off the chamber reveal and figure out who is stealing Oxford's magic. Then I can sit back and celebrate with my parents. I can almost convince myself that when I put it that way, it sounds easy.

# Chapter Thirteen

I wake up Monday morning determined that nothing is going to bring down my good mood. My cupboard is full of clean clothes and my refrigerator is overflowing with food. My hair has that perfect amount of spring to my curls and even the weather seems to have decided to cooperate.

My morning schedule is full of meetings with more of the Barnard female Eternals. I can't wait to show them the photos from Madame Tussauds. Hopefully my wax mannequin photo gallery will resolve their final concerns about taking part in the big Barnard women's celebration. The photos should give them plenty of ideas of how they could pose.

As we walk to work, H regales me with the story of his date night with Princess Fluffy.

"Wait, you got stuck in her owner's cat flap?" I turn my head to look at H and trip over the edge of the kerb. I barely manage to regain my balance and avoid a nasty tumble.

H shrugs his shoulders. "I wasn't thinking about it, Nat. Fluffs said her house was empty and suggested we take advantage of it. I was well up for some snuggle time on tha sofa. She went through tha flap and I followed right along behind 'er. 'Ow was I supposed ta know I wouldn't fit?!"

I stifle a laugh, making sure to watch my step as I reply. "I know regular people see you as a cat, but your wyvern form is a bit bigger. How exactly did you get stuck, and what did you have to do to get back out again?"

"It was my wings, mate. Fluffs trotted in ahead of me, her furry, white tail twitchin' left and right. She was taunting me, that's fer sure. I backed up a few steps and launched into a leap. My 'ead and shoulders made it inside tha openin', but that was it. Tha rest of me was still outside. Tha only good thing was that Fluffs was inside and couldn't see my backside hangin' thar catchin' the breeze."

This time the laughter overtakes me. I have to stop for a minute to catch my breath, with H glaring at me the entire time. Every time I manage to get a hold of myself, I look up, see him fuming and I break out laughing all over again.

"Iffen yer done now, Nat, I'd like ta get on wiff tha rest of tha story."

"Sorry, sorry. I'll stop now. Really." Snicker, snicker. "Tell me, how did you get out?"

"I couldn't get in, so thar was only one way ta go. But my shoulders and arms were wedged in tight. Thar was only one thing Fluffs could do... she is a cat, after all." H states with a straight face.

"She licked you? Ewwwww." I roll my eyes so hard, I start to worry they might fall out.

"Nat, mate! I'm a gentlemen wyvern. She didn't lick. She might 'ave given a few kisses to my shoulders before she shoved me back out again. But that's all I'm sayin'." Then H winks and I dissolve into another round of laughter.

When we arrive at Barnard, H and I split up, agreeing to meet at old library before lunch time. He has little interest in listening to a bunch of Eternals wax on about their lives. After promising to behave, he flaps off, chasing after a tiny mouse who has dared to poke its head out. I shove down any further thoughts about H's activities for the morning.

Inside the main building, I climb the stairs and follow the hallway to the Old Common Room where Lady Petronilla's portrait hangs. She offered me use when a few of the older Eternals seemed uncomfortable at the idea of meeting in my office. Since they regularly use the Old Common Room for their weekly gatherings, her Ladyship thought they'd be most at home in its familiar surroundings.

My first appointment is running a few minutes late, giving me an extra moment to organise my materials. An eight-person conference table takes up much of the space in the room, with the rest arranged in intimate seating nooks. I choose to sit at the head of the table, angling the chair to my right for my visitor. I want it to feel like a comfortable chat and not like an inquisition.

Lady Petronilla had given me an overview of each Eternal, helping me build out a timeline showing when they lived at Barnard. Settling into my chair, I review the list of questions I prepared on my train ride back from London the night before. However, as soon as my next meeting walks in the door, something completely different springs to mind.

A lovely little girl walks into the room and sits in the chair beside me. Her posture is perfect, her dark hair pulled back into a neat half-up style, with chestnut ringlets tumbling down her back. With her creamy skin and rose petal cheeks, she looks like a dark-haired version of Alice in Wonderland. Given her lifetime period, it's possible that the real Alice could have been one of her playmates. However, the scuff marks on her shoes and a dirty hemline reveal that she isn't as well-behaved as first impressions might convey.

I eye my notes, then her, then my notes again. After a small cough to clear my throat, I finally launch into the question which is sitting top of mind. "If I state upfront that I have no idea what the social guidance is in situations such as this, will you forgive me if I ask why you look like a preteen, given you lived well into your eighties?"

Thankfully, Miss Huntingdon doesn't take offence, instead giving me a cheeky smile. "Who would want to live out eternity as a doddering, old woman? I spent some of the best years of my life as a child here at Barnard, and I was happy to return to those times."

"Is that an option? I mean, can all of the Eternals pick any age they want?" I'm genuinely stunned by this revelation.

"Oh heaven's no. There are constraints. We can either return to the age we were when we lived within the college, or we can be the age we were at death." She pauses, raising an eyebrow, "If it makes you uncomfortable, I can switch to my older age..."

Shaking my head, I reassure her, "No, that's not necessary. You simply caught me unaware. Thank you for explaining it to me. As you can see, I still have much to learn about Eternal life in Oxford."

The morning flies by, lost in pages upon pages of notes I scribble furiously as the women share their insights into Barnard's history. Despite being barred from entry as students, women didn't withhold their generosity. Lady Petronilla set the stage by giving Barnard it's charter. Over the years, other women followed in her path, donating land for new buildings and providing funding for scholarships.

The stories of the women who worked behind the scenes are equally intriguing. Miss Huntingdon, with her unique view as a young woman living within the college walls, entertains me with tales of fellows misbehaving and childish pranks she pulled with her siblings. Stories such as these are priceless because they breathe life and humanity into what can seem like a staid institution.

I begin to see why Mathilde, Kate and my grandfather spend their waking hours thinking about the past. As I chart Barnard's history, it is easy to see how actions from hundreds of years ago laid the pathway for female students studying here now.

After my last interview leaves, I take a moment to breathe before setting to work organising my notes. As always, I haven't limited my jottings to the confines of a notebook. Oh no, I've got posters with timelines, sticky notes and bubble letters, diagrams and even a family tree, all of which I've been carrying to my Eternal meetings. Tidying up at the end of the day is far from simple.

I rise to my feet and stretch my back, moving around the table to loosen up muscles gone stiff from hours in the same wooden chair. After I spread all of my notes and papers on the table, I fall into the zone, focusing my full attention on organising everything correctly.

When a gruff, masculine voice breaks the silence with a hello, I nearly jump out of my skin. "My word, Master Finch-Byron! I didn't hear you come in. You startled me."

"My apologies, Miss Payne," he says, but his cheshire cat grin sends alarm bells ringing in my head.

I watch as he closes the door and crosses to the other side of the table, motioning for both of us to be seated. He settles into his chair, facing me across the table, and leans back with his arm draped over the top of the chair beside him.

"Did we have a meeting scheduled, Master?" I ask, trying desperately to remember what was on my diary for today. "If I'm late, or missed one, I'm so sorry."

Master Finch-Byron looses a hearty chuckle. "No, not at all. I had a window in my calendar and thought I'd check in with you. After all, you are organising two of our most important events this term. I've barely had a chance to speak with you. I thought we should get to know one another better."

"Sure?" My voice twists my response into a question. His words would look fine on paper, but there is something about the set of his shoulders and the gleam in his eyes that has me on edge.

"Tell me, Miss Payne. How long have you been employed here at the University?"

His tone gives me no clue where this is going, so I decide to keep my answers short. "Four months, or thereabouts. I started last term at St Margaret College."

"Excellent," he says, smiling. "And how are you finding it here? Is the job what you expected?"

I choke back an inappropriate laugh. Nothing here in Oxford has been what I expected, but I can hardly give that as an answer. "Yes, it's lovely. The job has its challenges, but then what job doesn't? The people here have been welcoming, which has helped with settling in and learning my way around."

"People like Harry?" He raises an eyebrow, his voice punctuating each sentence. "The young woman in the library? Even Kate who heads the Ashmolean. You've met a wide cross-section of people despite being here a short while."

My mind spins furiously, but no matter how hard I try, I cannot figure out where he is going with this conversation. "Well, I am in a centralised university role. I've had a number of opportunities to meet with staff both within and outside of the colleges."

Master Finch-Byron shifts his girth, moving his arm from the chair back to rest on the table. His smile doesn't shift, but his eyes narrow. He looks like a politician in the midst of complex negotiations. He appears perfectly comfortable, but leaves little doubt that he has an ace hidden somewhere up his sleeve. What I can't figure out is why me, why now and why here, in the Old Common Room.

"Would you say that you like your job, Miss Payne?" he asks, his voice laced with a hint of something other than simple curiosity. "What about your friends? Are they happy exploring the contents of our college's secret chamber?"

The alarm bells turn into full on sirens, blaring a red alert in my mind. The cheshire cat grin is back in force. I prevent myself from looking at the door, careful not to betray any hint that I am now desperate to get out of this conversation.

My voice is surprisingly steady when I reply. "Yes, of course, sir. I'm thrilled to be here. And the same for Mathilde and Kate. They are aware that it is an honour to be the only ones allowed to view the chamber contents in advance."

Master Finch-Byron stares, waiting to see if I have anything else to add. I shift uncomfortably under his gaze, my shoulders tensing when he places his other hand on the top of the table and leans forward. Part of me wonders if I'm in physical danger.

His stare hardens and a flush creeps up his neck and onto his cheeks. But still, he waits in silence, watching as I grow more and more nervous under his glare.

Just as I am about to make a break for the door, he opens his mouth, speaking in a furious whisper. "If you value your job here at Oxford. If your friends want to keep their access to the old library..."

He inhales before carrying on, his voice rising to a growl. "If I hear of you speaking with my wife, speaking with anyone in Oxford about me or my business, I will have your contract shredded. You won't work here in Oxford, or anywhere else I can reach." His voice lowers, his tone deathly, "You have no idea how far my influence extends."

With that, he pushes back from the table, rising to his feet to tower over me. His eyes are cold as he says, "I'm watching you, Miss Payne. One step out of line and you will be persona non grata in all of Oxford. Keep your focus on your little parties and ceremonies and keep your nose out of my business."

I gulp as he storms out of the room, the door slamming shut behind him, its bang punctuating his final words. I sit frozen, too stunned to think about what to do next. Before I can move, Lady Petronilla leans out of her portrait.

"How much of that did you catch?" I ask.

"I heard his speech in its entirety. The Master wast peering into rooms and asking for thee. I came to give warning, but he wast nigh here when I arrived."

I let loose a breath I didn't realise I'd been holding. "Thank you, Lady Petronilla. I had no idea you were there, but I feel better now knowing that I wasn't alone."

Her ladyship gives a nod of acknowledgement, brushing aside any further words of thanks. "It is why we Eternals art here, Miss Natalie."

I replay the scene in my head, zooming in on the ending. "So, he threatened me, but he didn't fire me. He thinks I could be dangerous, and he wants me here where he can control everything I do and say. Does that mean what I think it means?" I look to her ladyship for confirmation.

"Aye, Natalie. I strongly believe that thou hast unmasked our murderer."

I gather the last of my worksheets, shoving them into my bag. Forget my perfect organisational system. I've got to find evidence and get it to Edward before Master Finch-Byron decides to take a more proactive approach to ensuring my silence... permanently.

It takes me less than a minute to reach the old library. I

breathe a sigh of thanks when I make it inside without running into anyone else... particularly Edward. I need to put my head together with my fellow prefects so we can figure out what to do next.

After dropping my bag at the first table I see, I rush down the aisle towards the back of the library where everyone is camped out. I turn the corner in time to see H pick up one of the loose journal pages, its jagged edge testifying to its damaged state. Before I can ask what he is doing, he toasts the page in a jet of flame, sending a cloud of ashes tumbling down to the ground.

"Oh my god, H! What are you doing?!?!?! If Mathilde sees you, she's going to kill you!" I screech.

I stumble to a halt when Mathilde's head pops up from behind H. She isn't angry. In fact, she looks ecstatic. Huh?

"Watch this, Nat," she calls, holding her hands out in front of her. Like magic, the journal page reappears, floating through the air to land on Mathilde's palms. I look closely, trying to make sense of what I'm seeing.

I stutter, "Is that? Is it? But it's whole!"

What had previously been a torn remnant from an old journal is now a perfectly rectangular piece of paper complete with faded ink handwriting. H takes a bow while my grandfather claps on the other side of the room. "How on earth did you figure out that trick?" I ask.

"Not on purpose," Mathilde starts. "H was up to his usual antics, leaping around the bookshelves, flipping off the ladders and generally making a nuisance of himself."

"Oi!" interrupts H.

"Oh shush, you know it's true," Mathilde replies, unfazed by his hurt gaze. "Anyway, he did a particularly tricky manoeuvre, aiming to land on the sofa over there. But he misjudged the distance, overshot the armrest and ended up skidding across the floor, basically surfing on a stack of my papers."

Nodding, H jumps back in. "Tha flames were an accident. You know 'ow it is when I get nervous, Nat. When I saw tha look on Mathilde's face, the urge ta sneeze came over me and I couldn't stop it. Not fer anythin'."

Mathilde takes back over. "So I'm fuming over the mess, H starts sneezing, two of my journal scraps go up in flames, and then... voilà! The magic steps in, replaces the destroyed objects, and returns them in pristine condition!"

I raise my eyebrow and glance at H. "Wow, you really lucked out there, didn't ya, mate?"

"Oi. Tell me about it," he admits. "Now Tildy's got me ashin' all of 'er torn pages. Is it lunchtime yet? I'm starvin' after all this 'ard work."

Ignoring his question, I turn back to Mathilde. "Ok, I know that the magic replaces anything H sets on fire, but how come it repaired these old pages? Shouldn't it have returned them exactly as they were when he burnt them?"

My grandfather pipes up with the reply. "My best guess is that another Eternal was responsible for the original damage. But since the documents still existed, albeit torn, the magic didn't replace it. When H reduced the scrap to ash, the magic reformed it exactly as it had been before any Eternal laid a hand on it."

Rising to her feet, Mathilde dusts her hands on her jeans. "It's a mixed bag, if I'm honest. On the one hand, I'm thrilled to have the full pages back. But on the other, I feel a little sick knowing for sure that an Eternal must have been involved in their destruction."

I slump onto the nearby sofa, patting the seat next to mine in an invitation for Mathilde to join me. Kate emerges from behind another book shelf and joins us in the seating area. When we're all gathered around, I share my news.

"A mixed bag is a pretty good description of my morning as well. It started off positive with more interviews with Barnard's

Eternals. But then it took a weird turn right at the end when Master Finch-Byron cornered me in the Old Common Room."

"Cornered you?" Kate asks, her eyebrows raised in confusion. "What happened? Did he... I don't even know how to say this, other than to come right out with it. Did he come onto you?"

My immediate reaction is to scrunch up my face in disgust. "Ick, no. Thank goodness. I didn't even think of that. He went in the exact opposite direction, threatening to have me fired if I don't keep my nose out of his business."

Every face shares the same wide-eyed look of complete shock.

"I guess his wife told him about my visit, and he didn't take too kindly to me discussing rumours about him."

"My word," my grandfather exclaims. "You're lucky he didn't fire you on the spot."

"He can't fire her, Alfred. She doesn't work for Barnard, she works for the University," Kate reminds my grandfather. "But... he could request your dismissal."

"Exactly! If our suspicions were off-track, and he wasn't having an affair with Ms Evans, I'm sure that is the first thing he'd do. He'd have nothing to hide." I pause to make sure everyone is following my train of thought. "But he came to me, in a private room where no one else could hear us. He didn't call me into his office or send me an email requesting a meeting. He made sure there is no record of our conversation."

Kate still looks worried, but Mathilde's eye sparkle with mischief and she rubs her hands together. "Charles Graves was right! The Master was having an affair with Ms Evans."

I hold up a hand to slow her down. "I don't think that's the only secret he's hiding, Mathilde. Without Ms Evans here to contradict him, he could say that she came onto him, that she seduced him into breaking his marriage vows. Or he could always state that the relationship never went past the early stages. It wouldn't make him look good, but I think he could talk his way out of losing his job or being sanctioned."

My grandfather raises a hand, waiting for us to fall silent before he speaks. "Before we leap to any conclusions, I think we should back up a step. Start from the beginning, Nat, when the Master came into the room. Tell us everything you can remember about the discussion."

I close my eyes, re-envisioning the scene. "I was in the Old Common Room, tidying up my papers. I had moved around to the long edge of the table and my back was to the door. I didn't realise he'd come into the room. When he said hello, I nearly leapt out of my chair. He sat down on the other end of the table. There was something about the shape of his smile, or his eyes, something... it didn't sit right with me, although I couldn't put my finger on exactly what it was..."

I keep my eyes squeezed shut, blocking out the sights and sounds of my friends. I want to remember exactly what he said as much as what he left unsaid. By the time I finish, my shoulders are again tight with anxiety.

I open my eyes to see my grandfather's face glowing red with anger. "How dare he! He walked a fine line, never admitting to anything you could use against him. But equally, he made sure you understood his every word. From the moment he walked in the Old Common Room door, his sole purpose was to threaten you. Disgusting behaviour, certainly unbecoming of an Oxford Master."

I grab a hold of the last dregs of my anxiety and twist it into determination. "Don't worry, grandfather. I don't have any intention of letting him get away with it, whatever it turns out to be."

"But that's the problem, Nat," Kate says as she climbs to her feet and begins pacing around our group. "We've only got four days left on our original two-week time clock, and we still have more questions than answers. We cannot afford to accuse the

Master of anything unless we are absolutely certain and have the evidence to back it up."

I watch as Kate makes another loop past me, her mind clearly working in overdrive.

She pauses, running her hand through her hair. "We need to know exactly what happened on the night of the murder. Did the burglary happen before, during or after Ms Evans' visit? If she was pregnant, and the Master was the father, did he know? And if he did, why would he kill her? We have to remove any opportunity for him to cast doubt on our accusation."

"Ok, Kate. Then that's our plan. I'll lay low for the rest of the day, so he'll think his threat worked. And the same goes for the two of you." I glance at Kate and Mathilde, waiting for their confirmation. "Someone here at Barnard must know something that can help us."

"Someone definitely does!" H chimes in. "Simon, Barnard's Eternal monk. Remember, Nat? He said he saw tha murder. He knows exactly who killed 'er!"

"You're right, H!" I exclaim. "I'd honestly forgotten about him. He refused to tell us any information before, but he can hardly hold out on us forever. Right?"

"I'll take on that part of the assignment," my grandfather offers. "Simon has little patience for women, but perhaps he'll tell me if I can convince him it's in the college's best interests."

Kate, Mathilde and I all roll our eyes in annoyance.

I pull out my notepad and flip to a clean page. "Done. Kate and Mathilde - you're on burglary duty. Do whatever you can to try to put a timestamp on when it happened. Grandfather - you deal with Simon. Take H with you, he can always threaten to set him on fire if he doesn't come clean with what he knows."

Looking at my notepad, I add a final item to the list. "That leaves me to search for proof of a relationship between the Master and Ms Evans. I'll get in touch with Harry first thing tomorrow. With her access to the Master's files and records, surely we can find a trace or a hint somewhere."

As I scan the room, I notice we're all wearing the same expression on our faces: equal parts determination and nervous fear. If we're wrong, we've got a lot to lose.

# Chapter Fourteen

My mobile rings as H and I walk into Barnard the next morning. When I see the name on the caller ID, I speed through the entrance, aiming for a quiet bench in the garden.

"Hi Harry, you're just the person I was hoping to speak with. What's up?"

Harry's voice is barely louder than a whisper. "Where are you? I need to meet with you right away."

That was not what I expected her to say. "I just got to Barnard. I'm sitting in the Master's garden."

"Don't move," she hisses. "I'll be there in two minutes." With that, she hangs up.

"Okay, that was weird," I say to H, who is sitting on the bench beside me. "Harry sounded really freaked out, H."

"Do ya want me ta go get Mathilde or Kate?" H offers, his wings already flapping in preparation to take off. "I can fly up ta tha old library window, iffen ya want."

"Let's wait to see what Harry has to say. If she thinks they should be here, I'm sure she'll phone them. Now stop flapping, I'm freezing." I shiver inside my winter coat, my breath huffing out in a white cloud.

True to her word, Harry makes an appearance before I can think of moving to a warmer spot. She sees me shivering and waves at me to get up and follow her. "Not here," she whispers, and then her voice changes back to a normal volume. "Good morning, Nat. Fancy running into you here in the garden! Shall we take a walk, maybe get a coffee in the dining hall?"

I arch an eyebrow but decide to play along. Something is definitely up. "Yes, I just got here and I'm freezing. A steaming cup of coffee sounds lovely."

We cross under another stone arch, past the door to the chapel, and out into one of the college's famed quads. This one is busier, with a handful of students trudging past on their way to early morning tutorials. Harry's suspicious behaviour continues, her head twisting left to right as she scans our surroundings.

She waits until we reach the middle of the large lawn in front of the dining hall before she puts up a hand to halt our progress. "We can get a coffee in a minute, but first I have to tell you what happened this morning. I don't want to discuss this anywhere that we might be overheard."

I glance down at H, his wide eyes mirroring my own. "What is going on, Harry? You're starting to scare me."

"I came into work early this morning and went straight to the assistant's desk in the waiting area." Harry begins. "The inner door that goes from the waiting area into the Master's office was closed. Well, mostly closed. The door hadn't latched properly, and I could hear voices talking. I didn't want to interrupt a meeting, so I settled into my chair and began organising my work for the day."

Harry takes a deep breath and then carries on. "After a few minutes, I realised it was Edward inside meeting with the Master. Knowing we're curious about how his investigation is progressing, I tiptoed closer to the door so I could hear better."

"Oh!" I exclaim, "What did you hear? Did Edward speak with Charles Graves? Was he questioning the Master?"

Harry's face hardens. "No. In fact, Edward was saying very little. That was why it took me a few minutes to realise that he was the other person. The Master was all but reading him the riot act."

"What? 'Ow come?" H interjects.

"I only caught the tail end of the conversation, but the Master's accusations were clear. He told Edward that he thinks you and Mathilde have something to do with the burglary."

"WHAT?!?!" My shriek sends a flock of birds scattering. Harry shushes me before I can say anything else.

"Don't attract any attention! Master Finch-Byron said it was too much of a coincidence that the two of you would accidentally stumble across the scene and then Mathilde and Kate end up being the very people assigned to catalogue the contents. He's convinced you manipulated the situation so that you can cover up the theft."

I open my mouth but manage to stop myself before I shout again. No such luck with H. His sneeze sends the rest of the birds flying and sets a shrub on fire.

I decide to ignore it; I'm confident that the magic will sort out the shrub faster than I can. I turn back to Harry, my eyes glittering with rage. "Master Finch-Byron tracked me down yesterday. He cornered me in the old common room and threatened to have me fired if I said or did anything else regarding him and Ms Evans."

"I guess he didn't think a direct threat was enough, Nat," Harry replies, shrugging.

"What did Edward say?" I ask. "Surely he must have defended us, right? He knows we didn't have anything to do with the burglary or the murder."

Harry looks away for a moment. When she turns back, her

expression is a mix of sadness, frustration, and anger. I steel myself in preparation for whatever she is going to say next.

"I couldn't see his face or his body language, but his tone sounded... stoic? Resigned? He didn't try to argue with the Master." She reaches out a hand, resting it on my shoulder. "I'm so sorry, Nat. I can't tell you how disappointed I am with Edward. He should have come to your defence."

My emotions are in a turmoil, my stomach roiling as I try to make sense of Harry's words. "But he asked me on a date. He had lunch with us. He knows..."

An angry flush climbs up Harry's neck. "He should know. He should absolutely know better, and he is no shrinking violet. I've never known him to stay quiet."

By my side, H shoots a jet of flame from his nostrils. "Let me at 'im, Nat. I'll put 'im ta rights. Mathilde and ya, burglars? I've never 'eard anythin' so crazy in my life. Edward's a complete minger iffen 'e thinks ya two could be involved."

Harry is absolutely right. The first time I saw Edward, he was having a go at Dr Radcliffe, the principal of St Margaret College. He is not the type to tuck his tail between his legs and follow instructions without a word of complaint. As far as I can see, there can be only one reason he'd agree to do as Master Finch-Byron asked. He must have some niggling doubts about us as well.

I replay the last ten days in mind. Was it really a coincidence that he happened to be in Blackwell's at the same time as I was there? Did he come to lunch because he wanted a chance to observe us all together?

When I open my mouth, my voice cracks. "Do you think he asked me on a date as a cover-up? To distract me while he investigates me and my friends?"

Harry replies, her tone dripping with rage, "If he did, he will regret it for the rest of his tenure at Oxford. I'll make sure of it."

I tamper down my despair and harden my resolve. "Whatever

is going on needs to stay between myself and Edward for now. I don't want anyone else to speak with him on my behalf. I'm going to take the rest of today to think about what to do next. If I reach a decision, I can speak with him when I get home tonight. After all, he lives right upstairs from my flat."

H looks furious as he shadowboxes around us, but Harry nods her understanding. "Hopefully, I'm wrong, Nat. I didn't mishear the conversation, but I didn't catch the whole thing. If anyone is going to get to the bottom of this, it's you."

I shiver again as a cold wind whips past us. "Let's go get that coffee you proposed and then head over to the old library to check in with Mathilde and Kate. And please, don't mention anything about Edward to them. Let me do some exploring of my own before we get anyone else riled up."

❖

"Coffee's here!" I call out as we walk into the old library. "One triple shot Americano for Kate and a caramel macchiato with extra whip for Mathilde."

Mathilde bounces over from behind one of the towering bookshelves. "Thanks, Nat. You're a lifesaver."

"No worries. Harry and I were already in line, might as well pick up a drink for everyone," I reply. When my grandfather clears his throat, I amend my statement. "For everyone still alive, I mean. Can Eternals drink coffee?"

Shaking his head, my grandfather grumbles, "Ignore me. It's been twenty years since I've had a cuppa. I don't even like coffee, but I'd give my right arm for a pot of Yorkshire Gold tea."

I pat his arm, saying, "Poor Grandfather Alfred. Forced to live on as an Eternal but without any tea to warm him. There, there." He reaches up and squeeze my hand before giving a chuckle.

"Speaking of Harry," Kate says as she picks up her cup, "did you have a chance to ask her if she could look at the Master's email, calendar and correspondence files to see if there is any evidence of his relationship with Ms Evans?"

"I did speak with her," I reply, tamping down any thoughts about the rest of our conversation. "She's going to have a look around, but she said Edward had already gone through the electronic files along with Ms Evans' own notebooks."

Seeing the downcast look on my face, Kate gives me a smile, "Cheer up, Nat. It isn't the end of the world. Harry knows what to look for, she may have better luck than Edward did."

I force a smile onto my face. "Let's hope so, Kate. What about you? What's the latest on the contents of the secret chamber? Any other amazing finds?" I cross my fingers and hope she'll provide a distraction from thinking any more about Edward right now.

I follow Kate over to one of the seating areas. It takes me a few moments to get my coat off and get seated on the sofa. Once I do, I slide my feet out of my shoes and tuck them up underneath me. After standing outside, talking with Harry, I'm desperate to warm up.

"I do have some news," Kate announces before calling Mathilde to come and join us. "I was waiting for Nat to get here so I could tell you what I learned."

Mathilde flops down onto the sofa beside me, her long hair threatening to tumble out of her makeshift bun. She pulls two pencils out of her hair, makes a quick twist and shoves them back in again.

"Would you like a hair tie?" I ask, reaching for my handbag.

Mathilde shakes her head. "No thanks, I'm good. This is the only way I can keep from losing my pencils while I work."

This time when I smile, it's genuine. Seeing our unlikely trio come together always makes me happy. There's Kate, who only writes with a brand-name fountain pen. I've got a full pack of multi-coloured markers in my bag and Mathilde is dependent on her hairstyle to keep up with her writing instruments. Rather than keeping us apart, our differences make our group even stronger. Each one of us brings a unique perspective and approach to tackling problems. When that isn't enough, we've got an army of Eternals standing behind us.

"Right! Remember when I snuck those two carved statuettes over to the Ashmolean in my handbag?" Kate waits for us to nod in confirmation. "I asked a member of my team to x-ray them and report back."

The last few days have been so busy, I have to work hard to fish the right memory from my brain. "One was heavier than the other, and we thought the heavier one might have a copper rod inside. Is that right? Were our suspicions correct?"

"Got it in one, Nat," Kate replies. "We were exactly right, but it gets more interesting."

Mathilde and I look at one another with matching expressions of curiosity.

"After I got the report via email, I went over to the Ash late last night. I was intrigued to see if I could find any other items which might have something strange inside of them."

"Why didn't you ask one of your team to do that? It must have taken you ages," Mathilde asks.

"I couldn't exactly explain to an outsider why I suddenly thought a bunch of random, unconnected pieces of art needed to go through the x-ray machine, now could I?" Kate replies. "But don't worry, Bartie came along to help. It wasn't our best date ever, but I won't complain."

Rolling my eyes, I push the conversation back on track. "Ok, so you had an x-ray date with Bartie. What did you learn?"

"I was thinking about Sir Christopher's journal entry. He talked about setting up a number of rods, each acting as a reinforcement point for the magic. I started with some of the oldest items in our collection and managed to find several more statues and carvings with unexplained copper cores. But I didn't find as many as I thought I should."

Kate picks up her mobile and touches the screen before turning it around so we can see a photo gallery.

"Those are paintings," I say, confused.

"Bartie and I got to thinking about everything we've learned over the past few months. Why do some paintings, statues and books talk, but others don't? I don't know about you two, but I had never stopped to ask myself that question. Then Bartie reminded me about last term's gala at St Margaret. When the Eternals held older items from the college collection, they became strong enough to be seen by anyone."

My eyes widen as the implications set in. "Copper rods. Lots and lots of copper rods, scattered all across the colleges."

"Exactly!" Kate beams at me. "We made a second pass through the galleries selecting the items that can talk. What you see on my phone is a photo gallery of paintings which have copper strips built into their frames. The subject of each painting or sculpture provides expertise and insights into either a famous individual, or a historic time period."

Mathilde's brow is furrowed in concentration. "Do you think that's accidental? I mean, it can't be, right? Someone along the way must have selected which items would get endowed with the copper properties."

"I woke up at 3am with the same realisation, Mathilde. Brava for getting there so quickly!" Kate laughs before continuing. "I think this was originally part of the prefect's role, but the instruction, or the meaning behind the instruction got lost somewhere along the way."

"But that seems so important, how could we not know this?" I ask, genuinely perplexed.

"Think about our own training," Kate answers. "In four

hundred years, we can't be the first group of prefects who haven't had a proper welcome. Prefects are human, they get sick and die unexpectedly. The magic calls another person to come and fill in the prefect role, but there wouldn't necessarily be an instruction manual sitting there waiting for them."

My grandfather steps forward, his look serious. "My word, Kate. I think you've stumbled across the explanation. Before you three, we prefects were not such a close-knit bunch. There was no need for us to be. We'd meet up periodically, but for the most part, we kept our heads down and did our work."

Mathilde replies with a wry smile, "Hard to keep apart when the magic is on the fritz." She turns to Kate to ask, "Do you think we could put some of my books through the x-ray? I know exactly which ones I want to test."

"The book plates? Is that what you're thinking?" My grandfather's face lights up. "All those years, I pasted in bookplates identifying books as property of the library. I never stopped to ask myself why my predecessor had given me two different versions to use."

"Don't feel bad, Alfred, I didn't question it either," Mathilde confesses. "I thought it was some kind of cataloguing system - one sticker for general items and another to mark autobiographies and biographies of people of particular note."

I sit up straight, my feet falling to the floor with a thump. Everyone turns in my direction. "Wait a minute. This would explain how someone could stretch our magical borders down to London. If they knew which pieces of artwork and books to take, they could begin to build up their own magical community. Once they got a critical mass, the border would stretch and allow the items to come to life."

Nodding her agreement, Kate adds, "It would also explain why they raided the secret chamber here at Barnard. They needed more items, and they must have known of the stockpile hidden away all those years ago."

"They started their thefts at Iffley and St Margaret, but given both colleges were open and filled with people, they could only take an item or two at a time." I trail my gaze over the stacks of books and paintings spread around us. "But here at Barnard, during the holiday closure, they would have had plenty of time to take whatever they wanted."

Mathilde leaps to her feet, "Oh my! And since we don't have a record of what was originally put into the secret chamber, we have no way of knowing what, or how much they took."

"All is not lost, Mathilde," Kate waves her back to her seat. "Whoever they are, we are onto their game now. They won't be a step ahead of us any longer. Term is back in session, and the halls are once again filled with students, faculty and staff. We can have a quiet word with the college security teams and suggest they keep an extra close watch during the evenings and weekends."

I speak up, my tone grim. "We can stop them from taking more items, but we still have the task of finding the culprits and getting back everything they've stolen. We've seen firsthand what happens when Oxford's magic is out of alignment."

I glance at Mathilde and Kate, making sure they are paying attention. "We are the prefects. Chasing down criminals isn't in our formal job descriptions, but there is no one better placed to solve this than we are. Are we in agreement?"

Neither of them hesitates before nodding.

"The clock is ticking. We need to determine once and for all whether the Master is responsible for Ms Evans murder, and we need to do so as quickly as possible. We can't have his threats hanging over our heads. Once that is settled, we can move onto our bigger problem - finding out which Eternal is masterminding the theft of Oxford's magic."

# Chapter Fifteen

W hen I had organised my schedule for this week, I picked the wrong day to do paperwork. Reviewing budgets, updating spreadsheets, and reading proposals fail to distract me from Harry's news about Edward.

Back in the quiet of my office at Barnard, I replay my conversation with Harry over and over again. Try as I might, I can't come up with a single good reason why Edward wouldn't stand up and defend me against Master Finch-Byron's horrid accusations. I comb through every word we've exchanged since I returned to Oxford last week.

Does he honestly think I am a criminal? At what point did he begin to suspect me? When I ran into him in the library on his first day at Barnard? His concern seemed so genuine. I could say the same for his invitation to get a drink. But was he really 'too busy' to go now, or was he buying time to build up a case against me?

My mind replays the scene of us standing in the hallway outside the old library after Edward had lunch with us. He held my hand and asked to bring our date forward. I feel sick thinking about how tongue-tied I was. Did he think my nerves were due to guilt rather than insecurity? When he squeezed my arm, was he trying to reassure me, or was he apologising for what may come next? A formal accusation... a trial... Edward sitting on the opposite side of the courtroom? Is that what he had planned?

H gives a mouth-smacking yawn in his cat bed, jostling me out of my deep and worrying thoughts. I force my mind in a new direction. Why do I care so much? Why am I so upset? I haven't been on a date with Edward yet. It isn't as though we've spent months building up a close friendship or moved on to something deeper. Sure, we've had some nice conversations, but that's as far as things have gone. So far... but I had hoped for more.

On it goes for the rest of the morning, a ball of sorrow spinning in my stomach. My efforts to rationalise away the hurt fall far short, leaving behind an intense feeling of disappointment.

H wakes up in time for lunch, making a nuisance of himself until I agree to set my work aside and join the rest of our group in the dining hall. I don't know whether it is the cat or wyvern in him, but it is clear he can sense my emotional turmoil.

"Ya know, Nat, I've been thinkin'. 'Arry must 'ave gotten something about Edward's conversation with tha Master wrong."

I shake my head, replying, "I want to agree with you, H, because contemplating the alternative is driving me mental, but it's Harry. She's so dependable. She wouldn't gossip out of turn. And if she can doubt Edward, after knowing him for all these years, where does that leave me?"

H's expression is grim, but he struggles to hide it from me. We trudge along the garden pavement, our pace much slower than normal. When we reach the bottom of the wide concrete stairs leading up to the dining hall, H sweeps out a wing, forcing me to halt.

"Edward is no actor. Iffen Edward really does think ya and Tildy are criminals, thar's no way 'e could 'ide it from ya forever.

'Ave ya seen any signs, any 'ints that 'is friendship wiff ya is a sham?"

I tilt my head to the side, considering H's questions. "Well... no. Before Harry spoke with me this morning, I never had any doubts that Edward's interest in me was real. Interest in getting to know me as more than a friend, I mean."

Nodding, H pulls his wing back. "Thar ya go, Nat. I feel better already. Good thing, too. Didn't want ta ruin my lunch worryin' about Edward."

Satisfied with his own conclusion, H sprints up the stairs ahead of me. For my part, I find it harder to arrive at the same positive perspective on the situation. Last term, Chef Smythe's killer lived under all of our noses right there at St Margaret, with none of us the wiser. Every time I went into the dining hall, there she was. Sitting right in front of me, chatting with me, having lunch with me, and I was none the wiser. If I need a reminder of how wrong my judgement can be, I don't have to look far.

Over lunch, I sit quietly, letting Kate and Mathilde chatter away, none the wiser of the tumultuous thoughts passing through my mind. I push my food around on my plate, my appetite non-existent, until eventually passing it over to H to finish. For once, he doesn't thank me for the extra servings. Sensing my misery, he accepts my plate without a word of comment.

We gather our trays and carry them to the disposal racks before following a group of students out of the dining hall doorway. I'm barely out of the door when I hear Mathilde call out, "Hi, Edward!"

My head snaps in her direction in time to see Edward barrel past us. He waves off her hello, his attention focussed on his mobile. He walks past without saying a word to me, or even looking in my direction. It's as though I don't exist.

"That was weird," Mathilde comments as we head towards the

stairs. "Normally Edward would stop and chat for a moment. Must have been in a real hurry."

"I'm sure that was it," I mumble, silencing H with a look. He looks as gobsmacked as I do, suddenly far from certain that Edward is on my side.

In that moment, the feeling of anguish weighing on me morphs into anger. How dare Edward treat me that way! He's had plenty to say to me in the past week and a half while he was deliberately leading me on. Asking me on a date. Taking me by the hand. Squeezing my arm. The scenes flash before my eyes.

Now that he's moved me into the "presumed guilty" category, he doesn't have time for a simple hello? Master Finch-Byron points the finger at me and suddenly I'm unworthy of his time? If Edward is willing to take some blowhard's word for it, without even asking me a single question, then he is not the man I thought he was.

If he was truly attracted to me, or even if he simply saw us as friends or colleagues, he owes me a conversation at a bare minimum. But all day long, my phone had been silent, my inbox empty.

The longer I sit here without a word of explanation, the more I fume. I shift from wondering why to thinking of all of the things I'll say should Edward ever show his face in my doorway again. He might have judged me guilty, but I know I am innocent. Faking an emotional connection so that he can worm his way into my friend group is beyond the pale. Pretending to care for me while investigating me behind my back!

And has he given any thought to the damage he might do to my professional reputation? Or to Mathilde's and Kate's?

By late afternoon, steam is practically coming out of my ears. When I catch myself banging my desk drawer closed, I realise that I am in no mood for company.

I head out into the gardens to track down H. He abandoned the confines of my office earlier in the afternoon, choosing to make himself scarce rather than risk catching any of my ire.

"H?" I call out, pleased when I spot a black scaly snout poke out of a laurel bush. "I've got something I need to take care of this evening. Would you mind staying the night with Mathilde?"

H opens his mouth to argue, takes one look at my expression and decides to limit himself to a nod instead.

"Thanks. She's waiting for you in the old library. You can fly in one of the open windows when you are ready to leave."

On the walk home from Barnard, I debate the best place to confront Edward. Should I wait until he gets home and then go knock on his door? Or would it be better for me to text him and ask him to pop downstairs instead?

When I turn into our drive, I cast my eyes over the front of our building. The front porch light is the only illumination. Both mine and Edward's flat are dark, showing no signs of life inside. We're the only residents of the building.

I brush aside all thoughts of his flat or mine. This conversation requires a neutral ground.

Pausing on our doorstep, I stand under the wooden awning and look around. Right here. This is the place. If he wants to go inside, he'll have to get past me first.

I dash inside to drop off my handbag and grab a throw off of the sofa. After wrapping it around my shoulders, I return to my outpost under the awning. The last thing I want is for my teeth to chatter while I read him the riot act.

As the cars swoosh past our drive, I debate how to start the conversation. Is it best to go in hard, letting him know in no uncertain terms just how much he's hurt me? Or if I do that, am I no better than he is? Should I give him a chance to explain before crashing down on him?

The traffic gradually slows as Oxford's rush hour draws to a close. Other sounds filter in - a lone bird calling out, the fast-paced steps of passing joggers, the whistle of someone walking without a care in the world.

My eyes open wide as the whistle grows closer, the dark shape revealing itself to be Edward's broad shoulders and oversized winter coat. When I see him turn into our driveway, his form unburdened by the worries and anger weighing me down, my thoughts crystallise.

This jerk deserves every bloody thing he is about to get.

❖

"Hullo there, Nat. Are you heading out for the evening?" Edward smiles as he looks at me from the bottom of our drive.

I stand in silence, anger coursing down my spine. My eyes squinting, I search his face for any hint of mockery. His countenance is the same as always - caring, open, welcoming. This time, however, I know better. I won't be taken for a fool again.

Huddling deeper into my wrap, I imagine the blanket is armour, a physical barrier between anything Edward may say and my already bruised heart.

I wait until he reaches the bottom of the small set of steps and pauses. With me in his way, he can go no further. My voice is barely louder than a whisper, but seethes with fury.

"How dare you!"

He rocks back on his heels. "How da... What?"

"How dare you show up here and speak to me as though we are friends," I hiss. "As though you have any right to speak to me."

Edward's eyes circle wildly, confusion writ large on his face. He looks from left to right, hunting for any clue or explanation for this wild woman breathing fire on his doorstep. "Did something happen?" he asks, his tone sounding stressed.

"Did something happen?" I mock him, cackling with laughter. "Nothing happened, Edward. *Nothing!*" The last word comes out as a throaty shout.

I gather my throw, grasping the edges of the blanket in a fist. Edward takes one step back and then another as I sweep down the steps. I stride forward until I am barely a pace away. Looking up at him, I curb my rush of emotion.

"Last term," I begin, "I came to you when I needed someone to support me. You stood by my side when we confronted Beatrice about the death of Chef Smythe. When Santa failed to turn up at the Christmas party, you let me rope you into playing the part. I asked for help and you gave it, time and time again."

Edward stares, still confused. When it is clear that I am not going to say anything more, provide any additional context which might clarify the situation, he shrugs and replies, "That's what friends do, right?" He phrases it as a question, unsure of whether it is the right or the wrong response.

I snake a hand between the edges of the blanket, my finger pointing out to jab into his chest. "That is exactly what friends do! They *stand together*. They don't turn their backs and they definitely don't sit in silence when someone accuses them..."

Gulping in a ragged breath, my emotions threaten to overwhelm me. "I thought you cared about me, Edward. I was actually looking forward to our date. But now I know the truth. It was all a lie. I..." My throat closes up as I blink back a rush of angry tears and let my hand drop back to my side.

Edward reaches an arm out, but stops himself, sensing somehow that his touch will be unwelcome. "Nat, I don't know what I've done... what you're talking about. I can see you are distraught, but I have no idea how to correct or address whatever it is that is making you feel this way."

I wipe away a tear, still seething. "Don't play dumb with me, Edward. I know you are investigating me."

"What?" Edward replies, dumbstruck. "Investigating you? *You?* For what?"

"For the burglary. At Barnard. The secret chamber."

Shaking his head, Edward acts as though he is struggling to make sense of my words. "Why on earth would you think I'm investigating you? You said yourself that you weren't even in Oxford when it happened."

I glare up at him, refusing to accept the lies he is peddling. Silence stretches between us, my eyes narrowing as I dare him to continue on with his falsehoods. But he says nothing more. His gaze searches my own.

His hurt and confusion seems genuine, much more like the man I thought that he was. But I know what Harry overheard. I know he is lying. I gave him a chance to explain himself and he chose not to take it.

With nothing more to say, I spin and walk back up the stairs. The door handle refuses to give, the lock securely fastened. In my hurry to get back outside, I left my keys sitting on my coffee table beside my handbag.

"Natalie, stop. Stop!" Edward calls as he takes the steps in one giant leap, landing beside me. "Listen to me, please. I haven't the faintest clue what has happened or who could have upset you so much. I promise, on my honour, my interest in getting to know you better is entirely genuine."

I stare up at him in shock.

"I know you haven't known me for very long, but you are the first woman I've invited out for a drink in the last five- no, six years. I would never pretend affection with anyone, under any circumstances."

Exhaling, I twist in his direction and search his gaze, hunting for the truth.

"Please, Nat. Can we back up a step, start this conversation all over again? But this time, maybe you can explain everything from the beginning?"

The hurt in his voice breaks through the wall I was building between us. I nod, not trusting my voice.

"You're shivering, Nat. Let's go inside. Your place or mine, I'm not fussed. We can go wherever you feel the most comfortable."

He leaves one hand on my back as he leans forward with the other and unlocks the door. Nudging me forward, he waits until I am safely in before he follows, pushing the door closed with his foot.

On autopilot, I wander over to my own door, twisting the handle and stepping inside. Edward waits in the hallway for my permission before coming inside.

He leads me to the sofa, spreading an extra blanket across my lap once I'm seated, before settling into my armchair. Then he leans forward, resting his elbows on his legs, and waits patiently for me to decide where to start.

I straighten the blanket, using the moment to take a deep breath. When I'm ready, I look him straight in the eye. "I know Master Finch-Byron told you to investigate Mathilde and myself in relation to the burglary." I put up a hand to halt him when he opens his mouth to respond. "I also know that you didn't say a word, not one single thing, in my defence. So, tell me, Edward. Do you think I might be a criminal?"

Edward holds his arms out, pleading with me. "Of course, I don't think you are a criminal. How can you even ask me that?"

"Then why didn't you tell the Master to get in the sea when he suggested Mathilde and I might be involved in the burglary and discovery of the secret room? I know you're not a shrinking violet."

"Back up a step," he says. "How did you overhear this conversation? It was early in the morning and we were in the Master's office."

I shift in my seat. "I'd prefer to not say."

Edward cocks his head to the side, considering my reply. "Harry. No, don't shake your head at me. It had to have been Harry. Her desk is outside the Master's door. I can't believe she would run to you without speaking with me first."

"I'm not saying that it was Harry, mind you, but if she were involved, I'd imagine she'd react much the same as me. Why would bold, opinionated Edward Thomas sit in silence, listening to someone accuse his friends of a crime?"

Edward's head falls into his hands, a low groan emerging. "Is that your logic? Silence must equal agreement? There couldn't be any other reason why I'd choose not to argue with the Master? None?"

"What do you think I've been doing all day?" I ask, throwing my hands in the air. "I've asked myself the same question a dozen times and have yet to come up with a reasonable response. If you've got one, I'm all ears, Edward."

"I'm a Professor of Criminology at Oxford, Nat. I've spent years of my life researching criminal behaviour. It's not for nothing that I'm one of the foremost experts in my field. So, do you think I wouldn't recognise a classic attempt at misdirection when I hear one?"

Now it's my turn to sit dumbfounded. "What?"

"Master Finch-Byron has had me running all over Oxford and half of London searching for mystery criminals under every rock and behind every curtain. I was beginning to question his sanity when you, yes you, Nat, suggested I speak with one Charles Graves."

I lean forward, excitement clear in my voice. "You spoke with Charles? Did he tell you about seeing Ms Evans and Master Finch-Byron embracing?"

Edward arches an eyebrow, his tone droll. "I thought you said you didn't know him. That you'd overheard him talking with some friends? Isn't that what you told me when we had lunch with your friends in the old library?"

A flush creeps up my throat. "Um, well, I might have..."

Edward waves off my attempt at an explanation. "I know you spoke with him, and with the Master's previous assistant, Mrs Lucy James. Seems you've been one step ahead of me for this entire investigation."

I smile, deciding to accept his statement as a compliment. "Don't feel badly. I didn't have the Master sending me off on a wild goose chase."

He rolls his eyes at my response, before leaning back in his chair. "Haha. I will admit you've done well for an amateur, but I suspect that I have one fact in hand of which you are unaware."

"You mean, the fact that Ms Evans was pregnant at the time of her death?" I reply, smiling prettily.

This time Edward's mouth falls open. "You can't possibly know that! I haven't told anyone at all; I've never left the file sitting anywhere."

"As I said before, I couldn't possibly reveal my sources." I move on quickly before he can ask any follow up questions. "Was that what finally tipped you off that it might be the Master himself?"

Shaking his head, Edward answers, "I haven't made a final determination of whether it was him or his wife. After all, she had more to lose from the possibility of a child."

"You'd think so, but she didn't seem too fazed."

Edward leaps to his feet. "Didn't seem too fazed? Is that what you said? My god, Nat. Did you speak with her about this? Are you insane?" He strides across the room to look out of the window as he struggles to rein in his temper.

Straightening my shoulders, I huff, "I was careful! And I didn't blurt it all out in one go. She practically pulled the information from me." *A bit of a stretch, but what Edward doesn't know won't hurt him.* "Did you know that Master Finch-Byron threatened me after that?"

Edward spins from his position across the room. "Threatened you? When? How?"

"Sit back down and I'll tell you," I instruct, waiting until he follows my command.

Once he's calm, I recount my conversation, highlighting that the Master extended his threat to include both Mathilde and Kate as well. "So you see, when Harry... I mean *someone* overheard your meeting with the Master, we presumed he was taking another step to ensure no one looked in his direction. He must know that I am onto him. By pointing the finger at me, he'd ensure that it quickly turned into a case of 'he said, she said' - one which he expected to win given his stature here at Oxford."

Edward stares off into space for a minute, long enough that I can practically see the gears turning in his head. Finally, he reaches a conclusion and turns his attention back to me. "Assuming we are both correct, Master Finch-Byron is only going to get more desperate as the days goes by. He is intelligent enough to know that he can't hide his crime forever. It's a question of time - whether we can find the final piece in the puzzle, revealing exactly how and why he killed Ms Evans, before he makes a bold move to discredit one or both of us."

"Yes," I nod, "you're right. Now that we've put all of our cards on the table and know for certain we've both arrived at the same point, I can only see one way forward for us."

"Work together?" Edward asks, his eyes sparkling. "We've done it once before. As much as I'm loathe to involve an amateur, it seems I haven't got much of a choice, have I?"

"Amateur?" I reply, in mock consternation. "I'm two for two in my murder investigations so far. I bet even you can't match those stats, Professor Thomas."

"So, we're in agreement? No more hidden truths? No more rushing to conclusions?" His eyes lock with mine, ensuring I am hearing every word.

"Total and complete honesty. We're partners." I cringe. "Work partners. Not partner partners. Ugh, you know what I mean." And once again, I'm back to babbling. I bite my lip to prevent anything further from burbling out.

Edward shakes his head, trying desperately to hold back a laugh. The silence stretches, becoming uncomfortable. But neither of us seems to know what to say next.

I look around the room, hoping to find inspiration. The only thing I can see is the door. Abrupt, but I guess that will do. "Right, so if there's nothing else, I shouldn't keep you. It is a work night, after all."

Edward grabs the lifeline I throw out. He looks at his watch and leaps back to his feet. "Yes, look at the time. Nearly bedtime and I haven't had my tea yet. You either, I imagine. I'll get out of your hair."

I unwrap the blanket from my shoulders and stand to show Edward out. At the doorway, we pause, once again awkward.

"I'll see you tomorrow?" His voice is gentle and unsure.

"Tomorrow? Absolutely. Why don't you stop by the old library in the morning? We could grab a coffee, chat with the others, maybe put our heads together on next steps?"

"Put our heads together." He smiles, his blue eyes twinkling. "That sounds ideal. Good night, Nat."

He stares at me, his gaze gentle. A wayward lock of dark, wavy hair tumbles down his forehead, softening the sharp lines of his patrician features. Before I can say anything else, he leans in close and brushes a gentle kiss against my cheek. He turns and walks up the stairwell with a skip in his step, leaving me standing there, with my hand against my cheek.

"Good night, partner," I whisper.

# Chapter Sixteen

"**M**orning!" I call out as I walk into the old library. When no one responds, I shake the bag of croissants I'm holding, sending the scent of buttery goodness wafting out around me.

Unsurprisingly, H is the first one to stick his head out, his snout in the air as he follows the smell of breakfast. "Mornin', Nat. By any chance, 'ave ya got any cheese croissants?"

"Of course, I do! I've got cheese, almond, chocolate, plain, apricot..." I finish spreading the goodies on paper plates before waving H over. "Pick your pleasure."

Mathilde and Kate emerge from the depths of the library shelves and settle into the seating area. Harry follows behind, a pot of hot coffee in her hand.

"Morning, team!" Harry says as she makes her way around our circle, topping up our coffee cups. "I'm going to miss our breakfasts when I go back to St Margaret next week."

"Next week?" I raise my eyes in her direction. "So soon? Have you had any luck on finding a replacement for Ms Evans?"

"Soon? I've been here for almost two weeks. Dr Radcliffe can't spare me much more than that." Harry sets the coffee pot on a nearby table and pulls a chair over, joining the rest of us. "As for finding a replacement, all I've managed to do is get the job advert posted, and even that required me to call in a bunch of favours. The college recruitment process isn't known for its fast pace."

"Well, that's already something. I'm going to miss our morning catch-ups, too." I take a quick bite of my croissant and wash it down with a sip of coffee. "Speaking of catch-ups, there is a reason why I brought breakfast in this morning. I need to update you all on my evening. But before I do..." I pause to catch Harry's eye and make sure she isn't mid-bite. "Harry, could you tell the others what you overheard yesterday morning?"

Harry frowns, looking unconvinced. "Are you sure, Nat?"

Mathilde and Kate both perk up, their curiosity peaked.

I smile to reassure her. "It's fine, Harry. I've got the rest of the story, but it will make more sense if we start at the beginning, and that's where you come in."

As Harry recounts the conversation, I watch Kate and Mathilde for their reactions. Kate has a proper poker face but Mathilde is like an open book. Intrigue is quickly replaced by unease and then anger.

When she finishes, Harry puts her coffee cup down with a clatter and turns to me to fill in the rest. "Did you speak with Edward?"

Before I can answer, the library door swings open and the man himself walks in. Edward's smile falters when he's met with harsh silence and glares from everyone except for me.

"Err, hello all?" Edward's greeting turns to a question as he takes in the scene. He stops, looking to me for guidance on whether he should come further in or return later.

I pat the space next to me on the sofa. "Come on in. I'm in the middle of telling everyone about our chat last night. Why don't you take your coat off and come have a croissant while I finish with the story?"

Harry's sigh of relief is audible. "If Edward is here, that must mean I misunderstood what I overheard yesterday. Thank goodness."

"You're not off scot-free, Harry," Edward chides her as he unwraps his scarf. "You should have come to me straightaway instead of rushing off to tell Nat. I could have saved you all a day spent worrying."

Harry blushes, but remains silent, waiting to hear what I have to say.

By the time I'm done, the whole group is eyeing Edward with a newfound respect.

"Why, Edward! I didn't know you had a devious bone in your body!" Harry cries. "Pretending to agree with Master Finch-Byron so you could investigate him on the sly! It's bloody brilliant."

For his part, Edward looks chagrinned. "I typically prefer a more straight-forward approach, but in this case, discretion and deception were the better part of valour."

"Right," I interject, "unless anyone else has a question, maybe we should turn our attention to next steps. We're all in agreement that the Master himself is the most likely suspect in Ms Evans' death, but we don't have any evidence or hard facts which we can take to the police."

Edward finishes his coffee and places it on the table before leaning back and settling deeper into the sofa. His leg brushes against mine, setting off a tingle of nerves in the pit of my stomach.

For his part, Edward seems deep in thought. He props an elbow on the armrest, leaning his head against his hand. Staring off into the distance, he reveals, "I've been replaying all of my conversations with the Master and have noticed something. Although he ostensibly called me over here to focus on finding out who killed Ms Evans, everything he's asked me to do has been related to the burglary."

"What do you mean?" Kate asks.

"First, he was insistent that Ms Evans must have surprised the burglar. When the police review of the security tapes from that evening didn't turn up any evidence to support that theory, he next claimed that Ms Evans must have been involved." Edward grimaces. "That spun the investigation towards conducting background checks and looking into all of Ms Evans contacts. I personally spent a full afternoon reviewing all of the security footage of Ms Evans in the weeks leading up to her death. As a last straw, he decided to point the finger at Nat and Mathilde."

"He's been working against us this whole time!" Mathilde groans. "How are we ever going to get to the bottom of this?"

"Don't despair, Mathilde," Edward says, reassuringly. "We have one clear advantage - there are five of us and only one of him. Now that we've got everything out in the open, we can divide up the investigation and work through potential leads much more quickly."

"That's my Edward!" Harry cheers from her chair. "I'm sorry I doubted you yesterday, but if the end result is all of us working together, then maybe it wasn't all bad."

Edward turns his head to smile at me. "Yes, there've been a couple of positive outcomes."

Kate coughs, pulling us our attention back to the matter at hand. "Right, as lovely as all of this is," she says, waving her hand at Edward and I, "it doesn't get us any closer to proving the Master is at fault."

"That's where my divide and conquer idea comes in," Edward replies. "Have you found any evidence that someone inside of Barnard was involved in the burglary?

We all shake our heads. Edward's question reminds me of my weekend trip to London. I jump to my feet and cross over to where I left my coat hanging on the back of a chair. Digging in the pockets, I find the fish and chip shop flyer.

I return to my seat and hand it over to Edward. "Kate found

this folded up and tucked away between two crates in the secret chamber. We think the intruder, or one of the intruders, must have lost it while they were rummaging around in the secret chamber."

Edward's brow furrows. "Do I want to know why you didn't give this to me sooner?"

"I didn't want to run the risk that you'd toss the flyer without giving it proper consideration. You were so focussed on Ms Evans being at fault, I wasn't sure you'd listen."

"I can see that," he says as he folds the paper and puts it in his pocket. "Now that I've stopped letting the Master dictate my every move, I'm building a much clearer picture. Everything we know so far makes sense if we assume there are two crimes: the first is the burglary and the second is the murder."

Edward looks around as we all nod our agreement. "The burglary must have come first, as I cannot imagine anyone stepping over a dead body on their way to commit a theft. The thief would have been more likely to turn tail and try again another day, rather than risking getting caught breaking and entering and getting blamed for the murder as well."

"That makes sense," I agree.

Edward continues, "In that case, one group should focus on the burglary of the secret chamber. It must have occurred over the holiday weekend, between Friday, when the college closed at noon on New Year's Eve, and Sunday evening when Ms Evans was killed. The other group can continue to look for proof of the relationship between the Master and Ms Evans, and any reason why he would have killed her."

Kate interrupts, "We need three groups, actually. One for the burglary, one for the murder and one to try to stay focussed on the secret chamber itself. The Master gave Mathilde and I two weeks to catalogue the contents. If we can't prove his guilt before our time is up, we'll lose our chance to figure out what might have been stolen."

Mathilde adds, "We've made a lot of progress and it is becoming clear that there is a pattern to the items hidden away. But until we've examined everything and put all of the pieces we have together, we won't be able to make a guess as to what might be missing."

"That's our plan, then," I say. "Mathilde and Kate keep their attention on their current task. Harry and I should take on the challenge of finding evidence of the murder, and Edward, you should turn your investigation onto the burglary."

Edward's face darkens. "I'm not sure I like the idea of you and Harry risking catching more of the Master's wrath."

I glance at Harry to get her thoughts. Frowning, she replies, "I don't like it either, Edward, but I can't see that we have much choice. Think about it - I'm the only one who can access the Master's records without him knowing about it. Nat can use her connections around the college to see if anyone else saw anything important. Edward, only you can ask the security team for access to view the video footage from the weekend. You have to be the one to look for evidence of the break-in."

Edward opens his mouth to object again but stops as he realises the futility of the gesture.

"We're partners," I remind him, giving him no further room for argument.

I spend most of the day in meetings Will and Jill have organised. There are room layouts to approve, vendors to meet, and decisions that have to be made. Despite my efforts to delegate most of the work on Barnard's women's celebration, there are still some aspects of the project which require direct intervention.

I finally manage to extricate myself in the late afternoon. Harry rings, letting me know that the Master has left early, claiming to have a meeting to attend. We agree to meet at her desk outside his office, taking advantage of his absence to search his private books and files.

I arch an eyebrow at Harry as we stand before the inner door to the Master's office. "Are you sure he isn't coming back in today? We cannot afford to get caught in here. He'll have me fired on the spot."

"I'm positive, Nat. I wouldn't have called you over here if I wasn't sure. He left with his coat, hat and briefcase and said he'd see me tomorrow. I don't know where he is gone, but he won't be back in today." With that said, she turns the knob and opens the door.

Together, we survey the Master's office. It has all of the requisite signs of an Oxford master - looming portraits of white-haired gentlemen, a landscape of the Cotswolds and a wall covered in book-lined shelves. His desk is buried underneath towering stacks of files and paperwork.

"If I had any lingering doubts about Ms Evans' incompetence as an assistant, seeing the state of Finch-Byron's desk would sweep them away. Look at that mess! There must be months' worth of paperwork there. It will take us days just to go through the surface clutter." Harry shudders and frowns.

"Like it or not, we have to do the best we can. Why don't you start on his desk since you have a better chance of making heads or tails of the documents and files." I turn towards the other side of the room, saying, "I'll work on his shelves, checking to see if he's hidden any incriminating evidence inside any of the books. Who knows, maybe I'll find a book which triggers a secret door opening."

Harry rolls her eyes at my excitement. "I think we've had all we can handle of secret chambers here at Barnard. Try to stick to looking inside the book covers, okay?"

We work in silence for the next hour, keeping our ears attuned to the outer office where Harry's desk is located. Twice, Harry has to step out to greet visitors, sounding cool as ice as she apologises for being away from her desk. "Sorry, I was putting some files away in the Master's filing cabinet. I hope you weren't waiting long."

By six in the evening, we are ready to throw our hands in the air and give up. I stand up, my back creaking from being bent over for too long. "Why does the Master have so many books here? Couldn't he have interspersed some knickknacks or book-ends like a normal person?

Harry blows a lock of hair from her forehead. "I could make the same complaint about his desk. I've found papers awaiting his signature that date back to when Lucy James was his PA. They've been sitting here for months!"

Shaking my head, I scan the remaining shelves. "Fifteen more minutes. That's the maximum I'm giving us. I'll finish up these last three shelves and you go through his desk drawers. If nothing jumps out at us by then, I vote we call it a day and go get some dinner."

Harry rolls her head from side to side, loosening her neck muscles. "Okay, I'm in. But remind me the next time we have to search a room to do it first thing in the morning rather than after a full day of work."

"How about we hope that there isn't a next time?" I reply, arching an eyebrow.

"Good point," Harry concedes as she pulls open a desk drawer and dives in.

Before I can pick up another book, my mobile rings. "It's Edward, I should probably get it."

Harry nods as I touch the screen to accept the call. "Hi, Edward, any news? Really? That's fantastic! What's that? You can't see their face? Blurred? Huh... Okay, not as great as we'd hoped, but at least it shows that the two events are definitely not connected to one another. Harry and I are nearly done with our own investigation. Why don't we all meet up at my flat in an hour or so and decide what to do next? Dinner? I can order a pizza... Sounds good. See you later."

I don't try to hide my smile as I end the call. Harry clears her throat, reminding me that I need to clue her in on the other half of the conversation. "Good news from Edward. He reviewed the tapes from the long holiday weekend and found evidence of someone sneaking into the college grounds and leaving again soon after, struggling to carry out a cardboard box. Given the time of day and the person's strange behaviour, he thinks there is a good chance it is our burglar. It happened on the night before Ms Evans was killed."

"Finally, some progress. Did I hear you say something about blurriness? I'm guessing Edward couldn't see the burglar's face."

Shaking my head, I reply, "He said it was the weirdest thing. It was like there was a cloud around the person. He could make out their shape, but he couldn't see their features."

"Was there a problem with the cameras?" Harry asks, intrigued.

"He didn't think so. He seemed really perplexed. I can't help but wonder whether something magical was involved."

"Could it have been an Eternal?" Harry asks.

I mull over the idea but discard it as unlikely. "An Eternal wouldn't be visible on a video feed. I wonder..." my voice trails off as I process through potential explanations. "What would happen if you filmed a person walking in the middle of a group of Eternals." I get my phone back out and open up the Notes app. "I'm giving myself a reminder to try it out. I'm sure my grandfather and Bartie would be happy to help."

Harry pushes a drawer closed and slides open its neighbour. "Only three drawers left."

I put my phone away and go back to my task of checking the books. The bottom three shelves are blocked by a large armchair. "Harry, give me a hand with this chair, will you?"

Together, we manage to shove it over enough to make enough space to crawl behind it to where the books had been hidden in the shadow of the chair. Once again, I fish out my phone to use it as a flashlight. The narrow beam of light illuminates row after row of black leather-bound tomes, the spines blank of any identifying words. Harry and I look at one another and then back to the shelves. "Could these be Master Finch-Byron's journals?" I whisper.

"Forget the desk drawers. I'll give you a hand with these." Harry nudges me to crawl behind the chair. "Grab the first volume on the top of shelf and the last one on the bottom. One of them should be the most recent."

I pass Harry one volume, keeping the other for myself. I don't bother crawling back out again, waiting to see if we'll need to check more of the books. Setting the book on the floor, I hunch over, using my phone to light up the page. My eyes skim the scratchy handwriting, looking for a date or something else which would indicate the timing. "This one is from 2001. No luck here. You?"

When Harry fails to reply, I straighten up as best as I can. I find her bent over her book, frantically flipping through the pages. "Aha! Listen to this! *8 November. Intimate lunch with V.E. in my office. Threat of discovery made the event all the more exciting. 10 November. V.E. booked Cotswolds hideaway for the weekend, marking my diary out for a 'conference'...*" Harry pauses, shuddering with disgust. "I won't read any more, as it carries on in the same vein and I already feel like I need a shower. If you needed proof of their relationship, this is it."

"You're right. V.E. must be Victoria Evans. Quick, let's tidy everything up and get out of here. We need to get this over to Edward; he'll be waiting for us at my flat."

Harry backs up to give me space to crawl out and climb back on my feet. With our backs to the office door, we count to three and shove the chair back into place. As I reach down to fluff a pillow, I hear the sound of a man's voice behind us.

I breathe a sigh of relief when I spin around to find my grandfather standing there. Barnard's monk Eternal, Simon, stands at his side, fuming. I quickly realise the only reason he is there is because my grandfather has a firm hold on the back of Simon's robe.

"Alfred, you nearly scared me to death!" Harry holds a hand against her chest, breathing hard.

"My apologies, Harry," my grandfather replies. "I forget that you all can't hear my footsteps. I was in a rush to find you, Nat. After a long conversation, Simon here is finally ready to tell us the truth of what he knows."

I give Simon a hard look, but his gaze is impenetrable. "Not here, Grandfather. Between our discovery and your accidental fright, I need to get out of this office. Let's go to the old library. Mathilde and Kate should still be there, and I know they'll be just as curious to hear Simon's tale as we are."

Grabbing my handbag, I shove the Master's journal into its depths, zipping it up tight so there is no chance of it falling out. We wait for Harry to close the Master's desk drawers and erase any evidence of our search. When she's happy that the original disarray has been restored, we file out and let Harry lock the doors behind us.

We follow the stone hallway until it ends at a sharp corner.

One by one, we pick our way down the stairs and through the archway signifying the move from one wing of the old building to another. Before long, we see the familiar wooden door marking the old library.

"Mathilde? Kate? H? Are you here?" I call as we walk inside. Three heads pop out from different parts of the library - Mathilde and Kate from between bookshelves and H from above. When they see my grandfather manhandling Simon, they quickly drop whatever they were doing and rush to the sofas.

"I see no cause to involve these womenfolk, Alfred," Simon grumbles.

"Don't start that again, Simon." My grandfather's tone is fierce. "I've already explained that they are our Prefects. Your silence is doing no favours for this institution which you love so much."

"Is that why you refused to speak to us before?" I ask as I settle onto the sofa. "We know Master Finch-Byron is responsible for Ms Evan's death. Did you feel you had to protect him because he is the Master of Barnard?"

"Yea," Simon agrees, "I am loathe to bring shame upon these hallowed halls. But Alfred insists that the Master himself is rotten."

"You know he is rotten, as well as I do, Simon," my grandfather reminds him. "Now that we're all here, tell the rest of the group what you shared with me earlier."

H flaps down to perch on the armrest beside me. His dark eyes track Simon's every move. Should my grandfather require any further assistance to get Simon to talk, H sits ready to provide it.

Simon begins, "I was seeking a quiet place to say my prayers that eventide. I do not oft come to the old library, but I did on that night. The halls were empty, and I was sure the room would be vacant."

"But it wasn't empty, was it?" I ask.

"Nay, Master Finch-Byron was here, speaking with someone deeper inside the room. I could not see the individual, but the Master's raised tone attracted my attention. I moved closer, knowing that they would not be able to see me. That is when I saw the other person. It was Ms Evans."

"I knew it!" I cry in an excited whisper before Mathilde leans over to shush me.

Simon's voice lowers as he restarts, his tone weary as he forces out the confession. "She told the Master that she was with child and he was the father. She demanded he set aside his wife, refusing all his offers to send her away and pay for the upkeep of the babe."

Flames lick out as H flies off the sofa, hovering in front of Simon and my grandfather. "This is tha man ya've been protectin'? A man who would father a child outside of 'is marriage and then send tha woman away? Shame on ya, Simon! Yer unfit ta be an Eternal at Oxford."

Simon wilts, the last vestiges of his self-righteousness disappearing under H's harsh words. "I was protecting Barnard from scandal. The woman was no one. She threatened to bring down the Master, the whole college if he did not do right by her and the babe. Both the Master and I acted without forethought or malice."

"Acted how?" I shift in my seat, forcing Simon to meet my gaze. "What drove him to kill her? And how were you involved?"

"When the Master refused to accede to her demands, the woman became vicious. He reeled backwards under her verbal onslaught. She said she'd never had any feelings for him. He was simply a means to an end, with that end being her becoming the wife of an Oxford Master and all of the wealth and recognition which goes along with it. She gave him no choice... she gave me no choice! I could hardly stand by and let her achieve the outcome she desired. She would bring nothing but shame upon Barnard, no matter what the Master ultimately chose to do."

Shaking his head, my grandfather interjects, "If there is someone at fault here, it is Master Finch-Byron. Had he stayed true to his own marriage vows, none of this would have happened. Now finish up this sad retelling. How did Ms Evans die?"

"She grew louder and crueler, she laughed at him. She would not stop. The Master's face was florid with rage. He made a lunge for her and she picked up a book and threw it at his head." Simon sinks to his knees, his head raised towards the sky. "Forgive me, Father. I saw the candlestick sitting on the shelf. I gave it a gentle touch, enough that the moonlight would reflect on its wide, golden base, and catch Master Finch-Byron's eye. When she turned her back to gather another book to throw, he picked it up and smashed it against her head."

His confession made, Simon's head drops and his voice quiets to a murmur. "When she crumpled to the floor, the Master panicked. He reached down to check on her, but it was too late. She was dead. The Master swayed on his feet and for a moment I feared he would collapse as well. He steadied himself on the bookshelf, swallowing audibly as he muttered, 'Why did you make me do this, Victoria?' over and over again."

"How did Ms Evan's body end up covered in books and manuscripts? Was that you or the Master?" I ask.

"'Twas the Master, not I," Simon answers, raising his head to look me in the eye. "When he calmed himself, he looked at his hand and realised what it was that he was holding. A candlestick in an old library, it had to be out of place. He stepped past the body, walking to the end of the aisle, no doubt wondering why it was there. That's when he spotted the open door to the secret chamber. Seeing it must have given him the idea of blaming her death on the intruder. He rushed back and wiped his fingerprints from the candlestick before dropping it to the floor. Then he pulled a shelf of books on top of her."

Mathilde breaks in with a question of her own. "The book Nat found in the main aisle way? Did the Master put that there as well?"

"Nay," Simon replies. "That is the book Ms Evans tossed in anger... the one which set off the chain of events leading to her demise."

A hush falls over our group as we try to process everything we've heard. When it is clear that there are no further questions, Simon closes his eyes, folds his hands and prays for forgiveness.

# Chapter Seventeen

The trill of Harry's mobile echoes in the old library. She leaps to her feet and rushes over to her handbag, digging frantically in its depths.

"Hello?" Her greeting is more of a question than a reply, making it clear that she doesn't recognise the number on the screen. "Oh hello, Detective Inspector Robinson. What can I do for you?"

Mathilde turns to me, her eyebrows arched. She whispers, "Isn't that the police officer who interviewed us on the night of the murder?"

When I give a nod of confirmation, all of us in the library move closer, trying desperately to hear the tinny voice coming through the phone.

Annoyed, Harry motions us back to our seats as she continues with the conversation. "No, don't apologise. It's no bother, I'm still at the college. What can I do for you?"

Rocking in place, Harry listens to the caller, her face shifting from pleasant to a frown as she listens intently. "Tomorrow morning? I'm going to struggle with that as his diary is fairly well booked." She stops abruptly. "He asked for the meeting? Oh... oh, I see."

I peek at Mathilde, checking whether she is as confused as I am.

Harry waves her finger in the air, letting us know the call is wrapping up. "Yes, of course, I'll be sure to pass along the message. I have his mobile number. No problem. Thanks, and same to you, Detective Inspector. Goodbye."

Her eyes are wide as saucers as she ends the call. She shoves her phone back into her handbag and returns her attention back to me. "Nat, remember when I said that the Master left early today, with little explanation?"

"Yes?" I reply, the question clear in my voice.

"He went to the police station, apparently in search of DI Robinson."

Mathilde's eyebrows shoot up. "Why would the Master go to the police? He was the one who pushed them out of the investigation in the first place, demanding that Edward take the lead."

Shrugging, Harry replies, "DI Robinson was out of the office at the time. That's why he phoned just now. The Master left a note at the station requesting an urgent meeting tomorrow morning to discuss some new information about the crimes."

"What?" I squeak, my voice heavy with astonishment. "Master Finch-Byron wants to speak to the police? You don't think..."

"That he'd go to the police and suggest you and Mathilde are involved in the burglary? Or even go so far as to blame you for Ms Evans' death?" Harry looks pained by the thought. "If he was unhappy with Edward and felt he wasn't moving quickly enough, it would take some cheek, but he might," Harry confirms, her face grim.

"But that's ridiculous!" I exclaim. "Surely the Master must know that he can't possibly get away with pointing the finger at us for very long."

Harry settles back in her seat, tapping her finger against her lips. "None of this makes sense. However, the Master wouldn't have gotten where he is by being foolhardy. We need to take a step back and think this through."

"Let's start at the beginning," Kate suggests, rising to her feet to pace around the room. "There are two crimes: a burglary and a murder. From the moment Mathilde and Nat discovered Ms Evans' body, there has been the lingering question of whether the crimes were separate or part of the same event."

She does a lap of the seating area as she keeps up her stream of thought. "The Master obviously knew that the two crimes were separate, but he recognised the opportunity to use the burglary as a distraction. That's probably why he dropped the stack of books onto her body. He wanted it to seem as though she was killed by whomever ransacked the secret chamber."

I leap in, picking up the thread. "Next, the Master demands Edward take the lead on the investigation, knowing he had a better chance of giving him some heavy-handed guidance. He was the first to suggest that Ms Evans might somehow be involved in the theft."

"But he needed a back-up plan," Mathilde interrupts. "Eventually Edward was bound to figure out that Ms Evans had nothing to do with the break-in."

"Then I stuck my nose into things, talking to Mrs James and meeting with his wife," I exclaim. "Once again, Master Finch-Byron saw a chance to connect up the break-in with the murder... or rather the discovery of the murder. He's never come out and said he thinks Mathilde and I are responsible for Ms Evans' death." I shake my head, making my annoyance clear. "Oh no, he hints all around it, setting Edward off chasing another false theory of what happened."

"He can't keep this misdirection up forever," my grandfather states, stepping around Simon to rejoin our group. "At some point, he'll grow bolded, either manufacturing evidence or destroying the video footage from the weekend.

"So, what do we do now?" I look around the group, but no one leaps forward with an answer. "Do we take what we know to the Detective Inspector? Do we have enough to convince him to question Master Finch-Byron?"

Kate drops back onto the sofa with a frown on her face. "All we've got is the word of an Eternal - which we obviously can't share with the police. That's not enough."

"Wait, we've got one more thing. Between Simon's confession," I pause to glare at his still form, "and DI Robinson's call, I forgot to tell you what Harry and I found when we searched the Master's office." I rifle in my bag again, pulling out the leather-bound book. "He has years' worth of journals tucked away on his shelves. The latest volume includes coded reference to illicit activities with a certain V.E. That must stand for Victoria Evans."

Kate shakes her head. "That's helpful, but it doesn't prove he killed her. I don't think we can afford to wait. His visit to the police station is proof that the Master is clearly escalating. Our only advantage at the moment is that we can assume he hasn't taken his claims of our involvement to anyone outside of the college." She shivers, the thought clearly rankling. "As soon as Harry phones him to pass along DI Robinson's message, we lose our advantage. He must know that Harry will tell you and Mathilde."

"He's getting desperate, and that is never a good position for a criminal to be in." My grandfather scans our group, his face grave. "He's already shown that he's willing to go to great lengths to prevent facing a murder charge."

Silence falls back over the room as we contemplate my grandfather's last words. I try to imagine what a television sleuth would do at this time. They always find a way to get the suspect to confess, erasing all doubt that it could have possibly been someone else. But how on earth could we get Master Finch-Byron to tell the truth?

"We need professional advice," I announce while reaching into my purse. "I'm going to call Edward. Hopefully I can catch him before he leaves Barnard to return home."

The phone rings several times before Edward's voice comes over the line. I quickly update him on the latest news. Like us, he's shocked that the Master would go behind his back and involve the police, particularly since there is no evidence to support his claims of our involvement in any crime.

I mull over the best way to introduce Simon's confession of his involvement in the murder. My mind races through the options, until I land on the only one which seems like it might stand up to scrutiny. "Listen, Edward. There's something else you should know. I managed to find someone who witnessed the fight between the Master and Ms Evans."

"What! Why didn't you lead with that information?" Edward exclaims. "That solves all of our problems. Can you get them over to the police station?"

"Erm, not exactly. They told me in the strictest confidence and there is no chance of getting them to speak to anyone else." I mentally cross my fingers, hoping he will let the explanation stand. "I'm positive that they are telling the truth. There must be some way we can use what they told me."

Edward grows quiet long enough that I begin to worry he's going to demand more information on the witness. I hear the sounds of passing cars and a few bicycle bells before an intake of breath comes across the line.

"If we can't get the witness to come forward, we'll have to trick the Master into telling us himself. I agree with Kate, we can't wait a moment longer. Put me on speaker."

I press the button on my screen and toggle the volume to the maximum. Edward quickly outlines a plan.

"You and I can meet up outside of the entry to the Master's lodging, and go in to speak with him together," Edward says. "Our challenge will be to get him to confess to us that he committed the murder. We've both got mobiles, one of us can set a device to record and hope to catch the confession on the recording."

I start to nod but stop when I remember Edward can't see me. "I can do that. How do we get him to come clean?"

Edward pauses for a moment. "I think it would be naïve to assume he will just blurt out an admission of guilt. He is far too arrogant and cunning for that. We have to use his own ego against him. We might be able to goad him into making a mistake and accidentally give us some detail that only the killer would know."

"He just needs to be angry enough to lose control of his story," I agree.

"Then that's our plan," Edward states, his voice brimming with confidence.

"I can tell from the background noise that you aren't in your office here at Barnard. How quickly can you get back?"

"I was nearly at home, but I turned back as soon as you started speaking. I'm only two blocks away. I can meet you outside the Master's door in ten minutes."

I urge Edward to hurry before saying goodbye.

Looking around the room, I wait for someone to step forward, calling our plans to a halt. Mathilde's eyes are distant as she twists her hair around her fingers in a nervous gesture. Smoke seethes from H's nostrils, sure evidence of his unhappiness with the idea, but he remains otherwise silent. Kate, Harry and my grandfather wear matching expressions of worry tinged with fear.

As for me, all I feel is grim determination.

Edward and I have confronted a murderer before and wrangled a confession. We can do it again, even if most of me wishes we didn't have the task thrust on us again.

Standing, I bend over to gather my handbag. A voice shatters the hush. Simon rises to his feet and turns his head to look me in the eye. "I will come with you. I played a part in the woman's death. It is right that I should assist you in obtaining a confession."

My eyes narrow as I consider his offer. "You've made no secret of your disregard for women, particularly women prefects. Why should I believe you want to help?"

Simon remains steady, his gaze never wavering from my own. For the first time, his demeanour hints at respect. "I have prayed to my Lord for guidance. My loyalty is to Barnard and to the magic. My only chance for redemption lies in providing you aid. I know you would have no reason to believe me, but you can trust me in this."

I glance first at H and then at my grandfather. I don't know Simon well-enough to judge his honesty, but those two should. Simon tracks my gaze, his eyes imploring his fellow Eternals to give him approval to come along with me. My grandfather and H share a silent conversation, expressions flitting across their faces, before finally coming to a conclusion.

"If anything happens to my granddaughter, Simon," my grandfather growls dangerously, "I will ensure that you suffer for the rest of eternity."

Once again, Simon brings his hands together in the prayer pose and gives my grandfather a short bow of understanding.

I hitch my handbag onto my shoulder and cross the room in a determined stride. "Edward should be back in the college in a few minutes. If you don't have to rush off, please wait here. I don't imagine this conversation will take too long."

The entrance to the Master's lodging sits at the top of a stairwell, with a narrow corridor providing a small waiting area. I hadn't remembered about the tight space when I agreed to meet Edward here. If someone opens the door, I'll be hard-pressed to come up with a reasonable explanation for why I'm standing outside the door to the Master's home.

Simon takes up watch at the top of the stairs, leaving me alone in the corridor. I wipe my hands down my trousers once, and then again a minute later as my nerves make my palms sweat. Rolling my shoulders and neck does little to loosen the tight spot on my upper back. I pull my phone out as a distraction, checking the battery levels again and adjusting the volume and settings.

"Any sign of Edward?" I whisper to Simon.

"Nay."

Great, now he decides to be a man of few words. I tap my foot, keeping an eye on my watch as it ticks past the ten minute mark and then twelve. I'm about to set off on a hunt when a loud trilling noise fills the corridor, the multi-tone beeps echoing off the wooden floor and stone walls in a terrible ruckus.

I leap a foot into the air before I realise the noise is coming from my handbag. I bobble the phone twice trying to get it free, finally sliding the bar to answer the call. Before I can say hello, the door to the Master's lodging swings open.

I glance down to see Edward's name on my screen, but there's no chance to answer.

"What in heavens is this cacophony out here?" the Master grumbles to himself as he pulls open the door and sticks his head out. His eyes meet mine as I stand there like a deer in headlights, frozen with the phone halfway to my face.

He takes a step back in surprise, clearly not expecting to find me, of all people, standing outside his front door. His face morphs from anger to delight as an evil grin slides into place. "Well, well, Ms Payne. Standing outside my door. I can only presume you must be looking for me. Come inside."

Stepping inside his home without Edward by my side is the

last thing I want to do, but the Master leaves me no choice. I drop my phone into my handbag, the call still active. Hopefully Edward can pick up enough of the conversation to figure out what has happened. When the Master turns his back to me, I cast a quick look over my shoulder and mouth a final plea to Simon. "Help Edward get inside!"

True to his promise to come to my aid, Simon steps up behind me. The Master looms in the open doorway, barely leaving me enough space to squeeze past him. I can feel his hot breath on the back of my neck as I slip inside. He closes the door with a resounding thud, flipping the locking mechanism. When he is once again facing me, I watch as a ghostly hand slips through the door and twists the lock back in the other direction. Only then do I exhale. Simon has come through as promised.

The Master leads me through the now familiar reception and Drawing rooms, where only a few days ago I spoke with his wife. He doesn't slow, continuing on through another doorway, until we reach his private study.

The room is overbearingly masculine, standing in sharp contrast to the ostentatious femininity of the other rooms I've seen in the house. I imagine that his wife rarely sets foot in this space.

Heavy, dark grey drapes hang over the windows, obscuring the view of the street outside. The far wall is lined with bookshelves, separated in the middle by a stone fireplace. His family crest hangs above the mantle, with a set of antique duelling pistols on display below it. Paintings of hunting scenes and stuffed deer heads decorate the walls.

In the corner sits a small conversation area with two armchairs and a side table decorated with a pipe and box of snuff. The Master ignores the intimate seating area, moving instead behind his desk to take a seat in his executive chair. He waves me into one of the two wooden chairs arranged in front of his desk.

I sink into the chair and am caught off-guard when I fall more than I expected. The chair is low to the ground, leaving me at a distinct disadvantage compared to the Master and his oversized oak desk. I feel more like a child in the head teacher's office than a grown-up in a meeting. Somehow, I suspect the set-up is deliberate.

Master Finch-Byron leans back in his chair, his hands steepled, his arms resting on his bulging midsection. "What brings you up to my home so late, Ms Payne?" He grins like a snake as he asks, "Something you needed to discuss?"

I tug my handbag close to my chest, hoping against hope that Edward can hear me and hurry up. "Um, well..." I stall for time. "I, uh, I stopped by your office earlier to update you on our plans for the secret chamber reveal. Harry said you'd left early and you have a full day tomorrow. I didn't want to delay, so I thought I might catch you here at home." Initial stumbling aside, I'm fairly proud of my excuse. It almost sounds believable.

The Master stares at me, the smile on his face made evil by the cold look in his eyes. His fingers fan in and out, tapping a rhythmic beat. I will myself to sit absolutely still, but the urge to shift under his gaze is nearly overwhelming. My handbag is a comforting weight, reminding me that help is on the way. I just need to hold it together until Edward gets here. But just in case, I remain alert, ready to run at the first sign of movement from his side of the desk.

When I fail to say anything further, the Master places his hands on the desk surface and leans forward, his bulk looming over me, causing me to flinch. "Is that really why you're here, Ms Payne? To discuss a party plan?" He arches an eyebrow, doubt evident on his face. "Perhaps you were looking for my wife? Wanted to pass along another so-called rumour you heard? Maybe this time you'll be brave enough to say whatever it is to my face," he sneers.

My mind races as I weigh potential responses. None of this is turning out as planned. Edward should be sitting here beside me. We're supposed to have our phones set to capture every word said.

At this point, I can only hope that Edward and Simon will turn up soon, and in the meantime, I have to carry on. If I roll over now, tucking my tail between my legs as I take my leave, we'll never have another chance to confront him. Tomorrow morning, the Master will be in the police station, once again muddying the water.

I think back to what Edward said on the phone. We have to use the Master's ego against him. From everything I know about him, and all of my interactions, the one thing he doesn't take well is a direct challenge. If I refuse to back down, I have little doubt he will do whatever it takes to put me back in my place.

I put my feet flat on the floor and my arms on the armrest. I sit up straight, unbeaten and unbowed.

"You're right, Master Finch-Byron. I'm not here to discuss event plans or seating arrangements. There is a rumour going around, and it's been weighing on my mind."

Just like that, the chess match begins. The Master leans back in his chair again, a broad smile on his face. His voice drips with condescension. "Finally, we come down to business. Tell me, Ms Payne, about this rumour. Another alleged paramour of mine causing you trouble?"

I meet his gaze, my own expression shuttered. "Something closer to home this time. I've heard you intend for Mathilde and I to take the fall for the burglary and maybe even the murder of your assistant."

He cocks his head to the side, pretending to be puzzled. "Really? I presume you claim to be innocent. In that case, why would I do such a thing? What could I possibly hope to gain? Come now, Ms Payne. This seems ridiculous, but somehow I'm not surprised that you would come up with such an inane theory."

Forcing out a fake laugh, I look him dead in the eye as I reply. "I suspect it's part of your hastily assembled cover up of your own crime of passion. Pointing the finger at a pair of university employees is an excellent way to distract the world. It smacks of the exact kind of thing you would do."

Tilting his head back, the Master's face shows the barest hint of nerves. "Pity that it will be your word against mine."

He gestures around the room, "I am an Oxford Master, married to a peer of the realm. Look where we sit, look at the crest over the fireplace." He laughs, viciously. "Do you expect me to fear you, a new arrival, barely qualified for your role?"

He raises a hand, pointing a finger in my face as he carefully enunciates his final phrase. "Your word is worth nothing compared to mine. You have no credibility."

Before I can respond, a male voice booms from behind me. "Ah, but it isn't your word against hers, Finch-Byron. It's your word against ours."

With that statement, Edward steps into the study.

"How did you get in?" the Master splutters angrily, as he rises to his feet.

I look over my shoulder to see Edward leaning against the doorway. Despite the tension in the room, he seems perfectly at ease.

"Didn't Nat tell you I was on my way? I assumed that was why the door was left unlocked." Edward smiles at me as he apologises, "Sorry I was late. Someone deactivated my keycard. I was lucky to get in."

Unbeknownst to either of the men in the room, Simon strides

past Edward, his robe dragging across the floor, and takes up watch near me, standing in front of the heavy window drapes. I school my features, not wanting to betray a hint of his presence as I allow myself to relax in my chair.

"You cannot hope to continue this fallacy any longer, Finch-Byron." Edward challenges him, in a patronising tone. "We know that the burglary and the murder aren't connected to one another. I found video evidence that the break-in occurred on the evening of the first of January, before either Nat or Mathilde returned to Oxford from their holidays. You can't possibly make a case that they had anything to do with it."

The Master rises to his feet and walks around his chair. While he has no issue with looming over a woman, he clearly finds himself at less of an advantage when facing down a broad-shouldered man.

He pretends to dismiss Edward's remarks, turning his back to us as he runs his fingers along the books on the shelf behind him. "Very well, Edward. It was a simple mistake on my part. No harm done. You can begin a new inquiry into the burglary tomorrow. If you two haven't anything more to add, I would suggest you take your leave."

A tense line runs down the length of the Master's body. I watch as he glances towards the windows, as though he can somehow feel the heat from Simon's angry glare.

Neither Edward nor I move, all of us frozen in an angry tableau.

My mind dredges up the memory of the night of the second, of my visit to the library and the scene of Ms Evans lying dead in between the bookshelves. My brain forces me to remember how I found her, her body buried under a pile of books, with the instrument of her death tossed carelessly beside her.

My voice is steady when I speak. "There's still Ms Evans to discuss."

The Master's hand freezes in place, but his response is dismissive. "Ms Evans? What about her? Did you find evidence that she was involved in the theft?"

Edward and I exchange looks of disbelief. I harden my resolve and try again. "No, I meant her death. More specifically, the fact that you killed her. We know the truth."

The Master spins, his face looking like a gruesome mask from a greek comedy. "That's ridiculous! There is no way you could know any such thing. How dare you point the finger at me!" He grips the back of his chair, the leather creaking under his firm grip.

"I know that she called and asked you to meet her there in the old library." I speak with confidence, leaving no room for the Master to doubt that I believe every word I am saying. "You must have thought it was an invitation to another tryst, but she had other ideas. She told you she was pregnant and the child was yours."

My eyes dart to Simon, who gives a single nod of confirmation. I continue, "She wanted you to leave your wife, but you can't, can you? The money and the honours - those come from her Ladyship's family, not yours. If you divorced and took up with your assistant, you'd be lucky to stay out of the unemployment line."

"You're guessing." the Master interjects when I pause for a breath. "Making wild accusations..."

"Am I?" I ask sardonically. "You thought you two were alone that night. There was a witness to the entire scene. He told me how Ms Evans laughed at you, taunted you and said she'd achieve her goals of becoming your wife one way or another."

"You're lying!" he thunders, pivoting so he can see me. His cheeks are crimson with anger. "No one would ever have the temerity to laugh at me."

I straighten my back, unbowed by the threat in his voice. The angry slashes of red on his face confirm that our plan is working. I need to push a little harder to tip him over the edge into a confession. Hopefully Edward is recording this.

I point at him, "That's exactly what she did. She laughed at you as she confessed she was using you. She played you for the fool and threatened everything you hold dear, didn't she? When you lunged for her, trying to stop her rant, she tossed a book at you and ran."

"Stop it," the Master growls in a low tone. He sounds like a wild animal, cornered but not yet beaten.

"You followed her into the shelves. She grabbed another book, threatening you again." My voice rises on the last phrase. I drop it back down to a near whisper before I say my final lines. "A flash a light caught your eye. A candlestick sitting abandoned on a nearby shelf. You didn't question why it was there or what damage it might do if used. You picked it up and swung. Then it was too late for her."

Pointing a finger towards the Master, Edward says, "Your denial is pointless, Master. The truth has caught up with you. You need to turn yourself into the police. You wouldn't want the police officers marching through the college on their way to arrest you, would you? Nasty business being taken away in handcuffs in front of everyone."

The Master's chest puffs out as his rage grows. His head turns left and right, searching for a way out of this room, an escape from the truth which has caught up with him. But Edward remains upright in the doorway, blocking the only exit other than a leap out of the curtained third-story windows. In a split second, he reaches up and grabs one of the antique pistols from its mount on the wall, twisting to point it in my direction. I freeze.

"I told you to stop talking. But you wouldn't listen. Just like Victoria did in the old library. She was determined to get a rise out of me, same as you." His hand wobbles, but the gun remains centred on me.

I am terrified, paralysed in my chair. I don't dare to turn to look at Edward. He is too far away to save me. Any heroic efforts have more chance of backfiring given our positions in the room. I can see the edge of Simon's robe, but what help is a ghost at this point?

"Don't do this, man." Edward's voice is calm and soothing. "Put the gun down, Finch-Byron. We know Ms Evans' death was practically an accident. If you turn yourself in, you'll likely get no more than a slap on the wrist."

The Master's whole body is trembling at this point, matched by the pulsing vein in his forehead. Sweat drops bead on his brow, a sure sign of his growing stress levels. "I won't do it. I've devoted my life to this college and to my wife's tyrannical family. I've worked too hard to throw it all away. I won't give my life up."

My vision narrows until all I can see is the black barrel of the antique pistol. I catch my breath and hold it, fearing I will start to hyperventilate. I am as trapped as the Master, no way out of this situation for either of us unless he chooses to give up.

"Please," I whisper, letting my fear colour my words. "Hurting me..." I struggle to get the words past the tightness in my throat. "Shooting me won't help you."

Master Finch-Byron's eyes are wild, his breathing fast and shallow. His grip on the pistol tightens and becomes shaky. The red on his face deepens to an alarming shade.

I hear the sound of a single footstep behind me and watch as the Master's aim veers towards Edward. "Don't move, Edward. If you come any closer, I will shoot her."

Somehow, Edward's voice is still calm, as though he is unfazed by the enormity of the threat. "Let her go, Master. If it's an escape you want, I can get out of the way, clearing the exit for you. You can be on your way. You'd have a head start."

"A *head start?*" the Master shrieks, turning the gun back point at the centre of my chest. "I worked and sacrificed for my entire life so that I could be here. You want me to escape? Turn to a life on the run, always looking over my shoulder?" The tenor of his voice rises in indignation. "I will not give this up. None of it. I will do whatever it takes."

Before Edward or I can move, before we can take so much as a breath, Master Finch-Byron closes his eyes and squeezes the trigger.

❖

The Master's arm flies up as the kickback from the pistol reverberates up his arm. I hear the crack of the shot and Edward screaming, "NO!" at nearly the same time. In the split second, I brace myself for the searing pain I know will hit me any moment.

The next thing I know, I'm lying on my side on the floor, my body tangled in the wooden chair. My left arm burns, and I can't seem to breathe. I close my eyes, the last second flashing before me like an old-fashioned film reel.

I remember seeing the Master's finger turn white as he pulled the trigger. A brief cloud of gunpowder spraying out of the barrel of the gun, proof of the bullet flying my way.

Then someone rams into me with full force, knocking me out of the path of the oncoming shot.

"Simon!" I whisper. Then I remember the feel of his body landing across mine, followed by a sudden flash of light and then the weight was gone.

I open my eyes to see the Master gawking at the gun in his hand, seemingly shocked at its presence. He lets it fall out of his hand onto the floor and stumbles towards me. I watch as the stunned Master grips his chest and crumples to the floor.

Edward barrels across the room, picking up the gun from the

floor where the Master must have dropped it. Then he is at my side, on his hands and knees, his face deathly pale as he reaches for me.

"Did he hit you?" Edward reaches over to check me for injury, and quickly pulls back in shock. His hand is crimson with blood.

"Oh my god, you're hurt! You've been shot!"

I catch a glimpse of my left arm, still hot with pain. The sight of the bloody path running along my sleeve is too much for me. The world goes to black.

I wake again to find Edward still at my side, holding a cashmere blanket against my arm. I bark a laugh, hysterical at the thought of him using her Ladyship's expensive throw to staunch my bleeding. A security guard stands over him, muttering commands into a phone.

"Thank goodness," Edward mutters, turning to look up at the guard. "She's awake. Tell the ambulance to hurry."

His gaze returns to mine, his eyes shining with relief. I feel a squeeze as he tightens the pressure on my arm. "Stay awake, Nat. The ambulance should be here any second. I know it hurts, but you're going to be okay." He reaches out a hand to brush my cheek. "Stay with me. I'm here and I won't let anything else happen to you."

My vision blurs as grateful tears fill my eyes. "Harry?" I ask, trying to rise. "Did you call her? I left everyone in the old library. They must have heard the shot. They'll be frightened to death with worry."

"Sshh, she's on her way. One of the security guards went to get her. Lie back down, Nat."

I realise then that someone has tucked a pillow beneath my

head and placed a blanket over me. It must have been Edward.

"How long was I out?"

"A few minutes, long enough to scare the wits out of me." His face flushes as he stares deep into my eyes. "I thought I'd lost you. His aim... how did you get out of the way in time?"

Tears pool again as I think about what really happened. Simon came through in the end. Why did he disappear like that? I've never seen an Eternal do anything other than fade out.

Fortunately, before I have to come up with an explanation, I hear the sound of Harry's frantic voice shouting in the distance. "Nat? Edward?"

"In here, Harry!" Edward calls out.

Harry's eyes are wide with terror as she takes in the sight of me lying on the floor, a bloody blanket wrapped around my arm. She barely has time to do more than that before the paramedics shuffle her out of the way so they can get to me. A man and a woman drop to either side, their faces businesslike as they quickly assess my condition. I watch another pair move further in, disappearing behind the desk. A moment later, an unknown voice calls out, "We're too late. He's dead. Looks like cardiac arrest."

The man beside me says, "Bullet wound here, through and through." He picks up my arm and I black out again from the pain.

# Chapter Eighteen

"Stop fussing," I grumble at Edward as he hovers over me, checking on the ice pack. "I was poked and prodded enough in the A&E at the hospital. You heard what the doctor said. A week of antibiotics and I will be fine."

Edward ignores my complaints, much as he has been doing since he arrived at the hospital. Hours later we're back at my flat and he is still going. "I can't help it, Nat. I'm so sorry, it was all my fault. I was the one to suggest that we goad him on, and then you paid the price. Do you need some more water? Tea? Another pain killer?"

Realising that extreme action is required, I raise my voice in a command. "Sit down, Edward!" I punctuate the sentence with a glare, almost daring him to try to adjust the blanket on my lap again.

He backs up and takes a seat on my armchair, barely sitting on the edge of the seat so that he is ready to leap back into action should I need anything.

"Are you sure you don't want to go to sleep?" he asks. "It's after midnight... You really should have remained in the hospital overnight."

"Ugh," I shudder. "That was the last place I wanted to stay. All those people coming in and out, you apologising nonstop, and Harry trying to shush you. Right now, all I want is to sit here on my sofa and watch mindless TV until I can relax enough to fall asleep. Besides, I don't know how to lie down with my arm in a sling anyway."

"You want the TV on?" Edward jumps up and begins hunting for the remote. I bite my tongue, realising my efforts to get him to settle down are in vain.

H hops onto the sofa beside me, taking care not to jostle my injured arm. He circles around, just like a cat, before curling into a ball, his spiky tail wrapped around himself. I give his scaly head a quick pat of thanks. From the moment he flew into the Master's lodge, through the ambulance ride and hospital checks, up until now, he has been glued to my side. It's a true testament to the magic that no one questioned why I brought my 'cat' along with me to the A&E. Now that I am home again and he is somewhat reassured I am okay, he falls into an exhausted slumber.

"Do you want the BBC? ITV? Netflix?" Edward flips through the channels faster than I can register them.

"Was that Bake-off reruns? Go back," I call from the sofa, using my good hand to pat the seat next to me. "I bet you've never seen a single episode. Come sit and watch with me."

Cautiously, Edward lowers himself onto the cushion, taking exaggerated care not to accidentally jostle me. Once seated, he tucks his hands under his legs to make sure he doesn't bump against me.

The TV show begins, an episode from a few seasons earlier. I recognise several of the bakers but can't remember who ended up winning. As we sit in silence, watching the baking battle unfold, Edward slowly begins to relax, his shoulders lowering as he settles into a more natural position.

When the show pauses for a break, I ask one of the questions which has been lingering in the back of my mind. "Why were you late meeting me outside the Master's lodging? Did you say something about your keycard?"

Edward glances at me, "Yes, I practically ran the last two blocks, but when I got to the garden gate, the keycard scanner kept giving me the flashing red signal. The only reason I got inside is because I tried rattling the gate to catch the attention of anyone of someone within the college. Then it fell open of its own accord."

I realise it must have been Simon, opening the gate from the inside. I can hardly explain that to Edward.

After a moment, he speaks again. "The security guard later told me that Master Finch-Byron had asked him to deactivate all of our keycards. It seems he planned to block us all from getting back into the college after we left yesterday evening."

The theme song signals the episode's return, forcing us back into silence. When it breaks again, ten minutes later, Edward is the first to speak.

"Can I ask you a question?"

"Of course you can!" I chide him.

"I don't want to look a gift horse in the mouth, but how did you manage to fall over in time to avoid greater injury? It was the weirdest thing, but for a moment, I could have sworn I saw someone in a brown robe leap in front of you." He pauses, rubbing his forehead. "Never mind, that's impossible. It must have been the stress of the moment."

H cracks open an eyelid, giving me a serious gaze. I cough back my initial response, settling for simple agreement instead. "That is weird. I can't explain it. I guess I saw his finger moving to pull the trigger or something and my immediate reaction was to duck. Lucky I did, though."

I look at my heavily bandaged arm to keep Edward from seeing the tear in my eye. I haven't seen Simon since he disappeared after knocking me over. I owe him a huge thanks for saving my life. There's no doubt in my mind that I'd be dead if it weren't for him.

Thankfully, the programme resumes once again, saving me from any further questions about the robed man. When it ends shortly thereafter, another baker disqualified and sent home, Edward grabs the remote. "Are you getting tired? Do you want me to help you get to bed?"

"I'm a little tired," I confess, "but not enough to fall asleep just yet. If you are, you don't have to stay here, you know. I'll be alright on my own. I've got H here to keep an eye on me."

Edward eyes H, seeing a snoozing black cat instead of a fierce little wyvern. "I promised the doctor and Harry I'd keep watch over you tonight, making sure you take your pills on time. That's the only reason either of them agreed for you to come home, remember?"

I huff but stay quiet, not wanting to get into that battle again. Harry rode with me in the ambulance, refusing to leave my side for any reason. She harangued the doctors, making sure I got put at the top of the waiting list. Not that I needed help. A gunshot wound in Oxford, England is far from the norm. One of the nurses whispered that she'd never seen one before.

Edward clicks through the channels, searching for something else to capture my interest. I stop him when I see the preview for a home improvement show. As a round of advertisements begins, Edward lowers the volume, tuning them out. Out of the corner of my eye, I can see his head looking left and right, taking in my flat. He's been here once before, but he didn't stay long enough to really see anything. I wonder what he thinks of my choice of decorations and artwork.

The beep of an alarm on Edward's phone interrupts his viewing and sends him leaping to his feet. "It's time for you to take another dose of your pain medication, Nat. Hold on, I'll get you a fresh cup of water."

I take the proffered capsule and swallow it without any argument. Edward settles back onto the sofa, raising the volume on the TV show. Before long, we're cracking one another up by making disparaging remarks about all of the designer's choices. If it weren't for the swath of bandages around my arm, I could almost imagine that we were a typical couple enjoying a night in.

I lean my head onto Edward's shoulder as the pain medication begins to work, the drowsiness sliding over me like waves from the ocean. At the next advert break, Edward's voice startles me awake.

"The photo on your mantle... is that your grandfather?"

"Yes, that's him. Alfred Payne, former Bodleian librarian," I reply. "He had retired by the time I was born, but he used to tell me the most amazing stories about Oxford and its residents. He died years ago, but I never forgot them."

"And he's the reason you took the job here, right? Isn't that what you said on the day we first met?" Edward pauses as he rethinks his phrasing. "I mean, really met. The day we introduced ourselves out in the hallway and you realised I was your neighbour."

I shift to look at him, surprised at his words. "You remember that? It was an off-hand remark in the middle of a conversation about a murder investigation."

Edward gives me a gentle smile as he says, "I remember everything you say, Nat."

That shuts me up for a while.

When I find my voice again, I ask, "What about you? Any Oxonians in your family tree?"

Edward stretches his legs out, propping his socked feet next to mine on my coffee table. "No educators in my immediate family, I'm afraid. My father is a doctor and my mother is a photographer."

"A doctor and a photographer? So how did you end up as a criminologist at Oxford?"

"It's not a particularly nice story, I'm afraid," he replies. I can hear the frown in his voice.

My interest caught, I pick up the TV remote with my good hand and switch to a news channel before lowering the volume again. "Tell me anyway, Edward. Nice or not, you've piqued my interest."

"Fine, but only if you promise to close your eyes and try to get to sleep, Nat. You need your rest."

I snuggle deeper against his side, once again resting my head on his shoulder. He checks to make sure I'm following his instructions before he begins. "Like most little English boys, I dreamt of growing up to be a footballer or cricketeer, if I thought about a career at all. We lived in a little village and I went to a grammar school."

"Oh, how very middle class of you," I joke.

"Shh, this is my story," Edward gently chastises me. "Everything changed when I was in sixth form. One of the girls in the local secondary school disappeared. The whole village was in an uproar. I didn't know the girl, but nonetheless, my father and I helped with the searches."

"Did you find her?"

"No." Edward's tone is tinged by sadness. "A passerby stumbled across her body on the side of a field. Eventually, the police uncovered that she'd been kidnapped and murdered by a local schoolboy. I was at the right age to take an interest in the story, particularly since it happened on my doorstep. I couldn't help but wonder what would drive a boy my own age to commit such an atrocity."

I fight off another wave of sleep, desperate to hear the rest of Edward's sad tale.

"I was fascinated by the psychology behind the police work." Edward shrugs, the movement jostling me awake. "I guess that's how I ended up in academia instead of as a bobby on a local police force somewhere."

"I'm glad you're here," I murmur, my voice heavy with sleep, "even if you don't have any famous relatives tying you to the uni."

Edward reaches over to run his hand down the side of my cheek. "Rest now, Nat. We can talk more in the morning. If it's famous relatives you want, I'll tell you about my mother's family. She's convinced that we're somehow related to Sir Christopher Wren."

Sleep drags me under before I can ask anything else.

Throbbing pain yanks me out of a nightmare. I wake up confused and somewhat convinced that a lion is actually biting my arm. In the darkened room, nothing looks familiar. I raise my hands to wipe out my eyes, or at least I try to. As soon as I make the slightest movement with my left arm, sending a spike of pain shooting up my shoulder, it all comes back to me.

The Master is dead. I got shot. Edward is asleep on the sofa next to me.

I squint my eyes, struggling to make out the time on the clock, and am surprised to see it is six in the morning. That last pain capsule I took after midnight has worn off, leaving behind a drumbeat of agony in place of my bicep. With absolute care, I slide the blanket off my legs and scoot until I can stand without waking Edward. Even in sleep, his eyes are lined with deep shadows. He'll have to get up soon enough, no point rushing things.

I make one step away before a sharp talon catches the edge of my waistband, halting my escape. H's eyes glow in the darkness as he twists his head to the side in a silent question. I mouth 'pain meds', mimicking the motion of a glass of water. He removes his talon, flying up in the air to follow me as I slip around the side of the sofa.

In the kitchen, I close the door to the adjoining room so the light won't alert Edward to my movements. However, I quickly realise the futility of my efforts to open the medicine bottle one-handed. H huffs a whirl of smoke to catch my attention, and then makes quick work of the cap. I chase the capsules down with a glass of cold water, praying for quick relief.

As long as I stand still, H is content to sit on the counter, his gaze skimming my form to make sure I'm here and whole. Or mostly, anyway. My mind struggles to remember the last of the story Edward told me as I was falling asleep. In my sluggish state, the memories are swimming in a sea of treacle. I finally manage to capture the edge of the one I want. Sir Christopher Wren - that's what he said.

"H? Do you think Edward could be magical?" I whisper.

H glances down at the medicine bottle, unsure whether my question is real or drug-induced. Eventually he decides to humour me. "Like an Eternal?"

"No," I murmur. "Like a prefect. Like me."

H eyes me again. "Are ya sure ya were supposed to take a pain pill now, Nat?" He waves a clawed hand in my face. "'ow many talons am I 'olding up?"

"According to my arm, I am definitely due for more medica-tion. I haven't gone crazy, hear me out."

Frowning, H gives me the side eye as he motions for me to continue.

"I was almost asleep, but I'm sure he said that his mother's family tree includes Sir Christopher Wren. If that's true, he must have the same magic in his bloodline as Kate, Mathilde and I do.

Right? Maybe that's what called him to Oxford instead of some other university?"

"I don't know, Nat..." H hedges, "maybe, but we've already got three prefects. There's no space for another, even iffen 'e 'as tha right blood."

"Okay, but he also said that he saw Simon knock me over. Not Simon, but someone in a brown robe. How could Edward have seen him?" I raise my eyebrows a few times, daring H to disagree with my logic. "Wait, speaking of Simon. Have you seen him? I need to thank him for saving me."

Shuffling his feet, H refuses to meet my eyes. "I think ya better talk to yer grandda about that. 'E's outside, ya know."

"He is?" I walk over to the basin and peer out the window. Sure enough, I can see him sitting on one of the garden benches, a nearby lamp illuminating his bright white hair.

A quick rummage through my junk drawer produces the back door key, and once again H follows as I tiptoe out the door and into the cold, pre-dawn air.

"Ah, my darling granddaughter, you're a sight for sore eyes," my grandfather calls out when he spies me descending my back steps into St Margaret's gardens. "H, warm up the bench for her, if you will."

H swoops ahead, unleashing a fiery breath on the wrought iron frame before flying off to play in the gardens. I nestle in beside my grandfather and let the hot iron warm me through my layers of loungewear as I say good morning. A scattering of birds chirp around us, alerting us that night is coming to an end. Knowing I don't have long before Edward awakes and notices my absence, I jump straight to the issue sitting at the top of my mind.

I tap my grandfather on the hand to get his attention. "I know the Eternals have to stick to their colleges, but do you think Simon could make an exception and come by my flat? I'd like to thank him for what he did."

He stills for a moment and then slides his hand out to cover mine. With a gentle squeeze, he says, "Simon is gone."

"Gone where?" I ask, perplexed by this response. "He's an Eternal, where can he go?"

"Although the name suggests otherwise, the Eternals are not actually Eternal. Some grow weary and fade away into the after-life. In Simon's case, our best guess is that he sacrificed himself to save you from death. He knocked you out of the way, taking the full force of the bullet before it passed through your left arm."

Stunned, I open my mouth to reply but nothing comes out. My grandfather reaches over and tips it closed again. "Don't be sad, dear. He had hundreds of years at Barnard. The part he played in Ms Evans' death... I don't know if the other Eternals would have allowed him to remain. Saving you redeemed him."

I gulp down the lump in my throat. Knowing that my grandfather is no doubt correct doesn't make the truth hurt any less. I tuck away the rest of that line of thought for a moment when my arm doesn't hurt as badly. One wound at a time is enough.

When my eyes stop burning with unshed tears, I start again. "I need to talk to you about something. About Edward. He's a descendant of Wren."

"Really!" my grandfather exclaims as he contemplates this new piece of information. "That's interesting. I wonder how many other students and professors have been pulled here by a touch of magic in their blood."

I can't stop from rolling my eyes. "I didn't mean to start a hypothetical discussion. I had something more practical in mind - like letting Edward use my Head of Ceremonies key."

"Your key?" He splutters, twisting around to look me. "But it's yours! Do you want to give it up?" He shifts his focus to my bandaged arm, his face softening. "Oh, my dear girl, is it because of what happened?" His voice drops to a whisper as he asks, "Are you afraid?"

"Part of me is terrified of getting hurt again," I admit, "but that isn't what's driving my thought process. Ever since we discovered how many people are walking around with the potential to become a prefect, I've been wondering what would happen if one of them used my key to unlock their magic."

My grandfather stills and I can almost hear his inner wheels spinning. "You're thinking about the person behind the break-ins?"

I nod my confirmation. "Harry can see the magic, but that was only because Eternals agreed to give her that ability. It proved that more than just the three prefects could see the magic. What if the key will unlock the ability to see magic for anyone with the right bloodline?"

"You think another descendant, someone who isn't a prefect, used one of the three keys, and this person could be responsible for taking artefacts," my grandfather answers, this time with more conviction. "If someone did, that would certainly narrow down the field of suspects. Given the timing of the first break-in at Iffley, it must have been recent. It would take some time to identify everyone who had both the necessary heritage and the opportunity, but I bet the final list would be quite short."

"Exactly!" I declare. "In that case, we couldn't have a better test subject than Edward. Not only do we know there is a good chance he is a descendant, he's also a highly skilled investigator and criminologist. Imagine what he could do if he had access to the knowledge of the Eternals?"

I look over to gauge his reaction, but all I can see is a man who looks conflicted. "Your logic is sound, Nat, but I'm still not sure... perhaps we should wait, see what kind of progress we can make on our own. Bringing someone else into the fold should be our last resort."

"We're already at last resort," I reply wryly. "Since I arrived in October, we've been bumbling around with challenges well beyond any of our capabilities. As a result, I'm sitting outside in the cold nursing a gunshot wound."

My grandfather flinches as my words hit the mark. Sitting beside him, I can feel the exact moment he makes a decision. He straightens up and rolls his shoulders back, setting them in a determined position. "How do you want to do this, Nat?"

I sit up taller, wrapping my cardigan tighter around me. "Normally I'd suggest we consult with Mathilde and Kate, but I honestly cannot imagine that they'd say no. They know as well as I do that we need help and that resolving the issues with the magic is urgent."

My grandfather moves his head up and down, silently communicating his agreement.

With nothing left to discuss, I use my good arm to push myself to my feet. I spin around, looking down at my grandfather's face. No hint of concern or disagreement lingers there, only acceptance, love and support.

"Okay," I sigh. "If we're going to do this, there's no time like the present. My key is still sitting in the desk drawer in my office here at St Margaret. If I can convince Edward to come with me, there's a chance I can get in and out before Harry catches me up walking around."

"I'll come along with you," my grandfather offers, rising up. "You will need some help explaining everything to Edward if your theory proves true."

Using my good arm, I give him a quick hug. "Thanks, Grandfather. I'll go wake him now; I left him asleep on my sofa. Can you get Bartie? As the Head of St Margaret's Eternal Affairs, he should bear witness as well."

With a last shiver in the cold, I pick my way back towards my flat, searching for a convincing reason why I need Edward to come with me to an empty college office before daybreak.

❖

"There you are!" Edward blurts, his voice heavy with relief. "I woke up and you weren't there and..."

"I'm fine," I interrupt him as I close the door behind me and walk into the kitchen. "I woke up a little bit ago and took another dose of the pain medication, then I stepped outside for a breath of fresh air. Sorry if I worried you."

"That's okay, as long as you're alright." Edward points at his watch, saying, "It's almost time for your next antibiotic, but you need to take it with food. I might have some eggs and bread upstairs in my flat. I'm not a great cook, but I can whip up the basics. What do you think?"

"As lovely as that sounds, I've got a better idea." Leaning against the counter, I nod my head towards the back door. "What if we go over to the dining hall and have a full English? We missed dinner last night in all of the chaos. I don't know about you, but I'm starving."

Edward grimaces. "I'm not sure, Nat. Should you be up walking around that much? I can run up there and bring food back, if you want."

Waving at my legs, I remind him, "I got shot in the arm, not my legs. The dining hall is what, fifty metres from here? One hundred, tops?"

Edward still looks unconvinced, so I layer on another reason. "I'd love a cappuccino from the Senior Common Room. There's nothing like a hot cup of frothy espresso to heal whatever ails you, you know?"

When it looks like he's still trying to hold out, I play my last card.

"I'm going either way, so you might as well get on board with the idea." Then I tap my toe while humming the theme song to Jeopardy.

Edward barks out a laugh, raising his hands up in front of him. "Okay, I give in. Can you give me ten minutes to run upstairs and grab a shower?"

"Take twenty. After all, the dining hall isn't open yet anyway. I'm sure we can talk the new chef into letting us in early, but they probably haven't even fired up the ovens yet."

I shoo him out of the door and then make my way to my own bathroom. Thank goodness my left arm took the bullet. I manage to brush my teeth and hair, but draw the line at putting on make-up. As much as I'd like to look my best, I know that this breakfast outing is likely the only time today I'll get out of my flat. No point wasting mascara on a day spent sitting on the sofa.

Edward makes it back downstairs in exactly eighteen minutes, probably worried that I'd have left without him if he was late. Little does he know that this journey will be for nought if he doesn't come along.

His hair is still wet, the ends curling up despite a coat of gel. His simple white button-down shirt is tucked into a pair of dark brown trousers, reminding me that I've yet to see him wearing jeans. I wonder how long it will take me to loosen him up. He probably sleeps in proper men's pyjamas.

Edward's face lights up in a smile as he takes in my freshly washed face and damp hair. His tone is gentle as he asks, "Are you sure you feel up to going to the dining hall? You aren't saying it because you think I'm hungry, are you?"

My stomach rumbles before I can get a word out, providing a more convincing answer than any I could have given. Shaking his head in amusement, he grabs our coats off the hook on the back of my door and waits to follow me through to the garden.

Outside, my grandfather is nowhere to be seen, leaving me to hope that he has tracked down Bartie and is awaiting us in my office. H is also absent, probably off begging for sausages at the dining hall door. I make a mental note to keep an eye out for him.

If I eat a full English without him, there will be hell to pay. Even an injury won't grant me an exception.

Edward and I make small talk while we walk through the gardens towards the main building. After so many years working and living within the college grounds, Edward knows the history of every bench and building. Dr Radcliffe and Harry provided an overview when I first arrived, but Edward's stories include some of the more colourful aspects of the men and women behind the names on the plaques.

We finally reach the flower garden which surrounds the main building. The normally bright beds are dark, only a few evergreen plants to break up the dark soil and wood chips. Not even the college's famed gardeners are a match for the whims of Mother Nature.

"Do you ever wish you could go back in time and meet some of the people you've been telling me about?" I ask as Edward holds open the door, ushering me inside.

"Often," he admits, "although I imagine my wish list is a bit outside of the norm. I'd rather spend an hour interviewing Jack the Ripper than Winston Churchill."

"Why am I not surprised?" I mutter. "Oh, as long as we're here, I've been meaning to pick up some paperwork I left on my desk. You don't mind, do you?" Before he can reply, I turn off into the hallway where my office is located. I don't want to raise his suspicions, particularly if it turns out that he doesn't have a magical connection to the university.

In my nervous state, I fumble with the key. When Edward holds out a hand, I gladly surrender it, blaming my injury for my failure to unlock the door. The door opens to reveal two pairs of eyes staring out at me - my grandfather and Bartie, sitting comfortably around my office table. My grandfather gives a single bob of his head to confirm the plan is still on.

I pause in front of my desk and turn to Edward. "My arm is

starting to hurt a bit and the roller top is really heavy at the best of times. Would you mind opening it up for me?"

"Of course. Does it require a key?" he asks, unaware of the significance of the question.

"Yes," I reply, pointing a finger towards the desk. "It's in the top right-hand drawer. Not very secure, I know, but that's where I left it."

Edward passes beside me before making his way to the drawer in question. After he goes by, my grandfather stands up and moves over into position beside me. From his original seat, Edward would have blocked the view of his actions. Bartie, however, remains where he is, with a perfect line of sight to the desk and the man of the hour.

All three of us hold our breath as Edward tugs open the drawer and withdraws the key. I flashback to my very first day, remembering how the sunlight made the key look as it if was glowing. I had put the key in the lock, turned it to the right and felt the zing all the way up to my elbow. That was the moment my own connection to the magic was unlocked.

Edward barely gives the key a glance, flipping it over his fingers until it is in the right position to slide into the lock. I reach over and grasp my grandfather's arm, clenching my fingers around his forearm. I honestly don't know in that moment what outcome I want. Am I doing the right thing? Discovering Oxford's magic flipped my life upside down. Will Edward thank me, or will he resent me dragging him into a whole new world of problems?

Out of the corner of my eye, I see my grandfather freeze. My grandfather. Standing here beside me once again, as though the twenty-year absence was nothing more than an extended trip instead of death, mourning and moving on. What if the magic can give Edward a moment like this? Isn't that worth more than any of the other risks?

Edward inserts the key and turns it, without any comment or ceremony. The lock flips open with an audible click. Edward pulls his arm back abruptly, and his other hand flies up to rub his elbow. He prises open the roll top, commenting, "This lock has some kind of zing to it, almost like it shocked me. What did you say you needed from here?"

I release the breath I'd been holding and say, "I need to introduce you to someone."

"What?" Edward replies, tilting his head to look over at me in confusion. His eyes widen as he takes in the masculine form standing next to me. A form which definitely wasn't there thirty seconds earlier.

"Edward, meet Alfred Payne... My grandfather."

Edward's eyes narrow into a searching gaze until recognition hits. The man before him looks identical to the photo on my mantle.

Before I can say another word, Edward's eyes roll up into his head and he faints dead away.

# Chapter Nineteen

**M**y grandfather and I rush to Edward's side, falling to our knees on either side of him. "Edward, wake up. Wake up, Edward!" I say the words on repeat as I use my good arm to shake his shoulder.

"I think he's coming around," my grandfather reassures me. Indeed, his eyelids begin to flutter before opening wide.

"Nat?" Edward mumbles, confusion lacing his words. "What happened?" He picks up his head and looks around, still disoriented. "Why am I on the floor?"

Before I can reply, he spots my grandfather kneeling on his other side.

"Don't freak out," I order. "I'm going to explain everything, but first we're going to get you on your feet."

I motion to my grandfather. He stands and helps me back to my feet, and together we take a step backwards, giving Edward some space.

Somehow Bartie knows exactly the thing to say to break through the tension. He coughs, catching Edward's attention. "Professor Thomas, perhaps you'd like to have a seat at the table?" He asks, indicating the empty chair across from him.

Edward eyes all three of us suspiciously, his gaze darting between my grandfather and I and the door. But his curiosity wins out. He slowly rises up, crosses the room and takes a seat at the small round table.

I open my mouth, but Bartie silences me with a glare before I can make a sound. Apparently, he's in charge. My grandfather ushers me into my desk chair before taking up watch near the window.

"Edward," Bartie starts and then stops. "May I call you Edward?"

Edward nods, his face shuttered.

"Excellent. Edward, my name is Bartholomew Kingston, but everyone calls me Bartie. You may recall me from the autumn gala, which I had the good fortune to attend. I am the Head of Eternal Affairs here at St Margaret."

Edward's brows leap up his forehead. "There is no such role here at the college."

"Ahh," Bartie corrects, "there is, but few are lucky enough to be aware of its existence."

Still Edward shows no hint of his thoughts. "Who else knows about you?"

Bartie smiles and his face lights up. "Nat, as you might guess, along with Mathilde and Kate. Oh, and Harry. I mustn't forget her."

Edward turns to me and I give a small wave of reassurance. He twists back in his chair, ready with his next question. "What are the *Eternal Affairs?*"

"Exactly the right question to ask. I suggest you get comfortable, as this story starts more than four hundred years ago."

I look on as Bartie recounts the history, taking Edward through the discovery of Oxford's magic, the decision to keep it a secret and the subsequent creation of the roles of the prefects.

I cast my mind back to the day I unlocked my own connection. Instead of a personal briefing, I got a letter and a cat who turned into a mouthy wyvern. If my grandfather hadn't spent my childhood years planting the seeds of the story in my mind, I probably would have run screaming from the building. Now, I can admit that there is something to be said about being thrown straight into the deep end. Without any rules and limited background information, I had the freedom to explore all of the possibilities the magic can offer.

Bartie knew that someone so practical and staid as Edward would need a formal introduction from an authority figure. For his part, Edward slowly relaxes into the conversation, interrupting to ask for clarifications or to turn the discussion in a new direction.

"You want me to believe that in the last four hundred years, no one has noticed ghosts walking the halls?" Edward crosses his arms.

"How many years have you been at Oxford, Edward? Think of all of the times when just the right book would turn up or you had a sudden flash of inspiration. Did you ever suspect magic might be behind it?"

Colour flushes up Edward's neck.

When Bartie catches up to the current times, confessing his own role in the visit to the police station to snoop for evidence and Simon's ultimate sacrifice, I watch as Edward's eyes grow wide.

"That's how Nat knew about Ms Evans' pregnancy?" Edward asks, looking bewildered. "I never would have guessed... and your witness was a three-hundred-year old monk? No wonder you couldn't bring them to the station to give a statement."

Despite having shaken the foundations of his known universe, Edward seems open to accepting this new information. Given he is sitting across from a ghost, however, it would be challenging to continue to deny it.

Finally, Bartie reaches the end of his lecture. "Until this morning, we were unaware that anyone outside of the prefects could use the keys. It was Nat's idea to give it a try."

A hush falls over the room as we wait to see how Edward will respond. He sits quietly, tapping a finger against his lips as he considers everything Bartie has told him. His first words are not the ones I expected.

"You said this was Nat's idea. Was the plan to have anyone with the right bloodline test the key? Or did she specifically want me to be the first person to do so?" He looks Bartie in the eye, posing the question to him even though I'm seated a few steps away. Bartie glances at me, checking whether I want him to respond or if I intend to do so myself.

"I wanted you, Edward. Not someone else," I reply, my voice firm.

Edward shifts in his chair, turning to acknowledge my presence once again. His face and body language are unreadable. "Gentlemen, might I have a moment alone with Nat?"

I nod my approval before my grandfather or Bartie have a chance to ask my permission. If Edward needs to speak to me in private, even if it is to end whatever this *more than friendship* is before it starts, I owe him the chance.

My grandfather pats my good shoulder and then follows Bartie out of the room, closing the door behind them with a loud click. I tense up, as much as one can when their arm is covered in gauze and surgical tape.

Edward stares at me, the silence stretching as he hunts for the words he wants to say. He starts, stops, and finally leaps to his feet, pacing back and forth in front of my work desk.

His fingers muss his hair into further disarray as he nervously runs his hands over his head. He halts abruptly and turns to face me, his decision made.

"Magic... here in Oxford." His voice is full of wonder. "Right in front of me for all these years. Honestly, Nat, I don't know whether I should kiss you or shake you."

I give my arm a wry glance before retorting, "If it's all the same, I'd like to avoid any shaking right now."

He eyes me carefully, weighing my response. Slowly, he makes his way around the desk between us. His face is unreadable as he approaches. He comes to a stop a mere step away, his gaze searching. Then he bends over and plants a firm kiss on my mouth.

I sit there, stunned, having been sure his earlier statement was a joke. When the stupor fades, I use my right hand to grab the front of his shirt and pull him in for another, gentler but still insistent kiss.

Edward kneels in front of me, his hand caressing my cheek as he stares at me in amazement. "You are incredible. All of this... beyond my imagination."

"I'm sorry I didn't tell you sooner," I say, my voice rough. "But Oxford's magic isn't my secret. I hope you can see that. As a prefect, I have to protect it from all personal desires, even my own."

"Don't apologise. I understand. You must have been so conflicted. Is that why you asked about famous ancestors?"

"Yes," I admit. "When you said you saw Simon knock me out of the way of the bullet, I wondered if you might have a connection." My breath comes out in a relieved laugh, my shoulders settling back into a comfortable position. "Then you mentioned Wren and I knew we had to get you to use the key. Now we know for sure that it's your birthright as much as it is my own. The key confirmed that." I narrow my eyes, my tone growing serious again. "This doesn't come without responsibility. You heard what Bartie said. Something is wrong with our magical borders, and we desperately need your help figuring out who is behind our difficulties. For better or worse, you are now part of this."

Edward cups my face in his hand and whispers, "All my life

I've been alone. I thought I was happy living that way. Then you arrived, turning my life upside down. Practically since day one, you've been dragging me off to interview suspects, forcing me to dress up as Santa, and manoeuvring my investigations. I have loved every minute of it. How could I let that go?"

"And the magic?" I ask.

Edward barks out a laugh, his eyes sparkling in delight. "I know you won't believe this, but as incredible as the magic is, it comes in second place to you."

My stomach rumbles again, interrupting our tender moment and causing both Edward and I to laugh.

Edward arches an eyebrow. "I can see you weren't exaggerating this morning when you claimed to want to visit the dining hall."

"Well," I admit, "my main goal was to get you in here so you could try the key, but getting a full English was a pretty close second."

Edward helps me to my feet, taking great care to minimise any jostling of my arm. We cross the room, coming to stop before my office door.

"You know," Edward says, "today is Thursday. Tonight was supposed to be our first date."

"I think we skipped over a couple of steps a few minutes ago." I narrow my eyes in a mock serious look. "Don't think that this gets you out of taking me to dinner, although we may need to wait until I can hold both a knife and a fork at the same time."

Edward fakes a wounded look. "I'd never dream of doing anything of the sort. However, I have no intention of delaying our date any longer. You've managed to get shot and reveal a world of magic to me in the last twenty-four hours. If I give you another week, who knows what else you'll do!"

I can't help but laugh again, as his words hit home. "Then what do you propose?"

"Hmmm," he says, rubbing his chin as he mulls over the possibilities. "Leave it with me... and don't worry, I'll arrange it around your pain medication schedule." That settled, he takes my right hand in his own and opens the door, ushering us back into the real world.

I'm not surprised to see my grandfather and Bartie waiting outside wearing matching expressions of concern. As soon as they catch a look at our faces, they sigh in relief.

Bartie offers a hand to Edward, "Welcome to the magic of Oxford, Edward. I apologise for rushing off, but I need to update the Heads of Eternal Affairs at the other colleges about your ability to see them. If you have any questions, please don't hesitate to let me know."

"I've got nothing but questions, Bartie," Edward replies, "but I'll restrain myself from pestering you until I've had a few days to adjust to this new reality. Some things, I imagine, can only be learned through first-hand experience."

That settled, Bartie makes his goodbyes and disappears around the corner as the nearby church tower clock strikes seven.

My stomach gives another lurch, reminding me of my need to eat. "It's still too early for the dining hall to be officially open. What do you say to a walk through the gardens? We can see if we can beg entry through the kitchen door." When Edward agrees, I send my grandfather ahead, asking him to let the other St Margaret Eternals know about Edward's ability to see them.

"Who else is an Eternal here?" Edward asks as he holds open the garden door for me.

"You've met many of them at the autumn gala, not that you knew it at the time. Most of the major portraits come alive..."

Edward stumbles. "What? Portraits? Is that what you said?"

"Yes, there are portraits and books, statues and ghosts and even a few…"

Before I can finish my phrase, I hear a familiar voice shout from a treetop, "Oi, missie!"

H raises his arms and takes a swan dive from the topmost branch, bulleting straight for us.

Edward's eyes widen and he leaps in front of me, his arms spread wide. "Bloody heck, what is that thing?"

"No, Edward!" I shout. "That's H!"

Having missed all the excitement of Edward using the key and unlocking his magic, H has no idea what to make of Edward's antics. I watch in horror as he attempts to slow his speed and adjust his landing to account for the large man now standing in front of me.

Apparently, all of those hours spent practicing parkour in Barnard's old library weren't for nought. H grabs a hold of Edward's outstretched arm, somersaulting over it. He manages to rebound off another nearby tree before finally tumbling to a stop against my legs.

"Oh my heavens, H! Are you okay?" I ask as I use my good arm to brush him off and help him rise to his feet.

"Lor luv a duck, Nat! Wot's gotten inta old Edward? 'Asn't 'e ever seen a cat before?" H grumbles as he checks his wings for injury.

"I'm not a wildlife expert, but that is no cat." Edward declares, looking shellshocked by the events of the last thirty seconds of his life.

H does a double take when he hears Edward, of all people, respond to his question.

I clear my throat, blocking both of them before they can say anything else. "Edward, meet H, our four-hundred-year old wyvern. He originally harkens from the Bodleian, but more recently he's been living as my flatmate."

"Your cat is a talking wyvern?" Edward's voice booms across the garden.

"Ya don't need ta yell, mate. I'm right 'ere." He grumbles.

I skip my eyes back and forth between the two, wondering how they managed to get off to such a rough start. As hard as I try, I can't come up with any obvious way to diffuse the tension. I give a little moan of pain, rub my arm, and ask, "Can we sort the rest of this out over breakfast? My arm isn't handling the cold well and I'm starving."

"Of course. Let's get you inside." Edward offers me his arm and then uses his toe to nudge H out of my way.

In return, H singes the back of Edward's legs when he passes beside him. I cast a pleading look back at H, silently begging him to avoid further retribution.

At the kitchen door, the new chef takes one look at my sling and ushers us inside, promising to send three steaming plates of food to our table. I've eaten here enough for the chef to know that my 'cat' requires a plate of his own.

Within minutes we're feasting on eggs, bacon, beans, roasted tomato and hot, buttery toast. It's all I can do to keep from licking my plate clean. I don't, however, stop H from doing so.

"Do you think we have time to stop by the Senior Common Room for a cappuccino before Harry gets into the office? She was like a mother hen last night and I'm worried she'll start up again today if she finds me out and about."

"We do if we hurry," Edward responds, picking up our dishes and loading them onto the nearby tray. "Let me drop these off in the kitchen and we can be on our way."

Out the hallway, Edward again takes my hand. At the main entrance, he pauses to ask, "Do you mind if I pop out to the Porter's Lodge to collect my mail? I haven't been by in days."

"I don't mind... if you can collect mine as well. I'll wait here; H can keep me company."

As soon as Edward exits the building, H points a talon at a nearby portrait and suggests, "Let's go say 'ello ta Cathy."

"Good idea!" Together we cross over the main entranceway, coming to a stop in front of the portrait of Catherine Morgan, early benefactor of St Margaret College and one of my favourite Eternals.

"Natalie, my goodness! I heard the terrible news. I can hardly believe you're standing here in our hallways. Shouldn't you be resting in your flat?" Catherine wrings her handkerchief in her hands, her worry evident.

"I was desperate for a proper meal, but I promise I'm going directly back to my flat," I reassure her.

"After a cappuccino," H reminds me.

"Right. Breakfast and a coffee, and then I will go home and stay there until I'm fully fit and healed."

Catherine shakes her head at me, not giving my words any more credence than I do. "Could you stay put for a day or two, at least? Let someone take care of you for a change. Like this young man, I'm sure he'd be willing."

I look over my shoulder to see Edward re-entering the building, a bundle of envelopes in his hand.

"Grabbed it all," Edward calls out as he approaches. He comes to a stop at my side, curious to see what has captured my attention. "Ah, Catherine Morgan. I've always liked this portrait, such a kind and welcoming face. It's perfect for the main entrance."

I stifle a giggle as Catherine gives Edward a saucy wink. He leaps back, his hand over his racing heart. "Did she?"

"Edward, meet Catherine Morgan, another of St Margaret's Eternals." Catherine responds by offering her hand, sticking it out of the painting. Edward's manners come to the rescue. He grasps her hand in a gentle handshake before he can stop and question how a painting can suddenly become three-dimensional.

"I know Edward well, Natalie. From my position here on the

wall, I've seen him walking our halls every day for years." Catherine turns her attention to Edward and asks, "Isn't that right, Edward?"

Edward gulps, his eyes shifting left and right, likely wondering what behaviour Catherine has observed over the years.

Catherine decides to take sympathy on him, speaking up before he can worry too much. "You've had a rough morning, Edward, being thrust into our magical world. As long as you take care of our prefect here, I'll keep mum on anything I might or might not have seen. Deal?"

Edward gives a relieved smile. I make a mental note to come back later, on my own, and find out what tales Catherine is hiding away. Knowing Edward, he's more likely to be embarrassed by stories about his softer side than all the times he's acted like an arrogant arse.

"Stay in and rest, my dear!" Catherine calls as we take our leave and continue on our way.

Inside the Senior Common Room, Edward and H both insist I have a seat on one of the sofas while Edward turns on the coffee machine. H rummages in a cupboard, emerging with a box of biscuits. He buys my silence by offering me a chocolate digestive, flying it over to me so I don't have to get up. Within minutes, I'm happily dipping my biscuit in the foamy top layer of my cappuccino.

"Give me a minute to recuperate my strength and then we can go." I take a giant bite, letting the biscuit dissolve in my mouth, relishing the crumbly texture and taste of smooth milk chocolate mixed with a hint of espresso.

Edward takes a seat across from me, helping himself to one of the international newspapers lying on the table.

By the time Harry walks in, in search of her morning latte, Edward is several pages in and I'm on my third biscuit. She rushes across the room to flutter over me.

"Nat! What are you doing all the way over here in the main building? You should be at home, resting." She twists to glare at Edward. "And you! You couldn't have brought a coffee to her instead of dragging her up here?"

I gulp down my bite of biscuit, knowing there is only one thing which will prevent Harry from going into full mother hen mode.

"Harry, Edward knows about the magic!"

❖

I hear a knock at my front door at precisely seven in the evening. My reflection smiles back at me, barely visible in the glass front of a picture hanging on my wall.

This isn't how I envisioned I'd look for my first date with Edward. Fleece socks, flannel pyjama bottoms, a Breton stripe vest top and an oversized cardigan. I also hadn't imagined that I'd have one arm in a sling and be slightly loopy on pain capsules.

The knock sounds again, this time somewhat more forcefully. I quickstep to the door and open it before Edward gets worried enough to come in of his own accord.

There he stands, his dark hair slicked back, his eyes shining. He takes a half step back, his gaze sliding from my head to my toes.

"You're beautiful." There is no hint of sarcasm in his tone.

"I got your note saying the dress code was black tie, so I did my best to comply." I pirouette, allowing him to take in the full glory of my ensemble. "Fresh off the runway in Paris. It's the new thing. Everyone will be wearing it soon, you'll see."

"It suits you perfectly. If you're ready, we should get a move on it. I've made reservations for four minutes after seven. If we're late, they'll surely give our table away." He holds out his arm for me to take hold once I've said goodbye to H and pulled my door closed. The building door beckons from our left, the entryway light illuminating the world outside.

Edward points up to the right, leading me upstairs to his flat. My heartbeat speeds up as we approach his open doorway, the inside hidden in the shadows. It dawns on me in that moment that I've never been up here. It's strange how much time we've spent together at St Margaret and at Barnard, and yet so much of this is still new and exciting.

The first thing I notice when we walk inside is the array of candles. From tall pillars down to tiny tea lights, flames flicker from every corner of the living room.

"No candlesticks, you'll notice," Edward remarks.

I nod absently, my attention focussed on taking in every detail of Edward's domestic existence. The ceilings are lower, making the rooms feel slightly smaller than mine below. The furniture, however, is very similar: overstuffed chairs, a worn coffee table and a cushioned window seat. Where I have a television, he has lined the wall with shelves, books stacked two and three layers high, filling every square centimetre of space.

"Make yourself at home, Nat. I'll get us a drink. Be back in a second."

The books call to me, providing insights into the mind of Edward Thomas. There are plenty of textbooks and legal journals, which make sense for a professor at Oxford. I skip past them, more interested in reading the names of the paperbacks below. Dostoyevsky and Dumas are to be expected, but the worn spines of the Sherlock Holmes and Hercule Poirot mysteries testify to his real passion. Crime? Yes, but also the satisfaction that comes from identifying whodunnit at the end.

I realise that Edward chose academia because of his need to the guilty brought to judgement. A police inspector would have to live with the burden of unsolved cases and crimes too small to justify an investigation. I wonder if Edward knows this or if it was an unconscious decision on his part.

The sound of clinking glasses pulls me from further scrutiny of his book collection. Edward returns, holding two wineglasses in one hand and a plate of appetisers in the other. He places everything onto the coffee table before escorting me to one of the chairs, making sure I can sit comfortably and reach the food without putting pressure on my arm.

"Dinner is warming in the oven, so I thought we'd start here?" The implied question mark hints at his insecurity, the wineglasses and intimate setting making our date night very real. "Since you're taking pain meds, I skipped the wine and opted for a sparkling elderflower juice instead."

I take the offered glass and we cheers to our first date. Earlier in the day, I had promised myself that I would not succumb to my normal case of the nerves and end up babbling incessantly. I give myself a quick mental kick as a reminder.

"I've not yet been to the Natural History Museum here in Oxford," I announce by way of a conversation starter.

"Oh?"

"I've been meaning to go, but something always seems to come up with work or Mathilde will invite me over or I end up visiting my parents... Have you been?"

"Yes," Edward replies, still curious to see where I am going with this.

"You know the famous Oxford Dodo? The last Dodo that was allegedly to have walked the earth, it's stuffed remains now on permanent display in the museum?"

"Yes... I'm familiar with it. Why?" Edward asks.

I pause, letting Edward's curiosity build to a fever pitch. When I see him opening his mouth to say something else, I jump in with my big news.

"H told me that the Dodo is an Eternal!"

Edward jerks back, sloshing juice out of his glass. I pass him a napkin, trying desperately to hold in my laughter. I had no idea introducing someone to Oxford's magic could be so much fun.

Dinner turns out to be a smorgasbord of finger foods, all designed to be eaten with only one hand. We each relax as the night goes on, interspersing stories about ourselves in between discussions of what else in Oxford might be harbouring an Eternal.

"What do you like to do for fun, Edward?" I ask, eager to hear his response. Every time I have seen him, he's been working on one thing or another.

"For fun?" Edward tilts his head to the side, considering my question. "I attend most of the visiting lectures here at the college and in the department. Does that count?"

I shake my head emphatically. "No, that does not count. Don't you have a life outside of the college?"

"I... I used to meet up with my old school mates, but as they settled down, got married and started having children, our get togethers petered off." He frowns. "I didn't set out to make my whole life centre around the university. It happened, gradually, without me realising it."

"So you're saying you weren't always the gruff and introverted professor I met during my first week here?"

"Ouch!" Edward barks a laugh. "I guess I deserve that. But no. In graduate school, I was much more active. I played cricket, went to the theatre, met up with my mates for a drink. Then I moved here, started on the tenure track, and sort of lost myself." He pauses, lost in his memories. After a moment, he shakes himself, coming back to the present. "Watching you find your place here at Oxford reminded me that there is more to life than my books and papers."

I raise my glass in a toast. "Here's to us, then. To new adventures." Edward smiles as he clinks his glass against mine.

By the time we finish dessert, all of the awkwardness is long gone.

I don't want the night to end, but my tired body has other ideas. The combined exhaustion of the confrontation with the master, my injury and hospital trip, a night spent on the sofa and a day answering calls from concerned well-wishers takes it toll. I manage to stifle the first three yawns, but by the fourth, they're more powerful than I am.

Edward pushes back from the table and rises to his feet. "I promised myself I'd get you to bed early, and magic or no, I don't think I could forgive myself if keep you from getting the rest you need."

"At least let me help you tidy up," I offer.

"With one hand?" Edward points out, chuckling. "Leave it be, Nat. I'll sort it all when I get back upstairs."

At the bottom of the stairs, Edward opens my door, standing aside to allow me to step inside. I stop halfway inside, turning to face him.

Staring up into his eyes, I murmur, "I had a lovely evening. I hope we can do it again sometime."

Edward cups my face, leans in and presses a gentle kiss upon my lips.

"We can have dinner as often as you like."

# Chapter Twenty

Following the death of Master Finch-Byron from cardiac arrest, there was some discussion of whether it was appropriate to move forward with the planned event. I had to lobby hard to get the college leadership to agree to a postponement instead. Any thoughts of the revealing the contents of the secret chamber were immediately scuppered as the Barnard fellows focused their attention on electing an interim Master to fill the role while they put together a search committee for a permanent replacement.

Fortunately, my arm was well on the way to a full recovery by the time they elected Professor Margaret Lamb as the interim. In her early fifties, her experience of juggling academic responsibilities with motherhood made her the perfect person to help Barnard recover from the shockwaves left in the wake of the crimes. Although she claims it isn't true, I suspect Lady Petronilla played a key role in influencing the male fellows to raise a woman to the position of Master for the first time in Barnard's history.

When I wake up on the morning of Barnard's Celebration of Women, I feel hopeful. This March day is blessed with bright sunshine and a hint of spring warmth in the air, promising the perfect setting for our event.

I rush through my normal morning routine, pleased to feel only a small twinge of pain when I bend my arm to apply my mascara. In the first few days after I was shot, I had hoped the magic would somehow miraculously heal me, even though H told me time and again that it doesn't work that way. Indeed, it was the hours of physio that paid off in the end.

After opening the back door of my flat at St Margaret, I call out into the garden, "Come on, H. We need to get going if we don't want to be late." Together we make our way to Barnard where I'm scheduled to meet Will and Jill so we can oversee the final set-up before the start of the celebration later that afternoon.

Once inside Barnard, we follow the narrow pavements through the gardens until we reach the dining hall. Knowing we'll be lucky to sneak a few bites of cucumber and cream cheese sandwiches for lunch, I proposed we eat a large breakfast to sustain us through until the afternoon.

"Morning, team," I announce as I slide into the seat across from them. "We've got a long morning ahead of us, so don't be shy about asking for seconds."

The two mumble their hellos, their mouths full of food. I pass a plate of sausage links over to H and dive into my own breakfast. A quiet peace settles over our little group, interrupted only by requests to pass the salt and pepper or the tomato catsup.

Back outside again, we wind through the maze of archways and quads to finally reach the sprawling grounds where our temporary event structure sits awaiting the arrival of our first guests.

"I wouldn't have ever thought to combine a pavilion with domes," Jill admits, "but the end result is nothing short of amazing."

I think back to my first meeting with Master Lamb. Unlike the previous Master, she was keen to discuss the event plans. When I outlined my ideas for expanding the celebration to the beginning of the college's history, she gave her wholehearted approval. Together, we reviewed floorplans and event schedules, eventually choosing to forego a formal, seated meal in favour of afternoon tea. This allowed us to increase the guest list, ensuring Barnard's former students could bring along family and friends. Her inclusive attitude and open nature was a welcome change compared to the previous Master.

A long rectangular building sits in the middle of the grounds, the morning sun sparkling off its glass roof. Open doorways line the length, inviting people to pass in and out freely, popping in for a canapé before returning outside to bask in the sunlight.

Just beyond each of the building's four corners sit fabric-covered domes, each one housing a mini-gallery dedicated to honouring the history of women at Barnard. The white fabric diffuses the direct sun, filling the spaces with a warm, natural light. We put in a temporary wood floor, making the domes feel like actual museums.

"Would you two mind starting in the main room while I double-check the set-up in the galleries?"

My assistants quickly agree, splitting off to track down the catering manager and facilities coordinator to ensure all is well. H follows as I make my way to the closest gallery, which also happens to showcase Barnard's earliest history.

"Well met, Natalie," Lady Petronilla greets me as I walk into the dome. She circles around me, eyeing me carefully. "How art thee this fine morn?"

"I am doing great," I reassure her. "I expect Master Lamb to arrive in an hour for a walk-thru. Is everything arranged to your liking?"

"All is in good order here. If thou hast time, mayhap we can perform the final checks together?" Lady Petronilla steps further in, inviting me to accompany her.

To keep things simple, we used the same base layout in each gallery – four standalone display walls with three raised pedestals dotted in between them. We painted the walls in bright colours, letting them attract the eye and draw guests further into the space. The History and Literature departments assisted with the creation of informational posters and text, which we used to decorate the walls.

The pedestals are reserved for our Eternals, some including a piece of period furniture to help set the scene. Mathilde and Edward spent several late evenings alongside me, helping the Eternals perfect their waxen look. Now they can all stand for hours, no one the wiser that the people they see aren't wax sculptures.

As we make our way to the next dome, H and Ada, her Lady-ship's maid, follow behind us, ready to dash off should anything else be needed. Even though I spent hours sketching designs, thumbing through paint chips, and looking at floor samples, I'm still amazed at how incredible everything looks when put together.

Despite spending hundreds of years at Barnard, Lady Petron-illa seems equally impressed. Back outside, she stops to contem-plate the rectangular building. "Seeing this much reminds me of my childhood. My father would invite his knights to tourna-ments and my mother would oversee the construction of the pavilions. There t'was music, dancing and food as far as the eye could see."

I still beside her, letting my imagination replace the tempo-rary structure before me with old-fashioned wooden seating, colourful pennant flags flapping in the wind. I can almost hear the crash of the lance hitting the shield.

Wait.

I open my eyes again and turn to her Ladyship. "Was that a real crash I heard?"

H flies out of a nearby open doorway, a member of the wait-staff chasing after him. I spin around to look at Ada. "Wasn't H just here beside us?"

Ada wrings her hands. "Forgive me, my lady. H snuck away whilst thou wert conversing. I did not wish to interrupt..."

"That's okay, not your fault." Rolling my eyes, I admit, "I don't know why I expect him to behave at these events. I tried banning him and that didn't work. I'd hoped by giving him an invite, he'd be properly incentivised to behave."

Lady Petronilla and Ada fail to respond, too busy attempting to hold in their laughs.

I glance at my watch, hardly believing how much time as passed. "We'd better hurry up with the rest of our review. Master Lamb will be here before we know it, and I want everything to be perfect."

"Hiya, you made it!" I call out when I see Edward making his way across the main floor to join me on the other side of the room.

"I got caught up in my work, but someone set an alarm on my phone so that I wouldn't be late," Edward calls back. "You wouldn't happen to know who that was, do you?"

In truth, I set the alarm in time to ensure an early arrival. I knew I'd only get busier as guests arrive, and I didn't want to miss the chance to show Edward the end result of all of my hard work. Last term he got a hint of how much effort goes into organising an event of this magnitude when he read through a stack of my notes. This term, as my boyfriend, he's had a front row seat to most of the process.

While we both continue to put in long hours in front of our laptops and notepads, the magic has offered plenty of excuses to take a break and come up for air. With Eternals to meet, places to visit and let's not forget the weekend my parents came up, we've had a crash course in work/life balance.

Edward glides through the maze of tall cocktail tables, their bright white tablecloths reaching down to brush the floor. The perfect height to hide a certain mischievous wyvern, as Edward learns when a scaly black leg sticks out in front of him, causing him to stumble.

H pokes his head out from under the tablecloth, batting his eyelashes. "Oi, sorry, bruv. Didn't see ya there."

I rush over to straighten the table, glaring at H for his misbehaviour. "Aren't you supposed to be sitting with Miss Huntingdon? Are you really going to leave the young miss sitting on her pedestal all on her own?"

"Young miss?" H grumbles, "She's a 'undred and fifty years old, mate." But he does as I say, so I let him off without any further warning.

"That pet of yours is a nuisance, Nat," Edward mutters.

I point my finger at Edward's chest. "He's not a pet. He's only a nuisance to you because you keep treating him like a domesticated animal. He's a magical being, not a housecat."

Edward holds his hands up and backs up. "Okay, okay, I know. You've all told me, but I can't help it. I knew him for years as Lillian's cat and then your cat. I'm having a hard time making the transition."

I give him a stern look and then soften, planting a kiss on his cheek. "Now that you're here, why don't I give you a quick tour of the venue ahead of the hoard of guests descending upon us?"

We manage to visit three of the four domes before my walkie talkie goes off, Jill calling me back to the main entrance to welcome our first arrivals. I double-check that H is at his assigned post, curled up like a cat beside Miss Huntingdon, before I rush off.

The next two hours fly by, offering me nothing more than glimpses of Edward, Harry, Mathilde and Kate as they mill around the event. Small crises always emerge behind the scenes at events of this size, and this one is no exception. I barely make it back into my position in the rear of the main room in time to see Master Lamb step onto the raised dais and tap on the microphone to get everyone's attention.

Her British accent is crisp as she begins her welcome speech. "Thank you all for joining us on this important occasion, when we celebrate the forty-fifth anniversary of the day Barnard officially opened its doors to female students."

More guests trickle in through the open doors as the sound of clapping leaks out into the garden area. Master Lamb waits until the applause quiets down to continue. She introduces herself and gives a short speech about her twenty years of experience at Barnard and all of the changes she has seen. She has a talent for public speaking, moving comfortably around the dais, her gaze skipping around the room. Every person there feels she is talking to them personally.

I'm whispering instructions to a member of the waitstaff when I hear my name over the speaker.

"Natalie Payne, are you here?" Master Lamb scans the room, looking for my curly blonde hair in the midst of the mass. I wave a hand to catch her eye and she motions me to the front. Without waiting, she launches back into her speech.

"Natalie Payne is the Head of Ceremonies here at Oxford. As you can see, she normally stays behind the scenes, but today I'd like to bring her up to the front. When I saw this event on the college calendar, I thought in the back of my mind that it should include more than the last forty-five years. Natalie must have read my mind. Barnard's history is rich with examples of women who stepped in at critical moments, providing everything from the college charter to land for buildings to a mothering hand to oversee our students. It is right that we should honour this legacy, and no one could have done so more beautifully than what Ms Payne has orchestrated here today."

She pauses for breath, giving the crowd another chance to applaud as I step onto the stage. Out of the corner of my eye, I spot Jill stepping up from the other side, a large bouquet of flowers in her arms.

Master Lamb takes my hand and pulls me by her side. "Over the last two months, Natalie has given her body and spirit to Barnard, working many long hours to ensure that nothing would stand in the way of today's celebration." She turns to Jill, taking the bouquet from her. "Natalie, please accept these flowers as a small token of our thanks."

I stumble out a thank you, blinking furiously to stop the tears that threaten to fall. Edward meets me at the edge of the dais with a broad smile on his face, his hand out to help me with my descent.

I hear Master Lamb behind me. "Now, we've got one more special announcement before I let you return to your conversations. For this, I'll hand over to Kate Underhill, Director of the Ashmolean."

Kate gives my arm a squeeze as she passes by on her way onto the stage. She takes the microphone from Master Lamb, clearing her throat before she begins.

"Hullo, I'm Kate Underhill. As Master Lamb said, I am the Director of the Ashmolean. I don't typically get to make a speech at a college event, but a recent discovery has given me this extraordinary opportunity."

Voices murmur behind me, all wondering what is coming next.

"Two months ago, we uncovered a treasure trove of historical artefacts hidden away for the last several hundred years in a secret chamber in Barnard's old library. Few were told of the find, and myself and my colleague Mathilde Seymour from the Bodleian Libraries were the only two people allowed to review and catalogue the find. Based on our expertise, I can say without a doubt that the find is truly breathtaking."

I lean in close to Edward, whispering, "What is going on? Did you know about this?" He shakes his head no and stills beside me, as curious as I am to hear whatever Kate is going to say next.

"Barnard College does not have a single space large enough to properly display the paintings, statues, carvings, books and journals we uncovered. Therefore, Master Lamb has asked the Ashmolean to play host to their exhibition. I am pleased to announce that this May, we will unveil a two-month long special exhibit entitled *Barnard College: Three Hundred Years of Hidden Secrets*. I hope that you will all find time in your busy diaries to visit. I will look forward to seeing you there. In the meantime, on behalf of Master Lamb, I wish you all an enjoyable rest of the day."

# Chapter Twenty-One

I'm lying on my sofa, relaxing after the celebration event, when I hear a weird bumping sound at my front door. I open it to find Edward standing there, attempting to knock with his elbow as he juggles a stack of plates.

He comes inside, commenting over his shoulder, "It's a sad testament to both of our lives that neither of us has more than four plates to our name."

"Don't worry, I've got plates on my shopping list for when I move out of this flat."

As always, Edward ignores my reference to moving out of St Margaret. It's been a sore point for the last week when we realised I've only got less than a month to find a new flat to rent. Edward wants me to consider moving upstairs, but I'm not convinced. Our relationship is still new enough that I worry moving in might be rushing it.

After he sets the plates down on my coffee table, he changes the conversation topic. "The Barnard celebration today was outstanding. You should be proud of yourself."

I flop down onto the sofa again, putting my feet up on the armrest. "I am proud of how it turned out, but much credit goes to Lady Petronilla and the other Eternals. Their wax figures added the wow factor the event would otherwise have been missing. Now that it's over, I can admit I'm exhausted."

Edward picks my feet up and slides underneath them, taking my right foot in his hand and carefully massaging my arches. I let a small moan slip, catching H's attention in the other room.

"I'm still 'ere ya know!" he shouts from the kitchen.

Edward rolls his eyes and I snort with laughter. "Are you sure you want to take H with you when you go?" Edward asks, looking annoyed.

"I couldn't bear to think of leaving him behind. So be nice." I tug my right foot out of his hands and offer up the left one. "Could you do my other foot too? Our guests should be here any minute."

"Are you sure you want everyone to come over? We could still call them and arrange to meet at the pizza place instead."

"No," I confirm, "I am not leaving this sofa tonight for any reason other than to go to bed."

Edward barely has time to rub the aches from my feet before the intercom buzzes announcing everyone else's arrival. He motions me to stay where I am, getting up to buzz the building entrance lock and open my door.

Mathilde, Kate, Bartie and my grandfather come in, arms full of steaming hot pizza boxes. "Did someone order a delivery here?" Mathilde asks with a chuckle.

H swoops in from above, grabbing the top box off the pile before anyone can stop him. "I did, thanks fer stoppin' by."

My grandfather steps in to rescue the pizza box before H can inhale its contents.

I do a quick count, coming up short. "Aren't you forgetting someone? Where's Harry?"

Mathilde shrugs. "She said she needed to stop by her office to pick something up. She'll come in through the garden door." She turns to H, still hard at work trying to sneak out a slice of pizza. "H, can you be a dear and open the back door so Harry can come inside?"

"Iffen any of ya touches that pizza before I get back…" he mutters as he flies off to do as Mathilde asks. He must have arrived just at the right moment as I hear the door click and Harry's voice straight after. H flaps his way back to the front room with Harry following behind him.

"I had a feeling you wouldn't have a vase for those flowers," Harry explains as she rescues my bouquet from the window seat. "I popped into my office to pick one up. My husband sends me flowers often enough that I've amassed a collection."

Edward and Bartie exchange nervous looks at this comment, each looking worried that they are falling behind in the boyfriend department. I catch Kate's eye and we both stifle a grin.

Everyone pitches in to drag chairs into the front room and distribute plates, napkins, and pizza slices. Bartie and my grandfather take turns serving given neither of them can eat anything. One by one we eat our fill, settling into our chairs as we enjoy the combination of comfort food, friendship and a warm home.

My grandfather coughs to get our attention. "I hate to ruin a perfectly nice evening by talking shop, but now that the Barnard celebration is behind us, we really must focus on tackling our significant question. Who is stealing magical items from Oxford? We know they've broken into St Margaret College, Iffley College and now Barnard College."

Edward removes his arm from around my shoulders and leans forward, his elbows resting on his knees and his hands clasped together. "I don't have any teaching responsibilities next term, so I should have plenty of time to sit down with each of the prefects to gather a list of potential suspects."

"I don't know if we can afford to wait that long," I interject. "We've been lucky that things have stayed quiet for as long as they have. As we suggested, the security teams at all of the colleges have increased their patrols, but eventually whoever it is will find another way inside. We definitely need to test out my idea of whether you could use Eternals to make yourself look blurry on a security video."

"It seems they can get in and out without leaving any tracks behind, and that is what is worries me," my grandfather confirms.

Bartie stands, moving over to lean against the mantle. "I've called a meeting with the other Heads of Eternal Affairs." If you can let me know what you need, I will line up a team of Eternal assistants in each college and building around the university to help you."

Edward and Bartie agree to meet up Monday morning in the Fellows Garden to put together a plan.

Mathilde pipes up from the other side of the room. "Where will you be working next term, Nat?"

Raising my hands up, I admit, "I don't know yet. There have been a few requests from different colleges that have come into the team, but for some reason, none of them have been approved by the Vice-Chancellor's office."

"I know why." Kate replies in a sing-song voice. "I couldn't tell you until today, but since the cat is well and truly out of the bag, I can let you in on the rest of my secret. Come Monday morning, you should get an email letting you know you're being assigned to arrange the grand opening of a certain new exhibition at the Ashmolean."

My eyes grow wide as I process Kate's words. "Oh my, are you serious? I get to come work alongside you for a term? That's amazing!"

Kate catches sight of Mathilde's hangdog look. "Don't worry, Mathilde. We'll have need of you as well. Someone has to advise us on how to best display and care for the rare books and journals."

My grandfather beams at our circle. "Excellent, it sounds as though we have a way forward. Hopefully if we move quickly enough, we can identify both the person and the Eternal causing us so many problems before they do anything else."

With that agreed, Harry excuses herself, disappearing back into the kitchen. She returns with an oversized shopping tote to lay out an assortment of cakes and biscuits. There are so many options to choose from that no one complains when H sticks a talon into a small box of cheesecake slices, claiming them all for himself.

As we're passing around the packets, the ring of a mobile phone cuts through our chatter.

"Oof, sorry about that," Kate mutters, climbing to her feet to grab her handbag. She unsnaps a pocket and retrieves her mobile, answering the call before it flips to voicemail.

"Hullo?" She stills, her face draining of all colour. "What? I'm on my way." She ends the call and looks up at to find an audience wondering what has gone wrong.

Her normally solid voice trembles as she blurts, "The Ashmolean... It's on fire!"


Stay tuned to find out what happens next!

# Arson at the Ashmolean

OXFORD KEY MYSTERIES - BOOK THREE

**When the smoke clears, a man lies dead and a young woman looks to blame.**

The fire in the Ashmolean's archives reveals itself to be a cover-up for the real crime: dozens of valuables are missing from the shelves. Unfortunately, security guard Andrei Radu dies from smoke inhalation, elevating the crime to a homicide.

DI Robinson, Oxford's leading detective, is determined to see the guilty prosecuted. A witness puts Kate's young assistant Francie at the scene. She claims to be innocent but DI Robinson isn't convinced.

Nat and her friends know the likely perpetrator is the person behind the problems with the magic. Can they save Francie from going down for a crime she didn't commit?

Arson at the Ashmolean will be out on October 18, 2020. You can pre-order your copy now on Amazon.

# Let others know what you think

Indie authors like me depend on your reviews and recommendations to help us attract new readers. It only takes a minute to leave a review on Amazon, but it makes a world of difference to my success. So why not let others know what you thought of Burglary at Barnard?

Post a review on Amazon

# Mince Pies and the Missing Santa

AN OXFORD KEY MYSTERY SHORT STORY

Nat thinks helping Harry with the annual Children's Christmas party at St Margaret will be easy as mince pie. But when Santa fails to show, Nat has to call in favours from everyone she knows to save the event from certain disaster. Mathilde is happy to dress-up as an elf and H is wearing antlers, but Kate is more interested in getting Bartie to stand under the mistletoe than helping out.

If Nat can save the day, she needs to find a new Santa... can she convince a certain tall, dark-haired Criminology Professor to lend a hand?

This short story is available exclusively to my newsletter subscribers. Sign up on my website at lynnmorrisonwriter.com to find out what happens.

# Acknowledgments

I wrote a book during a global pandemic.

Those are not words I ever thought I'd say, but here we are. With my whole family at home for weeks on end, I had to figure out an entirely new approach to writing - one which didn't depend on hours of uninterrupted time.

As always, there are many people to thank. This time around I'll start with my husband. Finding time and space to write this book sometimes felt like it required an act of God. Together we learned how to balance out work, childcare, meal planning and home learning. We gave up on deadlines and threw away our task lists, making do with what we could accomplish without running ourselves into the ground. As always, he provided insights into the unique aspects of Oxford university life. Any mistakes are my own.

A big thanks goes to my editorial team: Inga Kruse, Anne Radcliffe and my dad. Under normal circumstances, I write a full draft before I share it with anyone else. My publishing timelines and pandemic schedule made it clear that wasn't going to work. We needed an assembly line.

Inga and my dad gamely worked through every chapter, providing feedback on each one before I started on the next. Anne followed right behind them with the copy edits. It was a leap of faith for all of us – sharing the risk I might write myself into a corner halfway through and send all of us back to start. Thank goodness that didn't happen!

To my mother, you're welcome for keeping dad busy for a while so you could get a break from the constant one-to-one time that comes from being locked in together.

Last time I somehow missed my amazing cover designer, Emilie Yane Lopes, from my list of people to thank. Emilie's incredible eye for design and skill with Adobe's creative suite are to thank for my gorgeous covers. As always, I am in awe of her work and cannot thank her enough for bringing my stories to life in such beautiful illustrations.

A special shout-out to my mother-in-law who calls my children every day to read with them in Italian. Those hours provide me with time to catch-up on my work and to think about my story.

My sister, Christy Wilson, sends me funny memes and doesn't complain when I when I whine via text message.

Last, but never least, my darling daughters. On the days when I wanted to give up, one of them would always turn up asking if I was done with my next book. Their desire to see what Nat and H would get up to next was the inspiration I needed to keep going.

Much love to my early readers, my author friends and all of the lovely people I've met in the last couple of months. Cozy readers are a warm and welcoming bunch, I'm so grateful you let me spend time with you.

# About the Author

Lynn Morrison lives in Oxford, England with her husband, two daughters and two cats. Originally from the US, she has also lived in Italy, France and the Netherlands. It's no surprise then that she loves to travel, with a never-ending wish list of destinations to visit. She is as passionate about reading as she is writing, and can almost always be found with a book in hand. You can find out more about her on her website LynnMorrisonWriter.com.

You can chat with her directly in her Facebook group - Lynn Morrison's Not a Book Club - where she talks about books, life and anything else that crosses her mind.

facebook.com/nomadmomdiary

twitter.com/nomadmomdiary

instagram.com/nomadmomdiary

bookbub.com/authors/lynn-morrison

goodreads.com/nomadmomdiary

# Also by Lynn Morrison

### The Oxford Key Mysteries

Murder at St Margaret

Burglary at Barnard

Arson at the Ashmolean (Oct 2020)

### Nonfiction (published by Fairlight Books)

How to be Published (August 2020)

How to Market Your Book (August 2020)